THE
LOST
PHARAOH

Also by Murray Bailey

Map of the Dead
Sign of the Dead*

Singapore 52
Singapore Girl
Singapore Boxer
Singapore Ghost
Singapore Killer

Black Creek White Lies

I Dare You
Dare You Twice

* previously entitled Secrets of the Dead

THE
LOST
PHARAOH

Murray Bailey

Heritage Books

For Barbara June Pope, the second star to the right.
And my wife, Kerry—you really are my North Star.

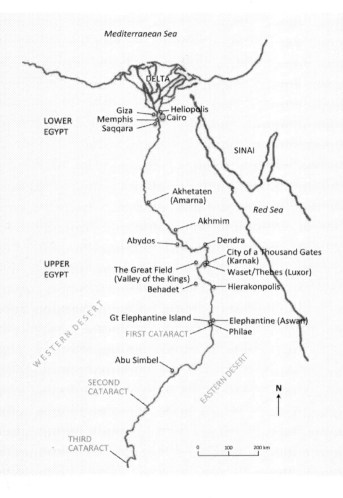

Mediterranean Sea

DELTA

LOWER
EGYPT

Giza — Heliopolis
Memphis — Cairo
Saqqara —

SINAI

Red Sea

Akhetaten
(Amarna)

Akhmim

Abydos — Dendra

City of a Thousand Gates
(Karnak)

UPPER
EGYPT

The Great Field — Waset/Thebes (Luxor)
(Valley of the Kings)
Behadet — Hierakonpolis

WESTERN DESERT

Gt Elephantine Island — Elephantine (Aswan)
FIRST CATARACT — Philae

Abu Simbel

EASTERN DESERT

N

SECOND
CATARACT

THIRD
CATARACT

0   100   200 km

ONE

I remember an expression from when I was a young boy: "Their fingernails have never seen dirt," the villagers would mutter if they saw a royal barge on the river or high-class travellers on the road.

I had been born a peasant and was now a magistrate in Akhmin, capital of the ninth nome of the Two Lands. People called me Lord Khety, although it had been my master's name. A great man, he had adopted me as his son on the same night I betrayed him. I'd joined the army, become a man and returned to find Nefer-bithia, Lord Khety's daughter.

We'd married and stayed in this town on the eastern bank of the Great River, roughly halfway between Elephantine in the south and the capital, Memphis, in the north.

We still lived in the lower noble's house of her father, with enough servants and slaves to be respectable, including my trusted Paneb.

He was by my side, his large semi-naked body oiled and impressive. I may not have the support of the city guard, like more favoured magistrates, but old Paneb was all the protection I needed. I always referred to him as old, but in truth he was probably only about ten years older than my twenty-six years.

However, he'd never counted the years, so either couldn't tell his true age, or he didn't want to.

"We should commence with the court, master," he said.

We were standing in the town square under an awning, shading me from the harsh sunlight. Afternoon prayers were past and we should have set up the stall for my court session, but I shook my head.

A group of men attracted a large crowd in the centre of the square. I took them to be actors. It was the beginning of Shemu, the low water or harvest season, and people had been celebrating—despite never having had dirt under their fingernails. Most of these people knew nothing of harvest or true hardship. They worked in the town as artisans or served in temples or the army or were higher nobles who had never done an iota of work in their lives.

The actors were not Egyptians and only one of them looked like he came from the south, possibly a Nubian. He was bigger and blacker than the others, who had wide faces and thin beards. Sea Peoples, I wondered, because of their unusual appearance.

The black man was the equivalent of Paneb, I decided, although he wore no slave rings. He moved about, looking at the crowd and saying nothing, so he was no actor. Did actors need security like a magistrate? I'd never considered it before because I'd never seen such a man.

Returning my attention to the play, I wondered which gods' story they were telling. Perhaps their very foreign nature meant they told the religious stories differently.

I sensed unease in the audience. A man in front of me started grumbling. Another began to pray.

What was this? I moved closer to hear and was shocked that this was not a religious play at all. It appeared to be some fantasy involving a sailor and monsters and made-up gods. No wonder I now heard more complaints. This was nonsense. No one told imagined stories. No one created gods. It wasn't right.

Someone voiced my own thoughts. "No!" he shouted, and others took up the call. "No, this is wrong!"

A loaf of bread spun through the air and struck the main actor—the sailor—on the head. The big black man glared into the crowd, but then a vegetable crashed onto the stage, and then another, the harvest celebrations having provided ammunition for the townsfolk.

More vegetables flew at the actors. Heavy ones tore into their banners and their awning collapsed. At that point, they realized their story was at an end and ran clutching their props out of the square towards the river.

The crowd had whipped themselves up into a frenzy now and gave chase. Paneb was ahead of me, and I realized he was howling as much as anyone. I'm an intelligent man in a position of responsibility, and yet I found myself swept up in the moment, sucked along with the crowd, driving the heretics out of our town.

As we neared the wharf, the actors appeared cornered, stuck between buildings, and that's when it turned ugly. Some of the townsmen had picked up staves. The foreigners were no longer just being pelted with vegetables, they were being beaten with sticks.

They in turn took the poles from their banners and slashed and poked to keep the braying locals back. I saw one actor's head split with a vicious blow as the attacker stepped inside his swing, struck and stepped back again. Blood quickly covered half of the actor's face, and like a pack of dogs the attackers' ferocity intensified.

"We must stop this," I said, coming to my senses. It was one thing driving the foreigners out, but quite another matter killing them. Despite the official law allowing it, my own morality said it was wrong unless they were clear enemies. There was a fine, ill-defined line.

"Stop it," I said to my slave, but Paneb wasn't listening. A sheen of sweat glinted on the back of his shaven skull and I could hear him panting. In his hand was his short ceremonial sword.

"Paneb!" I said, grabbing his arm. "Put the blade away."

He looked at me with surprise. "But, master, they're armed."

The actors had staves, that was all. And then I noticed that while the Nubian had a tattered flagpole in one hand, his other gripped a vicious-looking knife. As I looked, he seemed to stare right back at me; a moment frozen in time, two pairs of eyes locking as though he recognized me. Then the spell was broken and he was slashing with his pole again, forcing the attackers back with renewed energy.

He shouted something in a language I didn't understand and then went crazy, screaming and slashing. It was a clear diversion. As he attacked and the crowd backed off, the seven others dropped everything and ran for their lives.

Half of the crowd followed towards the quay, where I realized a boat was waiting for them just off shore. One actor slipped, went down, and was immediately surrounded, like flies swarming on dead meat. I saw bloodied sticks rise and fall and felt sick with the violence of it. The others didn't stop to help their fallen comrade. One by one they dived into the river and swam to the boat which was now edging away downstream.

The Nubian continued his frenzy. I saw his eyes now and again, red and bulging as he kept up the most incredible fight. And when they locked onto me again, I felt a shiver. It was as though he knew he would die and had selected me as his final target. Kill the magistrate and validate your own death.

Paneb had seen it too. "Get back!" he screamed at me.

I backed away, Paneb now covering me, and like this we retreated almost all the way to the square, with the crazed Nubian making headway. Locals lay on the bloodied stones and I sensed the mood was changing. This muscled black man was fearsome. Was it worth the people risking their lives to stop him?

Suddenly the Nubian was free of attackers and flung his pole at the two nearest men, giving him another few seconds. And then he was running. Running towards me.

"Run!" Paneb screamed, although he didn't need to. He may have been my slave but I also considered him a friend. His role was to protect me, and yet I couldn't just abandon him. So I stopped, maybe foolishly, and turned. Paneb stood his ground between me and the charging monster.

The Nubian's bulging eyes were still locked on me, his intention clear. I fumbled for my own pathetically small knife just as it looked like Paneb and the attacker would clash. But Paneb took a step to his left, out of the way. One minute a head-on collision, the next a vanished opponent. And like a man who dodges a charging bull, Paneb swivelled and lunged back in with his short sword.

The black man's momentum took the blade right through his neck. Paneb released it, but the man did not fall. He took three more strides, his eyes still wild and focused on mine. Only then did the impetus die. His legs buckled. His blade was no longer in his hand and he knelt two arms' lengths in front of me. The whole of his chest was slick with scarlet and blood foamed from his mouth. But he wasn't dead, and his eyes seemed to change from aggression to imploring me to come closer.

"Master!" Paneb warned as I shuffled towards the dying man.

"What?" I asked, but I wasn't speaking to my slave. The Nubian's mouth moved. He was trying to say something to me. I leaned closer, ignoring Paneb's warnings.

Blood bubbled and then gushed from the black man's mouth, and I had to step quickly aside as his body and face slapped onto the stones.

My retinue was suddenly there, fussing, mopping sweat from my face, dabbing at the spots of blood on my tunic.

"Enough!" I snapped, pushing them away. "I'm going home. No court today."

As I walked through the streets, my staff and slaves hurrying behind me, I fretted. In his dying

6

breath the Nubian had said something like, "You...
the boy."

I had no idea what he meant, but I sensed then
that we'd misunderstood. He'd never intended to kill
me. He'd needed to speak and now he never would.

TWO

Two weeks later

My court was less popular than the majority of magistrates mainly because of the punishments they handed out. As much as possible, I avoided chopping off thieves' hands or stoning cheats or flogging false accusers—although I confess to ordering the castration of rapists. However, my approach seemed to encourage both the accuser and defendant. Parties appeared prepared for frank examination and on the whole sought reparations more than punishment of the guilty party.

Paneb stood between the accuser and accused each time, and his presence was usually enough to keep order. My junior, a young man called Silthem, sat on the floor by my feet paying rapt attention. He came from a good family and his parents paid me a healthy fee for his training. He tried hard but was a slow study. His inability meant that I should have really employed an additional scribe because I only used Silthem's notes to write the reports after each court.

The two other members of my team were slaves, but lowly, unlike Paneb. Their job was to ensure I was cool and had everything I needed, including beer and food.

My purple court awning was more grand than I deserved, since it had come from Nefer-bithia's father and I knew my status as a magistrate was nothing compared to what his had been in his heyday, but I was contented. My court was fair and I was comfortably off with a beautiful and intelligent wife.

The first case was a simple one involving a young man called Sadhu, who had worked as an apprentice jewellery maker. His boss accused the boy of stealing a faience necklace.

"Did you steal it?" I asked the defendant.

I was well known for reading the truth in people's eyes, knowing when someone lied. Perhaps the boy was thinking about this when he delayed his answer.

Finally, he said, "Yes, I took it, but it wasn't theft, my lord. I intended to take it back."

I nodded. The truth.

"Explain," I instructed.

"My mother needed to prove that she had money. The rent was not due, but the landlord insisted that he see evidence a week earlier."

"What happened?"

"I showed it to the landlord but he threw her out of the accommodation anyway."

"Why?"

"I don't know, my lord."

I then enquired as to the boy's history, and his mother spoke for him. She appeared unwell, her legs weak, her pallor tinged with yellow, but she spoke clearly and passionately about her son's honesty.

"He had never done anything wrong before, my lord," she said. "Nor would he if I hadn't been so desperate."

"That's no excuse," I said.

"I merely borrowed the item, my lord," Sadhu said. "I was caught returning the necklace. If I'd kept it—"

"That's not the point," the boy's boss snapped, and he received a clout to the head for his interruption.

"Is the necklace now in your possession?" I asked the boss.

After he confirmed the item had been returned, I waved the three of them back to their seats and instructed Paneb to find the landlord. Normally, I'd wait for him to return, but this time I signalled for the next case.

A young man had killed a dog. Ordinarily this wouldn't have been an issue. Wild dogs were a nuisance, but this hound had been an official's hunting dog.

"I didn't know, my lord," the defendant claimed.

"Where was the dog when you killed it?" I asked.

"On the edge of the Eastern Desert."

I looked at the official, a fat man who had never done a day's hunting in his life, I was certain. "And you hunted with it?"

"I used to," the man said, "or at least intended to."

The statement had started as a lie but he'd saved himself with its conclusion.

Just as I was summing up the case, Paneb returned with a grumpy man. The landlord, I presumed.

The punishment for killing a man's hunting dog was death, but this dog had been out alone and was not his owner's livelihood.

The crowd were disappointed that there wasn't to be an execution, but I heard an excited buzz when I pronounced twenty lashes as punishment. The dog had worn a good collar and the man who killed it should have realized it wasn't wild.

I took a break and then reconvened the first case. When he took the stand, the landlord said his name was Ipuwer, a junior assistant to the town waterworks. He owned a number of properties, one of which had been rented to the mother of Sadhu, the boy who'd taken the necklace. When he spoke of the sickly mother I judged him to have all the empathy of a meat hook.

"Why did you ask for proof of wealth?" I asked him.

The man did not speak, and I nodded to Paneb. A sudden blow to the back of the head made the landlord start talking.

"Because I doubted they had it, Lord Khety."

"How long had your mother lived there?" I asked the boy.

"Five years, my lord."

Turning my attention back to Ipuwer, I said, "Had they missed any payments in the past?"

"No, Lord Khety."

Maybe I should have been honoured by his use of my official title, but I wasn't. This man was hiding something.

Unprompted, he said, "They are my properties and I have a right to rent them to whom I see fit."

I nodded sharply at Paneb, who hit the man.

Ipuwer grunted. "Sorry for speaking out, Lord Khety."

I said, "Tell me the real reason why you had the young man's mother removed."

"Because, Lord Khety, I had another tenant who would pay more."

I said to the boy, "Did he ask you to pay more?"

"No, my lord."

I shook my head. "Then it was unfair and unreasonable. You"—I pointed to Ipuwer—"will ensure that this young man's mother has accommodation as good as, if not better than, before and at the same price as before."

The landlord lowered his head. "Yes, my lord."

"And you"—I pointed to the young man—"are guilty of theft despite your good intentions."

Sadhu hung his head.

"And yet you have been otherwise trustworthy, and this gives me a dilemma." I signalled for a drink of beer and thought while I drank, then nodded. "The necklace was returned so you will not lose your hand." The crowd groaned in disappointment, but I ignored their blood lust. "The jeweller has suffered no loss except faith. I therefore decree that you will lose your job and find no further employment as an apprentice jeweller."

The young man looked at me with alarm which turned to disbelief.

I raised and then lowered my staff of office.

Paneb saw the instruction and came to my side.

"Ask the young man to come to the house between the seventh and eighth hours this evening."

My slave looked bemused but of course accepted my command.

We resumed and I dealt with three more cases before the final one. A woman called Senettekh accused Piye, a junior officer of the merchant quay, of taking her daughter.

"State your case against this man," I said.

Senettekh bowed, "My lord, five seasons ago, this man approached me about my daughter Leti. She was ten and the most beautiful thing in my life. So beautiful that men noticed despite her youth." She swallowed hard, as though her mouth had dried up. When she didn't immediately resume, I signalled for one of my staff to bring water.

She drank and forced a smile. "My lord, I needed the money and we made an agreement that this man could buy my daughter but that I could repay him and have her returned."

I looked at Piye. "Do you accept this?"

"Of course, my lord."

I figured he would since he was here under his own free will and so far he appeared to have nothing to answer for.

"For what purpose?" I asked. "The girl was too young for marriage."

He nodded. "My lord, as her mother says, she was beautiful. The reason for my purchase was to show her off."

Now I nodded. It was common practice for wealthy people to surround themselves with attractive girls—and sometimes boys—purely for show.

"Nothing else to it?" I asked.

"I never touched her, my lord," he said, and I believed him.

Turning my attention back to the woman, I asked, "How much did you receive?"

"Fifteen copper deben, my lord. And the agreement was twenty deben for her return."

It seemed reasonable.

"And you now have the twenty deben?"

"I do. I want Leti back home."

I shrugged. "Then the case is clear. Piye will return Senettekh's daughter for the agreed price."

Piye signalled that he wanted to speak. When I nodded he said, "It's not possible, my lord."

"Why not?"

"Because I no longer have the girl, my lord. I sold her."

"That wasn't the agreement," the woman said, her voice suddenly edged with despair. Paneb looked at me and I shook my head at him. Yes, she'd spoken out of turn but I allowed it.

"Was it the agreement?" I asked Piye.

He shook his head. "I never promised to keep her, my lord," he said, and I judged that he always planned to sell the girl on.

"Was there anything in writing?" I asked the woman. Tears were running freely down her face now.

"No, my lord," she said quietly.

"Where is the girl, Leti, now?" I asked the quay officer.

"I don't know, my lord."

"Who did you sell Leti to?"

"A captain of a merchant ship," he said. "With such beauty, he said the girl could make a fortune in the city. He paid me handsomely, my lord."

Despite the heat, I swear my blood froze. I felt sick, like I'd eaten bad meat. My focus went for a moment and one of my men mopped my forehead

14

with a towel. I breathed slowly and gradually my senses returned.

"How much... how much did this captain pay?"

"Thirty copper deben, my lord. I could hardly refuse. I bought three more girls with that money." He pointed to a group of girls standing off to one side. Young, pretty and wearing gay colours. I wondered if he was trying to show me how wealthy or maybe how reasonable he was. I don't know, but my powers of perception suddenly seemed blunted. He'd done nothing illegal. There was no contract and yet this poor woman wanted her daughter back.

I should have simply dismissed the case, but instead I asked the woman: "Can you raise thirty deben?"

She blinked away tears. "I can try."

"Then this is my judgement. If Senettekh can raise the funds, Officer Piye will locate the girl and ensure that she is returned to her mother."

I could see that the merchant wanted permission to speak, but with my mouth firmly set, I closed the case with: "This is the Law of the Two Lands."

Paneb didn't say a word as we strode back to my house. Nor did he speak as we entered the courtyard, but as my feet were being washed he looked at me enquiringly.

"It's not the law, is it?" he said.

"Let's not discuss this now, my friend," I said, and walked into my home.

THREE

My beautiful wife Nefer-bithia greeted me with a smile and a hug.

"You seem weary, my husband."

I kissed her cheeks and lips, felt her radiance and smiled. "Not now I have seen you."

She had a twinkle in her eye.

"What?" I asked.

"I've missed my second moon." She paused and gripped my hand excitedly. "I'm pregnant."

Joy of joys! I clapped my hands.

"Is something wrong? You don't appear that happy."

I blinked. "But I am, my love."

It was later, after we'd eaten and prayed, that she raised the issue again.

"You are bothered by something," she said. "Tell me."

"A boy at court today. He reminded me of myself. He'll be here shortly. I'd like you to meet him."

We drank wine until the courtyard door was opened by Paneb and Sadhu came in and looked around. When he saw me watching, he bowed.

"He's older than you were," Nefer-bithia said. "Nine years, weren't you? And his bow isn't as cute."

I trotted down the steps and greeted him.

His eyes were hard and his jaw set.

"May I speak freely, my lord?"

"You may."

"I am grateful for your judgement today and for saving my hand."

I nodded, waiting for the *but*.

He swallowed. "My mother cannot remain in the property because she is not well enough to work. The job as an apprentice was not much, but with additional employment I could have been able to provide food as well."

I nodded.

He said, "Not only have I lost my job but I will lose my other work. I may as well have been judged a criminal because no one will employ me in this town now. And, as you will appreciate, I cannot leave my mother and find work elsewhere."

"You would have struggled to find work with one hand."

He bowed his head. "That is true."

"Do you swear you will remain honest?" I asked, and when he replied, I believed him. "Then you will train as my second assistant," I said.

"But I cannot pay you, my lord," Sadhu said, understanding the usual arrangement for such a noble career. "And I am not high-born."

"Then prove yourself worthy," I said. "I will pay you"—I heard my wife's intake of breath behind me— "what you would have been paid in your previous work so that your mother can stay in her house. You will be fed and you may do additional chores to ensure there is enough food for your mother—at least until her health returns."

The boy bowed. "I am... you are most—"

"I've not finished," I interrupted. "You will appreciate your position, despite your pay. You are a servant, and below, in rank, to my master slave."

Paneb stepped forward, a smile disguised on his large face.

I said, "Before I hand you over to him, here are the rules: if you disappoint me at any time, the arrangement will end; if you cannot learn to write better than my first assistant within six months, you will be let go; If I ever suspect you of dishonesty—proven or otherwise—your role will be terminated." I rattled off more and the boy nodded his understanding each time.

"Good," I said, and I spun around and returned to our balcony, leaving the slave and the boy alone in the courtyard.

My wife wanted to speak but I asked her to wait as Paneb ran through the same process he'd taken me through some seventeen years ago.

He barked, "You need to learn your place. You are the lowliest. You do what you are told, when you are told. If I am not happy with you, you will be thrown out. Although I am a slave, you will not call me Paneb, you will always call me Master Hapuseneb. Is that understood?"

"Yes, Master Hapuseneb."

"Although you are not a slave, you are not the master's equal nor ever will be. You will never be familiar with his lordship. You will never be familiar with his family. Is that understood?"

"Yes, Master Hapuseneb."

"Now, hold still." The slave pulled a copper blade from his belt, tested it to show its sharpness, and gripped Sadhu's hair, pulling his head back. I remembered the sensation well. When he'd done it to

18

me, I felt like a goat whose throat was about to be sliced. But with a few easy strokes, Paneb cut away most of the boy's hair.

"Baldness is a great way to keep the lice away." Paneb laughed, and once there was just stubble, he began to shave the boy's head completely.

I still remember the feel of that blade as it bit my skin, leaving bloody lines that lasted for days. Perhaps I should have asked my slave to be less rough with the boy, but it was a way of Paneb establishing his status. Of course, it was also good entertainment.

"Can we talk now?" my wife asked, and I felt the lash of her tongue.

Paneb thrust the boy's head into the water trough and I tore my eyes away. "Sorry, my love."

Now I could see she was tense. She kept her voice low so that we weren't overheard, but the anger was no less for the volume. "What are you thinking?"

"About the boy? Well, I would have—"

"We can't afford it."

"We should be higher nobles," I said, "like your father used to be."

"But we aren't, and a magistrate's apprentice should not take a salary. We are paid by Silthem's parents—"

"And look at how bad he is!" I snapped, and then apologized for my temper. She was right of course. In a more reasonable voice, I said, "If I am to get a job in a better nome, I need a good assistant. Silthem is not my future."

"But it could take years," she said, "and with a baby on the way…"

I said, "I wasn't thinking. He reminded me of me. A boy who just needs an opportunity."

"We aren't a charity."

I took a long breath. "Can we give it a short time? If we can't cope then I'll let him go. But hopefully something will change." I hugged her and felt the tension in her ease.

"Maybe you're right," she said. "We're having a baby and I saw an ibis on the back of a hippopotamus this morning. A very good omen."

FOUR

Four days later, Nefer-bithia and I were at her father's tomb. We'd offered prayers and brought food. We sat beside his stele and ate his favourite meat and date cake while toasting the old man with sweet wine.

Despite it being against the rules, and foolish, I knew some of the visitors would leave food for their ancestors. No wonder scavenging animals waited until dark on the outskirts of the necropolis. One or two would find hunger drove them onto the grounds. The guards would spot them and those animals would never get the chance to try again, that was for sure.

"So, tell me," she said.

"Tell you?"

"You've been preoccupied. Are you now worrying about paying for the new assistant?"

"No—well, of course," I quickly added as I saw her frown. "It's that, and I'm not sleeping."

"Not sleeping, Yani?" She shook her head. "But I've heard you snoring. You're asleep when I've woken."

"Restless." I rubbed my forehead. "Dreams going round and round."

"What dreams?"

"Of me as a child. And Laret, my sister. That strange black man, whom Paneb killed, it's unsettled me."

"Because he called you a boy?"

"Or something like that. It was hard to tell exactly what he said as he died."

She shivered. "I'm so glad I didn't see."

I nodded.

She said nothing for a while, looking into my eyes, maybe searching for truth. Then she said, "It reminds you of your sister."

"The dying black man?"

"No, the case with the woman who sold her daughter."

"Leti," I said. "The girl's name was Leti."

"I knew it! You even remember her name. It reminds you of your sister doesn't it."

"But the memories aren't complete," I said. "In my dreams I'm running around the city and can't find my sister. And when I see her, she disappears. I chase after her and run into a wall. I find myself in blind alleys or lost. And all the time she's just out of reach."

My wife had her hand on my arm. I'd never talked about what had happened to my sister, Laret, not in detail, and now I couldn't remember properly. It was like my own brain was blocking the thoughts, putting up walls in my mind.

She said, "Can you tell me?"

"Not everything."

"Because you don't want to upset me, or you just can't."

"I can't," I said, and I knew she could see tears in my eyes. I brushed them away and smiled. "Anyway, this day isn't about me, it's about your father."

"Your father too," she said.

She meant the fact that Lord Khety had adopted me, rather than my real father. I didn't know where he was and couldn't remember him except as a vague figure who was sometimes around during harvest. The rest of the year he was away, working in the city as a builder. He wasn't alone. Most peasant men did the same. Only, my real father rarely returned, and I never saw him after our mother died.

"You should go to the dream temple," Neferbithia said.

"We're saving money, remember?"

She raised her eyebrows in a way she did when there would be no further argument, and a day later I was on the road south to the dream temple.

Paneb came with me and insisted he would wait outside the gates until I returned.

"One night," I said and he nodded.

I was greeted by a priest who washed my hands and feet and asked whether I had an ailment or wished to visit my ancestors in the Field of Reeds.

I'd never been here before, but I soon realized that the temple was split into two depending on one's dream requirement. He frowned when I described the need to recall my dead sister but he finally decided it was a problem with my head rather than communion with the dead.

I was guided deeper and deeper into the temple, with oil lamps and incense giving the spaces a strange depthless—or was it infinite?—quality.

A girl in a silver-edged robe took over and she made me sit for a long time as she swayed and chanted around me.

Despite being a little mesmerized by her form, I didn't feel sleepy, if that was her intention. And I was sitting, which started to make my back ache.

Finally, I was about to interrupt her when she raised a hand and a second girl brought her a bowl. She handed it to me and I took a tentative sip. Warm milk that was slightly bitter.

The girl motioned for me to drink it all and then asked me to lie down.

I stared up at the dark stone ceiling, the lights playing with the cracks and crevasses. The girl knelt beside me a placed a cool hand on my forehead. The contact made my eyes close. I heard her chanting again but the words soon lost meaning and I could no longer smell the incense. Instead, I could smell warm earth and bedding reeds.

I opened my eyes and realized I was staring at the ceiling of our hut in the village. I'd been crying. My chest hurt from the sobs, and at first I couldn't recall why.

I must have been about seven, and there was just me and my sister then. We slept in a hut on the edge of the village.

Laret comforted me.

"They're only words," she said.

"But our cousins are so nasty to me. They say horrible things in my face. They throw stones at me."

"Who does?"

"Mostly Nabetu." He was an older boy.

She shook her head, angry. "They're jealous of you."

I turned to her in the darkness but her face was just a shape, a suggestion.

"Why are they jealous? They say I am an extra mouth to feed. But I work as hard as any child."

"Yes, and you can bake bread."

"So why?"

"Because you're different."

"And that makes them hate me?" I said, not understanding.

"You are better looking than them."

I touched my forehead. "But I have a scar."

"Even with your little scar! And you're smarter than all of them. In fact, you are the smartest person I know. That's why they hate you. Children can be cruel. You're special."

"I don't feel special."

"You were a miracle, Yani. That's special."

I had stopped crying, but the depth of sadness was great—like it had been two years earlier.

It seemed natural that the thought of that time should transport me to the earlier period.

A breeze played across the wheat field like ripples on the river. My hands hurt, my neck baking in the midday sun. I pulled up a handful of grass and looked at it. I could see a bug in the soil.

"Yani."

My sister's voice snapped my attention from the bug.

She was crossing the wheat, careful not to stand on any. "Yani," she said again as she stopped.

I was about to complain that pulling the weeds out of the wheat field was cutting into my young fingers, when I realized she was crying.

Laret put her arms around me. "Yani."

I was only five and didn't understand these things. I should have hugged her back and comforted her, but instead I pushed her away.

"What?"

He gulped. "Mother is dead."

I knew she'd been very ill. The plague, the other children said. We hadn't been allowed to stay in the same hut for the past two weeks and no one else would come close to us.

"What does it mean?" I asked, reflecting my own confusion rather than a real question about the future.

Laret was almost three years older and much wiser than me. She moved her mouth but no words came out.

"What does it mean?" I asked.

"I will look after you now, and then, one day, when you are big and strong, you will protect me."

She handed me water to quench my thirst but I couldn't taste it. Instead, my mouth filled with sand. I coughed.

"Water."

I felt a hand on my forehead and opened my eyes.

I was back in the dream temple, the lights playing on the ceiling, the girl over me. She placed a hand under my head and raised it. I took a drink of water and then another.

"How are you?" the girl asked.

"All right," I said, and wondered whether I'd spoken out loud.

"Did you see your sister?"

"Yes." Although quiet, this time I heard my voice.

Another girl appeared, and I was given a morsel of compressed fruit, although I couldn't say what it was.

A mixture pressed into a ball. I had another and then another sip of water.

Afterwards, I said, "But I haven't finished. I still haven't found her."

"Ah," the girl said. "You need a deeper dream."

Moments later I was being given another bowl of warm milk, only this was much more bitter—like eating crushed palm leaves—and I had to be encouraged to drink.

When I lay back and closed my eyes, it was as though my *ka* had left my body. I was nothingness itself.

FIVE

The moon hadn't yet risen and so the only light came from the stars. However, the man took no chances at being recognized. No one was around at this late hour except for a couple of guards and their baboons. He'd watched and waited until they were too far away to see him as he slipped from his hiding place on a boat and crossed the quay.

A dark hood covered his face and he bowed his head like an acolyte walking solemnly to the great temple. But he didn't head for the temple. That would have been too risky: a noble entering the temple of Amun at this hour? If he was seen, if he was arrested... he shook the negative thoughts from his mind. This was no time for such thoughts. He had good news and tonight was the turning point. Tonight would be recorded as the date that the balance of power shifted. And he was the messenger. He would be recorded as the bearer of the news that changed everything.

He moved through the city, keeping to back streets and avoiding the occasional drunk he spotted. And finally he reached the inauspicious building with a wooden door and no windows.

He knocked once, paused, and then knocked again three times.

"Go away," a grumpy voice hissed from the other side of the wood.

"Water dries more quickly on a stone," the man in the hood whispered back.

The door swung open and he darted inside. Immediately the door was shut behind him and a bar slotted across. The man there had a short sword.

"Put it away," a second man said. He was sitting at a table and the light from a candle barely showed his features.

The man at the door remained there with his sword unsheathed. The man who had entered noticed a third man standing at the back in the shadows. There would be a second door there: the escape route if they were discovered.

The man at the table said, "You weren't followed?"

"No, my lord. I have been most careful. I arrived at the city docks five hours ago and have waited this long to be sure."

"I wasn't here five hours ago," the seated man said.

The man in the hood knew why his superior was irritable. Their plans had been failing. There hadn't been any good news for weeks. It looked like Pharaoh Horemheb would remain in power and continue to corrupt the great legacy of the Two Lands.

His heart pounded in his chest and the words barely came out. "Good news!"

The seated man shifted. "Careful."

"Of course." His superior meant to use language that would not incriminate them. They could take no risk of being overheard and understood. They would

29

surely go to Behadet prison or worse if they were found out.

The conspirators had been told about the boy they sought. He had been taken from Waset and briefly raised by a nobleman's family loyal to the crown. And then even that was too risky and a slave had smuggled him away and hidden him in a peasant's village. Few knew what the boy looked like and everyone had been looking. But they had recently learned that the man who knew him best, the Nubian slave, had been killed.

"The slave died with a sword in his throat," the hooded man said.

"We know this."

"But not before he saw the boy."

"How can you know this?"

"He told one of the foreigners he was with. He travelled with a group of actors. He told one." He knew he was gabbling now, such was his excitement.

"And you know who the boy is?"

"Yes, my lord. The actor told me."

"Where is this actor now?"

"Dead, my lord."

The man at the table nodded. They couldn't risk this vital information reaching the other side.

The hooded man breathed in and out to calm his racing heart.

"Yes?" the seated man prompted.

The man in the hood leaned over the table. "The magistrate of Akhmin," he whispered. "He is the one."

SIX

The smell of river silt clawed at my airways. I was hiding in the reeds waiting for a duck to show me where she'd laid her eggs. My empty stomach ached with the thought of food.

But the quiet was broken by laughter from the river. A boat, but not a merchant. There was too much jollity.

And then I saw it, a royal barge with a golden prow flashing in the morning sun. A giant blue pennant, almost as long as the barge itself, fluttered in the wind like a hunter's arrow, pointing the way downstream.

When she was close, I counted fifteen oars on each side that dipped in and out of the water with slow, casual grace. And yet the noise from above deck rose and fell with shouts and screams and a melodic noise made by men with instruments. It was the first time I'd heard real music rather than the banging and clacking noises we made in the village.

The laughter came mostly from girls, who I could now see dancing in clean white skirts, their breasts jiggling between necklaces of gold, emerald, turquoise and lapis.

I am nine, I thought, and I had never seen anything so rich; it was a life of music and happiness that was alien to my own world. Perhaps this was a glimpse of the afterworld where my mother now lived. I liked the idea of her dancing with the other women and wondered whether she was able to laugh now. She surely knew I was well and strong and that Laret cared for me.

Yesterday, my sister had seen another royal barge. She'd chattered all night about it, saying that something big was happening. She wondered whether it explained why the soldiers had been in our village. It was the wrong time of year for taxes, and a scribe with them took note of everyone's name, age and patron god.

"Who is my god?" I had asked her.

"Anhuris," she'd said, smiling. "You are strong and good and above all you are a protector."

"But I am so small, and it is you who looks after me."

Again she smiled and held me close under our blanket. "One day, my Yani, one day you will be my protector."

When the barge had gone, the river became still once more. The duck I'd spied at sunrise returned to the reed bed. I waited another fifteen minutes, barely breathing, watching the reeds and picturing the duck as it found its nest and settled. I felt the sweat prickling the exposed back of my neck. A black insect crawled up a stem close to my nose, but I didn't move. Then I saw it, the twitch of a reed that told me the duck was settling. Still careful, in case I was mistaken, I eased myself into position and pulled two sticks from my belt. With the smooth motion my father had taught me, I parted the reeds. "Imagine you are the breeze, Yanhamu," he had said, and I heard his voice now.

For a moment I thought I was back in a time when he was with me, but then I heard the distant sounds from the royal barge. I was relieved, because this was the time I needed to witness.

I breathed to calm my beating heart and pressed on. And there she was, a golden duck squatting low over her nest, unaware she'd been found.

The need for stealth over, I thrashed at the reeds. With a jump, the bird scurried into the undergrowth and seconds later burst through the far side, skittered across the water and into the air.

I stepped into the silt and waded to her nest. Seven eggs. The rule of ma-at said: always leave three eggs behind so that Het will not be angry.

I reached through the thicket and picked up the first, warm with life and of perfect form. After placing it carefully into my satchel, I did the same with the next and the next. When I placed the fourth in the bag, I found myself reaching for the fifth, the sixth and then the seventh. I held the final three, cupped in my hands.

Did the goddess make the rule to protect the bird? If all eggs were taken, birds wouldn't reproduce and so there would be no future birds to give them eggs. It made sense, although I knew other animals took the eggs and sometimes the duck produced another batch.

My stomach growled at the prospect of eggs rather than bread and onions. Surely the goddess would understand. I could feed myself and Laret for days.

After convincing myself of the justice, I said a prayer to Het asking her to understand and grant the bird great fertility and many offspring. Satisfied, I

33

stood, scraped the Nile dirt from my legs and hastened back to the village.

"Laret, Laret," I called as I neared the outskirts, then pulled up and stared. A soldier was standing at the main hut talking to the matriarch.

Laret was by his side, a tether around her wrist.

Before my unbelieving eyes, the soldier handed something to the matriarch and walked away, Laret, a step behind, her shorter legs hurrying compared to the big man's stride.

Laret had been arrested! It must be a mistake. What could my beautiful, caring sister have done wrong?

I called her over and over but she didn't look back. By the time I reached the gate, she was over sixty paces away and heading for the river.

I caught hold of a cousin's tunic. "What has happened? What did she do? Where is he taking my Laret?"

Nabetu was older than Laret and tried to shrug off my grip and pull away, but in desperation I hung on as though fighting him would stop it all happening.

He hit me but I didn't let go. Then he grunted, "She's going to be trained."

"Trained?"

"As a palace dancer."

"But, she would never... I need her!"

Nabetu finally jerked out of my grip and laughed. "You simpleton, Hamu. She will be much better off... and the family is better off too." He nodded towards his mother, the matriarch still standing in the doorway.

I guessed that she weighed a purse in her hands.

Nabetu said, "Since your mother died and your father left, you should think yourself lucky." He laughed again. "I myself would have sold you both as meat to the butcher."

I barely heard this last remark. I was already running, my desperate feet kicking up dust like a sand viper.

"Sister, don't leave me!" I said as I neared.

Laret looked at me with tearful eyes but didn't stop. "I have no choice." She forced a smile. "But, my clever brother, I will be happy. There is a big festival and I am to be a dancer! I will dance like a princess at a palace."

I stayed with them, half walking, half jogging beside the path. As they neared the river, I saw a boat with more soldiers and a gaggle of young girls on board. It was happening. This nightmare was really happening!

Rushing ahead, I stood directly in the soldier's path. The man stopped and glowered.

I wanted to tell the man that there was a mistake, that the matriarch didn't really let my sister go, that Laret really wanted to stay with me. Only the silver payment to the family had persuaded her. Maybe Laret thought I would benefit. I swallowed, my mouth dry. The words wouldn't come.

The man's face was like chiselled granite, his eyes almost as cold. He spat, "Stand aside you insolent pup or feel the lash of my staff across your peasant face." He raised his stick so suddenly that I flinched in expectation of a blow, but I stood my ground.

However, instead of striking me, the soldier snarled, then lunged. Snatching me around the waist, he then flung me aside like a rag doll.

"No!" Laret jerked her leash from the soldier's grasp, dived to my side and helped me up. She brushed dirt from my face then kissed my forehead. "Take care, little brother."

"Laret!" Tears sprang from my eyes and stung my cheeks.

"Promise me you will think of me and pray for me. One day perhaps you will see me dance." She kissed me again and rushed along the path.

"Let me come with you," I pleaded with the soldier, but he just took up Laret's leash and pulled her away.

"I work hard," I shouted, but we were at the gangplank and my sister was boarding. Another soldier barred my way and then the gangplank was raised and I was alone on the riverbank.

Immediately, the granite-faced soldier barked an order and the boat pushed into the current, forty oars lowered and ready. Then with the precision of a many-legged creature, the boat pulled smoothly away.

I noticed symbols on the side and I knew this represented the boat's name. Committing them to memory, I was determined I'd find this boat again.

SEVEN

I ran along the bank, scattering birds with my wails. I slipped on mud and stumbled over tussocks and kept going but my heart and legs were not strong enough to keep up with the boat.

Eventually I had to stop. Gasping for air, the fear of never seeing my sister again pulled tight around my heaving chest.

I could still see the boat, maybe a hundred paces distant, and was surprised to see the rowing stop. In unison, the oarsmen raised their oars to the sky. Despite the pain in my chest, I forced myself to hurry, to close the gap.

I could hear low chanting that increased in pitch and volume. The distance was now halved and I saw a man in a flowing white gown at the prow of the boat. He raised his hands in prayer to the sky.

Following his gaze, I froze, for in the sky I saw that the edge of the moon had turned a dusty orange. As I watched in horror, the moon began to shrink, as though a cloud of locusts swept across its surface, devouring all life. Then, when the whole surface was covered, the moon was dark mud-red.

Instinctively I felt for the satchel hanging at my side. I had broken the rule. Het was angry with me and had destroyed the moon. My sister had been taken away from me as a punishment by the gods. I had defied them and there would be no Field of Reeds in the afterlife for me. On Judgement Day, before the great god Osiris, my heart would fail the test and be tossed to Ammut—to be eaten by the Devourer.

I clenched my teeth. A strength coursed through my muscles like never before as I realized that without Laret my earthly life meant nothing either. Breathing in deeply, I forced myself to walk again, and then, as fortitude returned, I began to run.

The redness of the moon faded, to be replaced by orange once more—the swarm of locusts seemed to be moving away.

Before I could get close enough, the boat carrying my sister had dropped oars and was moving swiftly with the current again.

My intense focus on the soldiers' boat and strange occurrence had led me to ignore something behind me. Another boat, a small merchant vessel, had tied up, its crew also raising their arms in supplication to the moon.

They too began to move away again.

Without considering the dangers, I made a decision and rushed into the water. At the boat's side, I called up to the man at the tiller. "Passage, my good man."

The sailor looked over and waved me away. He called to another man who poled the bow further away from the bank.

I splashed and jumped and held onto the side.

"I can pay you!" I called, not daring to climb aboard.

The first man looked thoughtful as he steered into the river. From the corner of his eye, I could see him watching.

"You can't hold on for long, and when you are finally weak you will drop and be food for the crocodiles."

"I'm strong. I won't let go," I replied.

The man nodded. "So how much can you pay me, urchin?"

"I have seven large duck eggs."

The man waved me to climb on board and I swung my legs out and over. Then I opened my satchel and stared with horror at the mess. Only two eggs remained unbroken. I handed them over and showed the snotty residue of the rest.

The man shook his head and took the two eggs. "If you are strong, can you also work?"

"I work very hard. By Horus, I am the hardest worker for my size!"

"Good, because you may have passage as long as you work. Stop working and you are over the side and may Sobek protect you."

He set me to work at once, instructing me to scrub down the timbers. I cleaned the dirt from the boards for two hours in the sweltering sun before the sailor handed me a gourd of water.

"Now go below and check the fruit. Polish them and remove any which are rotten or wormed. And mind that you don't eat any, urchin. It is all counted, and even the rotten fruit must be accounted for."

"I would rather work in the sun," I said.

The sailor frowned. "Has the heat made you lose your senses?"

"I need to follow the soldiers' boat, the one with the forty oars. My sister is on board."

The sailor waved towards the hold. "I know the one. It is called The Heliopolis Black Bull. *Go below and I will watch for it. Don't worry, I won't pass without telling you.*"

This was an honest man, I could tell from his face, so I nodded my thanks and scurried out of the cruel sun.

When I was eventually called to the deck, the sun had set and its parting still touched the encroaching night with a gentle light like a mosquito bite on pale flesh. Nedjem—for that was the sailor's name—had steered to the bank and told me to jump ashore and tie them up. When he had finished, Nedjem patted me on the shoulder like a man. "The Heliopolis Black Bull *is two hundred paces that way, after the merchants' quay.*"

"Where are we?"

"Between the twin cities of Waset and the City of a Thousand Gates."

I shook my head. The names meant nothing. Despite seeing travellers along the road past the village and selling them fresh water and bread, I knew very little of the places outside my village.

I bowed my thanks, first touching my knees and then reaching out. I'd seen someone do this once and it seemed a good way to show genuine and extreme gratitude.

This made the sailor laugh. "Good luck, urchin, and Horus protect you."

I ran along the public quay. People were tying up boats for the night and closing up warehouses. The first section smelled of beer and then there was a cattle enclosure followed by a timber yard and pottery warehouse. The final section was a storage area for wheat and barley. Men looked at me suspiciously as I hurried past and a few called lewdly with the tones of drinking men.

Beyond the public wharf there was a grove of bushes and then a long quarried-stone quay. Five boats were moored, and in the rapidly fading light I realized three of them looked like the one Laret had been taken on. Just as I recognized the symbols on the side of The Heliopolis Black Bull, a man called out.

I swivelled and saw a watchman with a fearsome beast on a chain rushing towards me. Heart pounding, I backed away but then stood my ground.

"Clear off, urchin!" the guard shouted as he stopped a couple of paces away with his animal straining at the leash. "Run now or my baboon will bite off your manhood." The creature showed its wicked yellow teeth as though it understood its master's warning.

"I don't have a manhood," I said, straightening my back. "I'm only a child."

The watchman's face mellowed and he jerked the baboon back so that it sat obediently at his side. "You are brave for one with no manhood."

I did my bow—hands to the knees and then out.

It had the desired effect. The guard laughed. "What are you doing here?"

"The Heliopolis Black Bull." I pointed to the ship. "Has everyone gone?"

"Disembarked? Yes. Why do you—?"

"Where is the palace dancing school? My sister has been taken there."

The guard laughed again. "All right, all right," he said when he could get his breath back, and then he gave directions.

As I ran off, the watchman called out, "Since you don't have a manhood, if I see you on the military quay again, I'll let my baboon have his way with you!"

Once off the quay, I made my way through narrow streets. The sky was fully dark now, for the moon had been awake during the day. However, this was an artisan section lit by torches. Inside buildings and sitting at tables on the street I saw men of supreme skill working glass and pottery and painting pictures that made me gawp at their beauty. But I did not dally. I ran along the side of a long wall and at the end turned right past a temple. I noted that the way seemed to lead away from the centre of the town, and at first I thought I was heading for the residential area, but then I found myself on the outskirts, faced by another long wall.

Working my way around this, I reached a wooden gateway with braziers burning on either side. The great Pharaoh Ahmose was said to have been more than twice the height of a normal man and even he could have walked without ducking his head through this entrance. Two soldiers knelt by the closed gates and leaned on their spears.

"Sir, is this the palace dancing school?" I asked, approaching one.

The man laughed. "Some call it that. Now piss off!"

"But, sir…" A stone struck me on the arm. I looked at the other soldier and saw he was about to let another fly.

The other soldier said, "You heard him. Piss off, dung heap!"

I stood my ground and let the second stone strike me on the chest. I didn't flinch at the sharp pain.

The first soldier took a step forward and lowered his spear.

"Please..." I began, uncertainly, "what do you mean people call it that?"

Both guards laughed. "It's the bloody garrison, isn't it!"

"But my sister... I was told she was here!"

"Oh she'll be here all right," the second soldier said, and he made a rude gesture and laughed again.

I staggered backwards into the darkness. The night closed in as though Nut herself had come down and swallowed me whole.

EIGHT

I awoke before dawn, my bones aching with cold and from sleeping on the stone ground. I had dreamed of a hawk that terrorized my village, attacking the women and girls and making them cry out. It took a few moments for me to remember where I was: outside the garrison in Waset.

After stretching and rubbing my limbs I climbed a tree as high as I could go before the branches bent too much. As the sky lightened with morning, I could partially see over the garrison wall.

The whole enclosure was bigger than my village and most buildings were two storeys high. From what I could see, they formed an L-shape along two sides of the walls.

Animal sounds suggested a third shed, with at least one horse and some buffalo. They must have been hidden from my sight beneath the nearest wall.

Still before the sunrise, a cart laden with bread trundled through the gate and two young men unloaded it into a store and left. Soldiers began to emerge and, after a period of relative quiet, began training in the open courtyard, wrestling, some fighting with short sticks and others practising with spears.

I saw no sign of any girls.

Had the guard at the quay lied? Maybe this was all a cruel joke and Laret was elsewhere. With some hope, I climbed down from the tree and retraced my steps into the town. There I asked people about the school for dancing girls. With each negative response, my heart sank again until I became convinced that Laret was inside the garrison walls.

Returning to my tree, I watched the soldiers, hoping to spot my sister or any of the girls I'd seen on board The Heliopolis Black Bull. At one point I saw the man who had taken her away—the man with the face like granite. He shouted and pointed a lot and I guessed him to be in charge. He also seemed to have a room to himself—the only part of the building that was three floors high.

By mid-afternoon, weak with hunger, I slipped and almost fell from my perch. I dropped down and headed to the artisan sector looking for work.

A man said he'd pay me if I won a game of sticks with him. If I didn't then I'd sweep his yard for free.

I won and swept for half an hour. When I finished, the man didn't pay me and left me stunned as he swore that I had lost the bet. Either he fooled himself or he was the best liar I have ever met, such was his conviction.

Despite this bad experience, when a potter welcomed me in and offered me work, I swept the floor of his studio. He rewarded me with bread and cheese, a pat on the head, and praise for working so hard.

I cried at his kindness and told him the story of the man who had tricked me in a game of sticks. Afterwards, the potter insisted that I wash with warm water and a bar of natron. Then he gave me a pale *blue smock in place of my rags. He said I was more likely to find work now that I looked less like a waif.*

I went on to explore the workshop area behind the quays. Everywhere was swept clean and organized with each section clearly demarked. In places the air smelled like flowers, not the usual acrid smell of living quarters and animals. I noticed that there were no farm animals in the town except for an area by the quay penned off for cattle.

Over the next three days I spent time watching the garrison from my tree and found labour for food. I asked everyone I met about a dancing school but the answer was always the same. There was no dancing school for common folk.

I learned where the palaces were and which temple was which. I also learned that this was a special time. There was great excitement about the coming festival. Osiris was about to rise into the heavens, signalling the arrival of the inundation. But also, Horus had returned to human form as a boy. They called him Tutankhaten.

One of the jobs I got was running a message for a warehouseman. I delivered it quickly and found I was sent on with another message. This one took me to a bakery where I was given a scrap of bread, for it was always the receiver of the message who paid.

I hung around and was allowed to watch the baking since I had some skill myself. I quickly saw that the knowledge I'd gained in the village was inferior to a professional's skill.

Later, out of interest, I followed a laden cart to the warehouse of the first merchant. His message had been an order for bread. When he saw me he nodded in recognition. However, I was surprised that he didn't know the young man from the bakery who pushed the cart. In my village, everyone knew everyone.

That evening, now emboldened by strength from good food, I decided to return to the garrison and confront the soldier who had taken Laret away.

The guards eyed me suspiciously as I approached.

I did my bow, hands to the knees and then out, which made them laugh. "Are you hungry?" I asked as I straightened.

The men stopped laughing and I could see in their eyes that they were. "I have sweet bread," I said, and from the blue smock I pulled two hand-sized triangles of cake.

The nearest guard reached out. "What do you want in return?"

I stepped out of reach. "To speak to the soldier with the granite face who shouts a lot."

The second guard laughed. "You are out of luck. The captain prefers girls to keep his bed warm. And he has a new girl to do that."

I swallowed. "What's her name?"

The first guard stepped forward. "The bread first."

I handed over both triangles and the man tossed one to his colleague.

After they had both taken a bite, I asked again, "What's her name?"

"Don't know," laughed the nearest guard. "But if the captain's true to form, we should get a go at her before the next season is out."

The second grabbed his groin. "Then we can show her how real men do it."

After they both finished laughing, the first guard said, "Got any more bread?"

"No."

"Then piss off."

I stood my ground. "Wait," I said as both men picked up stones. "Just tell me when the girls come out. Tell me that and I'll bring you bread tomorrow."

The first one said, "You're a bit young to be sniffing after pretty girls."

I forced a laugh, "Never too young, eh?"

The guard chuckled. "All right, horny boy. Sometimes they are allowed out in the morning before the men get up. Sometimes it's in the evening." He looked at me hard. "You promise to bring bread?"

I nodded.

"They'll be coming out very soon. Make sure you're downwind if you want a good sniff."

The other guard said something lewd, but I was already running to my tree. It was barely light enough to see, but when the girls came into the courtyard I heard their voices, subdued and sad.

At the top of my lungs I shouted, "Laret!"

"Yani!"

My heart leapt. It was my sister's voice, although I couldn't see her.

A commotion ensued, with female screams and shouting men. I thought I saw sticks being used to thrash the girls, round them up, and then they were gone.

Over the next four days, I watched and worked out the pattern of activity. I also discovered that these were known as the Hidden Days, the extra days in the calendar that Ra had provided before the rise of Osiris and the start of a new year. During this time, the wealthier people stopped working. They prayed and drank and fornicated.

Between short visits to the garrison, learning their routine, I worked incessantly, running messages and helping at the bakery. On the day before the New Year, I delivered the morning bread to the garrison and hatched a plan. The girls exercised at the time of a watch change. The bread was delivered by two boys after the new watch.

The celebrations continued all day and night. In the early hours I was with another baker's boy and walked a donkey pulling the laden bread cart through the dark streets. Drunken men staggered between buildings and others lay where they had collapsed, either passed out or still praying incoherently to the sky.

The older boy moaned about them delivering too early. Truth was, he'd been up all night and had drunk too much beer.

"Then go home," I said.

"And deliver on your own?" The other boy was clearly interested.

"I can manage."

The boy looked me up and down. "I'll miss out on any tips."

"I'll split them with you."

"I know you are trustworthy, but it's not fair on you."

"It is fair—I want to do this alone."

The other boy didn't need to hear more. He scurried off to bed calling, "Thanks. See you tonight, Yanhamu."

It was a struggle to goad the donkey the final five hundred yards, but I made it to the gate just before the watch changed. Inside, I took my time unloading the bread so that I was about done when the girls appeared. With my heart beating in my throat, I watched as they filed past. And then I saw her.

"Laret!" I whispered.

She looked at me, but her eyes were hollow and unseeing. Her lip was cut and her cheek glowed with the early stages of bruising.

"I'm getting you out," I said, and from the cart I pulled a spare baker's cloak. Throwing it around her shoulders, I pulled the hood over her head. Checking that the guards weren't looking, I gripped her arm and pulled her in the direction of the cart.

"Walk!" I whispered as I struggled against her indifference. We made it to the cart and I placed her hand on the side and made her grip. Then I took hold of the donkey's reins and eased the empty bread cart towards the gate.

Keeping my head down, sure the guards would hear the drumbeat in my chest, I walked through the gate and past them. At that moment, the pealing of a hundred bells began, announcing the start of the New Year worship and parades.

Then one of the guards shouted, "Hey!"

I swung around and gaped. Laret had fallen to the floor. I rushed to her side and helped her stand.

The guard shouted, "She better not have the plague." And I realized he hadn't recognized her.

I grinned. "No, it's too much bread. Extra poison for you today!" I made a choking sign and then waved. "See you tomorrow."

The guards laughed.

As soon as we were out of sight, I stopped the donkey and checked on my sister. Her eyes were empty.

"Are you hungry?" I asked. "Can I get you something?"

Laret didn't reply, and I felt tears prickle my eyes. My excitement at getting her out was turning to fear for her condition. We sat in the shade and I hugged her long and hard.

I told her I would have to leave but I would be back soon. I needed to return the donkey and cart to the baker. All the time, I had a strange voice in my head saying, "Don't leave her alone," but I couldn't stop what I was doing.

I hurried, all the time wondering what we should do, where I could take Laret so she would get better. I decided to find a temple dedicated to Het and explain that it was my fault for taking the eggs. She had nothing to do with it, so I should pay the price, whatever the goddess needed to make amends.

I hurried back to the spot where I'd left my sister and my heart turned to ice.

She was gone.

NINE

Frantic with worry, I ran through streets and alleys until I was lost. But I kept on running and the city walls closed in, the light being snuffed out until I was running blind. I collided with shadowy objects, bashed my shoulders and arms on stones. I stumbled, got up and kept running. Until I collapsed, dizzy and sick.

When I opened my eyes, looking up I saw a swirl of lights, which were strangely mesmerizing. There was a voice too.

"I can't hear you," I said, but my voice was soundless.

The sounds grew louder and my neck muscles strained as I tried to raise my head.

"Lord Khety," the soft voice said.

"My name is Yanhamu," I managed to say, my voice sounding other-worldly.

I felt a hand behind my neck, lifting so that the strain evaporated. I blinked. There was a face over me. Familiar...

"Lord Khety, it is time to wake."

I saw him clearly now as I was raised to a sitting position. The priest.

"Where am I?" I asked, even though it dawned on me that I was in the temple.

"You are back. It is time to end the dream." He gave me water and helped me to my feet. I took juddering steps as my bones and muscles remembered their purpose. He guided me out of the sanctum.

I saw people sleeping and girls attending to others' needs. As we left the room and crossed the shadowy hypostyle hall, I got my senses back.

"I haven't finished."

"You have stayed long enough," the priest explained gently.

"No," I said, stopping. "I need to continue. My dream isn't complete. I still haven't saved my sister."

He looked at me and bowed.

"How do you feel?"

I blinked and tried to assess my state. "Vacuous," I said, shrugging. "Like a husk. My body is empty and my mind is floating."

"Yes," he said, placing a hand on my arm and guiding me again towards the exit. I found myself complying.

When he spoke again, the priest said, "When you arrived, Lord Khety, we understood your needs and explained the risk. You agreed to stay a maximum of three days."

Three days? But I'd only been here a night!

He said, "Time is meaningless to the person in the dream world. You have been here for three days. This is your first time. Any longer and you would feel worse when you awoke. Sometimes people never wake up—which is acceptable in the other sanctum where they visit the afterlife and wish to remain. But your request was to travel back to see your sister. Did that not happen?"

"I never agreed to three days."

He smiled kindly. "You have forgotten. The dreams can do that, and that's another reason for limiting your visit. Too long and you may also forget yourself." We were at the exit now and I could see Paneb sitting in the shade of a tree playing a game with another man. As soon as our eyes met, he jumped up and ran towards me.

The priest repeated: "Did you see your sister?"

"Yes."

"Then be grateful for that, and you may return in a week—but no sooner."

I knew it would be a long week. The dream world had taken me to a place where previous fragmented dreams had left me frustrated.

When she saw me, Nefer-bithia was alarmed by my pallor. "You've lost weight and look sick," she said, ushering me to the dinner table and fetching meat and beer.

After I had eaten only a small amount for fear of being sick, she asked me about the experience.

I told her what had happened, and added, "It was real, Bith. I was there. I could touch the earth, smell the wheat and river silt. I saw a black insect crawling up a stem close to my nose. I touched the reeds."

"And your sister?"

"I touched her too and she held me."

"Then why are you frowning, my love?"

I took another drink of beer. "Because my memory is already fading. It was real while I was in the temple, but with each passing minute I find the details recede into a fog."

"Then write it down," she said.

Of course! My Bith was always so practical and smart. I would write down as much of what had happened and I would prepare myself for when I returned. Despite my anxiety, I would go straight back to the time when Laret had disappeared.

Last time, I had ignored the voice from the future that told me not to leave her alone. Next time, I would remember. I would change the past.

I wrote then and took more than a day until I was content that I'd got down as much as I could.

"How is Sadhu doing?" I asked my wife when I saw the boy studying in the courtyard.

"He tries hard," she said. "You'll soon have an assistant scribe—that is, so long as you need him to write that there's muck on the duck or a stone on the throne."

I laughed.

"He does remind me of you," Nefer-bithia said. "A young boy trying to better himself, prove that he is something special and worthy."

I raised my eyebrows.

She said, "You are special. I never told you that I would secretly watch you at your studies. I fell in love with you that first week you came."

"Don't fall in love with Sadhu," I said, faking concern.

"Lucky for you, he's too young," she said, smiling. "Also, you had a better teacher. My father spent a lot of time ensuring you would be as good as he was."

"I will teach the boy," I said. "And anyway, I may not be your father, but I have my own attributes."

"Hmm," she said. "Having a pretty face is not a legal attribute, my lord."

"I'll teach him," I said again. "I'll teach him the law as I see it."

I was about to call the boy to my study when a knock came at the courtyard door.

Paneb opened it and then came to tell me that a messenger was here.

"With what message and from whom?" I asked.

"He won't speak to me, my lord. Only you."

"Formal?"

"I think so. He carries an official scroll."

I made the man wait until I'd dressed in my noble's robes. It was unseemly to be seen in anything else outside my home. Only my family, staff and friends would see me without my magistrate's robe.

When I was prepared, the visitor was shown into my office where he presented me with a scroll. I didn't immediately recognize the blue seal, and read the name: Lord Userhat, Nomarch of Elephantine. So, the messenger had travelled far. Elephantine was in the first nome, the furthest south before the land of Kush.

I'd been there once before as the assistant of Lord Khety.

I opened the papyrus and read.

The nomarch was requesting my presence. He used a lot of words, praising me and my adopted father, and our ability as magistrates. He said that there was a legal case that required my skills and I should prepare to travel immediately.

Immediately?

I was mere days away from revisiting the dream temple and finding my sister there. Also, despite the extreme flattery of the letter, I felt no inclination to make the trip.

I wrote a short reply expressing my gratitude at the honour but declining. As my excuse, I used the demand for my work here and an alleged shortage of staff.

While I doubted the messenger could read the papyrus, I was sure he could read my reaction.

After he had left, Nefer-bithia asked me about the message. When I told her she was astounded.

"It would have paid handsomely, my husband!" she said. "This could have been the breakthrough we needed. This could have been our road to upper nobility."

"I'm sorry," I said. "I couldn't do it."

"Your sister?"

"I need to finish what I started. Once I have found her again, I promise I will not turn away another opportunity."

She nodded and smiled. "Don't worry," she said. "If I judge your letter correctly, Nomarch Userhat of Elephantine won't accept no for an answer. That messenger will be back."

And as usual she was right.

TEN

I started teaching Sadhu by asking him about the law. "What is it?" I asked.

"The Law of the Two Lands," he said, which was no answer, but seeing my face, he then added: "Rules?"

"All right, but what is it in essence? Why do we have these rules?"

"To punish people who do not follow them."

"Is that what you believe?" I said, dismayed.

"That's certainly how it seems, my lord."

I nodded. There were times in my youth when I saw the inequity of the law, and it was something I abhorred. It made me reflect on the message from the Nomarch of Elephantine and the flattery he'd used about my skill as a judge.

I said, "There are three sets of rules, Sadhu."

He looked at me wide-eyed.

"You mentioned the Law of the Two Lands. This is the law of man, the laws as decreed by Pharaoh. And as such these rules can change. The second is the Law of Ma-at"—Sadhu's head bobbed with realization. Of course he'd known that, he just hadn't associated it with the law of the land—"which is about the balance of the universe, is it not?"

"Nature?" he asked.

"The law of nature, which is distinct from the final set of rules: the Law of Ra."

Now he shook his head. It was an old expression that few used these days and few understood, since the pharaoh's laws were supposed to be based on the old laws.

I said, "The Law of Ra is the original morality. It is the determination of what is right and what is wrong and has been preordained by the gods themselves."

"But the pharaoh is the living god, the Follower of Horus."

I didn't want to get into that debate because it questioned His divinity since I did not agree with all of His laws. Instead I continued: "The original morality is what is contained within your heart. Your task is to come back to me within two days and recite those laws."

"But where shall I look, master?"

"Within your heart."

After he'd left I found myself remembering the tuition that Nefer-bithia's father had given me. He believed more in practical experience than debate and didn't like me challenging his beliefs. Not at first anyway.

Later, after sunset prayers, I was talking to Paneb about those early days. He loved to rib me for my naivety—as well as my dirty sandals.

I'd been searching for the Law of Ra when I ran a message to a young scribe in a beautiful white tunic and scarf with gold symbols. When he offered me more than I'd ever been paid before, I handed it back.

"Payment if you can tell me about the Law of Ra," I said.

"You are cute," he said, laughing effeminately. "Has anyone told you, you look like Tutankhamen when he was your age? What, you are a bit younger, I think?"

I shook my head. "The Law of Ra, please, my lord."

"It's an old expression. I can't imagine where you heard it. The city magistrate is the man who executes the law. We call it the Law of the Two Lands these days. Run me a message tomorrow and I will tell you more." He raised his eyebrows and smiled girlishly. "No charge."

I thanked him and scurried out of the royal enclosure. I hadn't needed the scribe to tell me more, I knew exactly who the magistrate was: the man with the shaven head and purple sash who sat under an awning. A crowd always gathered when the magistrate was sitting, and I had assumed he was just another priest telling his news from the gods or from far-flung cities.

I spotted the magistrate's flag amidst a crowd close to the wharf. I squeezed through until I was able to squat at the front of the semicircle. The magistrate squinted over his hooked nose at two men who stood before him. Two soldiers stood either side of the magistrate and a slave with an ostrich feather fan stood behind.

I tried to make sense of what was being said. First one man spoke, and he seemed to be the manager of a grain store. He accused the other man of stealing from the store. He called for a boy who passed a papyrus roll to the magistrate.

"See," the manager said, "the records are thorough. It shows all the grain recorded both in and out. And yet two sacks are missing. Nekbhet has taken those sacks for his personal use."

The other man shook his head violently but didn't speak until the magistrate pointed a golden rod towards him.

"I am Nekbhet. I am the record keeper of the grain store. I swear, my lord, that I did not take the sacks. I was the one who discovered the discrepancy."

The manager indicated he wanted to speak and the rod was waved towards him. "Nekbhet is the only one with access to the store, the only one with opportunity to remove the sacks."

The magistrate asked, "And what would his motive be?"

I noticed the manager started to scoff but managed to suppress it. "Either for food or to sell, my lord."

The rod swung to the other man. Nekbhet said, "I did not take them. If I planned to steal the grain, I would have falsified the records!"

The crowd took a collective intake of breath and began to mutter. Someone close to me said, "An admission of guilt."

The magistrate stood. "Falsification of documents is a capital offence!"

Nekbhet quaked and started to speak. One of the soldiers lunged forward, his spear levelled at the accused's chest.

"Halt!" The magistrate raised the golden rod. "I have yet to rule on this!" When everyone quieted, he waved at the soldiers and had them part the crowd. "I want to see the grain store." He began to stride away from his chair and porch.

I was swept along by the enthusiastic mob. They stopped suddenly by a circular wall with spiral steps which descended into the dark, and I saw the manager lead the way into the depths. In my effort to see, I leaned over the side. A sudden surge from behind sent me over the wall and I landed heavily on the steps. I rolled and found myself at the feet of the magistrate. A spear immediately prodded my side and a soldier shouted.

As I stood, my eyes met the magistrate's and saw a kindly man. It wasn't until much later that I learned Lord Khety had a terrible temper, especially when he was drunk.

With the spotlight on me I blurted something that had troubled me.

"The accused is innocent."

The soldier with the spear prodded me again. "Get out, urchin!"

"No!" Lord Khety raised his hand and bent so that his ear was close to my mouth. "What do you know?"

"That the accused didn't do it, my lord," I whispered.

"How?"

"I read it in his face, my lord."

"And what do you read in mine?" he said menacingly, gripping my shoulders.

I smiled at his act. "An honest man, who would rather listen to me than see me harmed."

"That is true." Lord Khety beckoned me close and asked me to whisper what I'd seen in the other man's face.

"My lord, the manager is hiding something. I think perhaps he knows where the grain sacks are."

The magistrate stood and motioned to the guards. "Take us to the manager's house."

They remounted the steps and the crowd once more hushed as the magistrate was led to a large house nearby. The accused and the manager were told to kneel while one soldier entered. After a few minutes, the magistrate also entered. There was no shelter in the courtyard at the front of the grain manager's house but no one moved away, too desperate to see the outcome of the case. After ten minutes, the magistrate emerged, followed by the soldier carrying a sack under each arm.

I'd been right, and as payment had asked Lord Khety to teach me about the law.

Later, after I'd been washed and shaved by Paneb, Lord Khety had asked me questions.

"So, you can tell when someone is being truthful. A magistrate is required to have this skill, to judge the guilty from the innocent, and it is something I... it is a talent I was born with. You want to learn the law, my boy, so be it. You will learn by being my assistant. Is that agreed?"

I'd nodded enthusiastically. "You won't regret it, my lord."

"I regret it already," he'd said.

Paneb remembered this story well and said his master constantly questioned his judgement in those early days. People must have thought him crazy, taking on a peasant boy as an assistant.

Paneb laughed. "I certainly did. But then people didn't talk because once you were presentable, you didn't have the look of a peasant."

"Nor you the look of a slave," I said. I rarely drank with him, but tonight we shared beer.

He said, "Do you remember my test?"

"I remember you took my precious amulet!"

He took a swig of beer. "It was reasonable. I thought you'd stolen it. After all, what would an urchin be doing with a silver Eye of Horus?"

I'd been given it by the same unusual noble I'd met who'd told me about the Law of Ra, but Paneb said he'd keep it until he knew the truth.

"You kept it for years," I grumbled, because it was the one thing I'd never forgiven him for. It wasn't the physical removal, it was the lack of trust.

He ignored me. "My test was to tell you two stories, one of which was true and one of which was false. I wanted to see if you could really tell."

"I remember," I said, finishing my drink and thinking that was the end of it.

"Now I will tell you two stories and I want you to tell me which of them is the truth. Understand?" he said, using the same words he'd used all that time ago.

I thought that was the end of it, but he continued, enjoying the reminiscence. "I told you that I had lost part of my ear as punishment for stealing bread as a teenager."

I nodded.

"My second story," he said, "was that I was sold into slavery as a baby, because my mother died in childbirth."

I nodded again.

He said, "You questioned whether my parents had been slaves, which clearly they could not have been, but I suppose I hesitated at the surprise question. When I said no, you then asked what their jobs had been."

I got another beer and drank it down.

Paneb kept on talking. "It was clever of you to ask questions. You then said that the second story had part of a lie. You said my parents had both been slaves so I hadn't been sold; I'd been born into slavery. However, you believed the part about my mother dying in childbirth was true."

"You never told me whether I was right," I said, finishing the drink.

He laughed. "I gave you the amulet back, didn't I?"

"Eventually," I said, starting to feel the effect of the beer.

He shook my hand then, something he'd never done, nor would have expected me to return. But I did.

I went to bed hoping that the beer would stop the dreams. Since returning from the temple I'd had nightmares every night. I was still running around the city looking for Laret and crashing into walls, finding myself in blind alleys.

Two more days and I could return.

ELEVEN

I held an uninspiring court the following day and blamed a hangover for my lack of enthusiasm.

Later, Sadhu came to my study. "You tasked me with reciting the Law of Ra, master," he said.

I tore my eyes away from writing up my cases from my other assistant's bad notes.

Sadhu continued: "You gave me a big clue when you told me to look within my heart. The laws can be implied from the Book of Gates, the instructions for the deceased when imploring the Foremost of the Westerners, Lord of Abydos, Lord of Djedu—"

"Lord Osiris," I said, cutting him short.

"Yes, Lord Osiris," he said, as though the name were challenging to pronounce. "In essence, it is the weight of the heart."

Then he said something that astounded me for such a young man, something I had taken years to understand. He said, "The weighing of the heart by Anubis is figurative, isn't it?"

"It must be as light as a feather."

"But the Foremost of the... Great Lord Osiris must know. The deceased has journeyed through the gates and faced the challenges. He has defeated the demons because he has a good heart. He has lived by the Law of Ra."

I clapped my hands and the sound made the poor boy jump. But when he saw my grin, he relaxed.

"Well done. Now tell me the laws," I said, suddenly serious again.

He ran through them all from memory: "I have not committed sin. I have not committed robbery with violence. I have not committed theft—"

"Stop there," I said. "Interesting that theft and robbery are different. We'll come back to that, however, please continue."

"I have not cursed any god. I have not shut my ears to the words of truth. I am not violent. I have killed no man." He continued, and I stopped him now and again asking him to think rather than have me explain.

When he'd finished, I said, "So those make up the Law of Ra?"

"Yes, my lord."

"Let's go back to robbery and theft. The robbery refers to theft from a person. It appears to be acceptable without violence."

He thought for a moment. "Is this where the Law of the Two Lands comes in?"

"Yes," I said, "but it also shows the flaw in the rules, because no type of theft can be acceptable, can it, Sadhu?"

The young man lowered his head, clearly reflecting on his own case.

"It's all right," I said. "You have not committed your soul to the Devourer. Mistakes can be made in life, and the important thing is the symbolism, not the words. I'll tell you why. Remember the promise that you have not killed a man?"

"Yes, master."

"It should be that you have not killed a man righteously. Otherwise no soldier could find his way to the Field of Reeds, could he?"

"No, master."

"So what is the Law of Ra?"

"Justice and truth?"

I nodded. "The feather on the scales is clever symbolism, Sadhu. It represents *ma-at* as balance rather than the law of nature but those laws are intertwined with justice and truth of the law of the gods."

He thought and finally nodded appreciation.

I said, "If you should ever become a magistrate, you will find the Book of Gates is a good foundation for your judgements, but they are again man's interpretation of what makes a good and weightless heart."

"And this is what all magistrates do?" he asked as I indicated the lesson was over.

"No," I said. "I'm afraid I may be quite unique." In truth, the word unorthodox would have been more fitting.

TWELVE

On the morning Paneb and I were preparing for our journey back to the dream temple, a young noble appeared at my door.

He was furtive and I immediately took a dislike to the stranger. From his clothes I judged that he'd come from one of the big northern cities, maybe Memphis or Heliopolis.

"Tell him I have answered the Nomarch of Elephantine's request. I am not available."

The slave at my door said, "This gentleman says it is most urgent and secret that he speak with you, master."

I took another glance at the young man below before turning back and picking up my silver amulet. I hoped that holding it in the dream temple would take me back to the right time so I could relive my past and find my sister.

"Send him away. Tell him I will be busy for three days. Perhaps after that, if his message is still urgent, then I will see him."

On the road to the temple, I thought about the visitor I'd refused. The nomarch had sent a messenger and then a lower official. Who would be next? The nomarch himself? Maybe there was change in the wind.

"What are you chuckling for?" Paneb asked.

"Happy," I said, gripping the amulet. "Just happy."

"No more than three days, my lord," the priest said, recognizing me when I arrived. I accepted and Paneb found his spot under the sycamore tree.

I was shown to the same cot I'd been given before and hungrily drank the milk before lying down and closing my eyes.

"It's not working," I said after a long time of listening to my heartbeat and imagining lights swirling in my mind's eye.

"You've been asleep for many hours," a girl whispered.

"But I have not dreamed!"

"You surely have," she said.

Could I have been asleep? Could I have been looking for my sister but not remembered my dream? Disaster!

"More," I insisted. "Give me a stronger potion."

A second girl appeared above me and I was given a bowl of bitter milk. Again I gulped it down and closed my eyes.

Remember, I told myself. Stop it happening and change the past. I gripped my amulet. I had a good idea of where to find Laret and I would remember.

The priest came into view above me and said, "Focus on my prayers, my lord. Don't force your dream. Let the dream world come to you."

I relaxed and listened to his chant and let the incense enter my nostrils and fill my lungs. There, the smoke danced like...

I was suddenly transported back to the City of a Thousand Gates. I could hear chanting and music—the tinkling bells of religious musicians and the sound of singing and clapping. People streamed in processions led by priests. The air was filled with curling smoke and intoxicating smells.

I gripped something that had been in my hand but my hand was empty. What had been there? What had I been holding? Did it tell me where to find my sister? My head was groggy from tiredness and anxiety. I couldn't think and the incense was making it worse.

There was a pylon in front of me, a giant stone gate proclaiming some sort of story to the gods, I'd been told. They were built by pharaohs and important people, although I didn't understand why.

I felt my legs carrying me towards it but had to stop as a procession of priests with flowing white gowns and shaven heads crossed my path. They carried the god Amun aloft in a litter. Behind were the musicians I'd heard and then the noisy crowds.

I could not wait here. I felt compelled to move forward as though a force could draw me towards Laret. Forcing my way through the body of people, I found myself swallowed by another crowd, this one worshipping Tefnut. Followers imitated lions with their growls and hand movements. I was swept along with musicians clicking bone castanets and singing.

When I could, I ducked between and through the snake of people only to find another crowd following Khnum, the god responsible for the Nile inundation. It was like a bad dream. I was no longer running blindly through city alleys, I was trapped amid endless processions.

Were they even real? Would I now wake up?

And then I briefly saw a blue flash—the blue of another baker's gown standing out against the mainly white and ochre colours of the worshipers.

"Laret!"

I pushed my way through more people and found myself swept towards a temple. Inside, the priests were performing a ceremony and guards posted outside stopped people gaining access.

I saw the blue gown briefly again and worked my way in her direction, along the temple wall, and reached the front of the crowd. To my horror I realized the soldier was not just a guard. He was the captain.

Bile leapt to my throat and I found myself heading for the man, forcing my way against the flow of people. Ahead, I could hear the soldier shouting orders to his men, trying to corral the good-natured masses, preventing them from entering the temple. The crowds didn't seem to care, for they sang and clapped, and even when one of their number was struck with a stick, it seemed to increase the fervour of their celebration.

Then, through the crowd, on the far side of the soldiers, I saw my sister again.

"Laret!" I called, but my little voice was lost in the noise of a hundred people. The bodies moved closer, and looking through a gap, I couldn't make sense of what I saw.

Weak though she was, Laret was running towards the soldier; raised in her hand was a copper grappling hook. While the soldiers were distracted, she lunged at the man who had brought her to this city, slashing at his face.

In a swift motion, the soldier pulled his short sword, twisted and plunged it deep into her belly. As she fell, the soldier kicked her away and waved to one of his men. I forced my legs to move, although no sooner had I taken two steps than a soldier drove me back.

"No entry to the temple!"

Blind with distress, I blinked tears from my eyes and pushed forward. My reward was a blow to the head from the soldier's stick.

I could no longer see her body. "Laret!" I cried, and I pushed back through the throng, circling the temple entrance to get closer to where she had fallen.

When I reached the point, the blood on the ground was already vanishing under trampling feet. The granite-faced soldier was still there, although his bloodied hand was pressed to his cheek, staunching the flow from a gash caused by the grappling hook. Then I saw another soldier carrying a body—Laret's body. The crowd parted to let him pass and then closed ranks as though he had never been.

I elbowed my way after the soldier, desperately trying to gauge which way he'd gone. The tears had dried, replaced by a fear for my lovely sister that gripped my throat.

Finally, I was through the crowds and found myself on the merchants' quay. The water had risen almost to the level of the stone blocks. The soldier was at the end by the flooded reeds. He looked at something in the water, adjusted his tunic and turned.

I shoulder-charged him with the cry of a wild hawk. I felt the impact and then I was spinning, tumbling into the river. When I came up, gasping, the soldier glowered at me from the bank before spitting a curse and hurrying away.

My sister lay face down in the water. Pulling her towards me, I rolled her over. Her eyes had the gaze of the dead, and the howl that came up from my stomach scared geese into flight.

Shaking, I tried to calm myself. I knew I had to get her out of the water quickly in case her blood attracted a crocodile. So I tugged her through the reeds, but the silt made me slip and the reeds seemed to be trying to drag her the other way.

I got her to the bank but could not lift her over. I called for help but the handful of people within earshot ignored my pleas. Climbing out, I ran to the nearest man.

The man waved me away. The next listened to me briefly but then excused himself. After six more failed attempts, I collapsed. When I opened my eyes, I realized I was kneeling beside a shrine to Het. The irony of it made me scream.

I picked up a stone and threw it. With a puff of sand it disintegrated, leaving but a smudge on the red granite shrine.

"No!" I yelled, and with all my might I picked up a larger rock and charged. It thudded against the granite and fell from my hands and struck my shin as it fell. Enraged, I yelled again and struck the shrine with my fists.

"It should be me!" I cried. "I'm the one who did wrong. I'm the one you should take!"

I continued to pound and shout at the stone until a hand touched my shoulder.

A kindly voice said, "You'll damage your hands if you continue much more."

Tears blurred my eyes but eventually I focused on the man. He was an elder, upper class from the look of his tunic.

The man smiled kindly. "What's wrong?"

"My sister…" My voice caught, and suddenly the rage I'd felt melted into sobs.

"Sit down," the elder said, and he eased me to the floor. With his hand still on my shoulder, he continued to talk softly until the sobbing subsided. "Now tell me what is so terrible that you wish to anger the gods, my child."

"They are already angry with me, my lord."

"Perhaps, but why anger them further… unless your life is over and your ba longs for the Devourer."

I studied the noble. He had a white tunic in a style different from the other nobles I had seen. He wore a scarf with gold symbols, the writing of the gods. His hair was shaved except for a ponytail on one side. I told the man my story, that my sister now lay dead in the river, killed by the soldier who had taken her.

The noble didn't question the story, just said, "I'll help you. We must be quick."

I hurried back to the reeds by the merchants' quay with the noble following at a swift pace. When I arrived, my legs gave way. I sank to my knees and wailed. Through my tears I sobbed, "She's gone and her soul is lost. Anyone who drowns will not find the Field of Reeds in the afterlife!"

The noble placed his hand on my shoulder. "Was she beautiful but also good?"

"Yes." I looked up at the man, unsure why he asked. "She was the best sister… looked after me since the plague took our mother."

"Take a good look. There is no sign of her, no sign her body was taken by a crocodile. No sign an animal has dragged her body out."

"No…"

"Then I think the gods have taken her. Sometimes it is not only the ba that ascends to Heaven. In special cases, when the gods so choose, the body may also leave this world."

"You think?" I stood. "You really think she is with the gods?"

"What was her name?"

"Laret."

"Come, I will walk you to a temple and you should talk to her. Tell her you will be all right and that you will think of her every day and attend to her should she need anything." He steered me away from the river, but instead of heading for the main temple—of the god Amun, he led the way to the small temple of Isis.

"What about the soldier?" I asked as the noble bid farewell. "What about the man who killed her?"

"You know about the law?"

I said, "I know about ma-at."

"Well, there is ma-at," he said, "but that is really the harmony and balance of the world. No, I mean the Law of Ra." He bowed his head in thought and then said, "A good man has nothing to fear of the gods or the law. A man who has spilled Egyptian blood should beware both." He nodded as though his words meant something more to him.

After that, he gave me the silver amulet and said, "Your face has been opened. Be true to your heart and the gods will be true to you."

THIRTEEN

After rushing home from the dream temple, I wrote up my story. I had blocked so much from my memory that, despite my sorrow, I was relieved that the veil had been lifted.

I'd been amazed to find that I hadn't been the full three days, despite the time it took to enter the dream world and relive it.

"Are you happy?" Nefer-bithia asked.

I shook my head. "I learned that you cannot change the past in the dream world. Not really. But you can learn from it, and I am contented. I now recall the detail of what happened and must hold on to that memory of my sister. After all, despite my hatred of the captain, I learned that my sister had been chosen by the gods and she is in the Field of Reeds."

"Contented then?" she said.

"In a way. I mean, I don't need to go back to the dream temple. I know I can't save her and I will see her again one day."

"What about ambition? Are you now content with your life or do we still want to improve our status?"

"Of course we do," I said.

"Just checking, husband of mine." She had a little smile in her eyes.

"Why? What are you up to, Bith?"

"The messenger returned."

"Not the nomarch himself?"

"No, the messenger, and—please forgive me, but I took the liberty of reading the scroll." She suddenly had it in her hand.

"You did what?" I barked, and then I laughed at my pretence. We had no secrets, my wife and I. She was my equal, my other half. "What does it say?"

"Read it."

I unrolled the papyrus sheet and hastily read through the same obsequious words that the nomarch had written before. But this time he named a significant price.

"Enough money to buy a better house in a better nome," Nefer-bithia said.

"More!" I exclaimed. "Possibly enough to buy a nome. But he insists that I leave right away, and the message arrived how long ago?"

Now she laughed. "I've already packed your bags, my love."

A higher noble would have undoubtedly travelled by litter, if not a royal barge, but that would have to come after this job.

I took Paneb and the young man Sadhu, who had already surpassed his senior with his writing skills. Accompanied by the messenger, we went to the quay and I paid for passage south.

The journey would take three and a half days. If the pilot had been willing to sail by night we would have arrived much sooner, but he could not be persuaded since there was no moon and he feared robbers. Larger boats travelled with armed guards, but none had available space at short notice. Paneb tried to insist that he could defend us but the pilot was taking no risks. So for the three nights that we moored, we stopped at guarded town quays along with many other small boats.

On the first night we stopped at Dendera. We'd been sharing our ride with a group of Hathor acolytes on a pilgrimage to the giant temple dedicated to her. They disembarked when we first docked and our pilot informed me that he'd be picking them up on his return journey.

However, it wasn't all good news. I was fretting because of our slow progress and asked Paneb to investigate whether we could buy horses to complete the rest of the journey. He spent half the night looking and in the morning said he couldn't buy a horse but plenty were willing to sell him donkeys at twice the going rate.

We continued by boat.

I spent the days talking about the law, educating Sadhu, who was like a sponge to the knowledge.

I told him about the two philosophies we called the Wisdom Texts and instructed that he should learn them by rote as I had once been told by the old Lord Khety, my teacher.

The first was Ptahhotep's dealing with advancement in life. It instructed the pupil to hold his tongue, to listen carefully before speaking, to put forward logical arguments and stay cool and calm. It also provided the rules of etiquette that a young man must know if he was to advance through the ranks of society.

I found his most powerful tenet to be: the power of truth and justice is that they endure.

"The Law of Ra," I concluded.

"What does he mean by *Learn from the ignorant as well as the learned man*, master?" Sadhu asked me.

"I take it to mean that all situations provide learning opportunities. However, you should also be wary that the teacher may not know everything."

"Surely *you* do!"

He was being serious, and I caught Paneb smirking as he listened in. I frowned at him and then laughed. "Dear boy, I know far from everything. Only the gods can know how the universe truly works and what the future holds. I am a mere mortal—and a flawed one at that."

Paneb leaned in. "Lord Khety is humble."

Sadhu nodded. "One of the wisdoms, am I right?"

"Yes," I said. "Do not let your heart become swollen with pride."

"Why?"

"Because a proud man can be a fool. A fool to others and a fool to himself."

"I will learn and follow this guidance, master. And the second philosophical text?"

"Were the words of Pharaoh Kheti," I said, "who focused more on judgement. Therefore it is a good foundation for the study of justice."

I recited the philosophy and my student asked good questions. My favourite section was about *The Judges who give judgement on the downtrodden* and the phrase *Where these judges are concerned, a lifetime lasts but a single hour.*

Sadhu said, "What is time, master?"

"I wish I knew," I replied. "I have noticed that it can run at different speeds, sometimes fast and sometimes interminably slowly. I have also experienced travel back in time—"

"Master?"

"You are too young," I said, thinking of the dream temple and powerful milk drink that aided my journey. "One day you may be able to have the same experience. You cannot change the past but you can relive it."

He nodded as though I had explained, although, in truth, I didn't understand.

I said, "But the point is that the gods live in a realm where they have existed forever, and so our short lives are a mere blink of their eyes. Like an ant's life is this"—I clicked my fingers—"to you and I."

Sadhu gawped when he saw the mountain where Horus had been born and beneath which many pharaohs had been buried.

I could have told my young assistant stories about the necropolis we called the Great Field, but he was too young and my knowledge too damaging. Sadhu had never seen Waset and the City of a Thousand Gates before and gawped as we sailed past the great temples on either side of the river. It was also the busiest part of the journey, with boats docking and launching and crossing our path.

We saw royal barges and rowing boats for soldiers.

Then after the great city we passed through a stretch of land where peasants scratched a living. This should have been a time of harvest with the villagers out in their fields, but instead of abundance, I saw ruin.

I saw crops burned and occasional huts destroyed.

Almost a day's walk south, I asked the pilot to pull over to the bank.

"There's nothing here, my lord," he said with a deep frown.

"Give me half an hour," I said. "We'll still make Heirakonpolis before nightfall and I'll make it worth your while." With this, Paneb tossed him a small purse and the pilot quickly pulled over to the bank.

Without my slave or assistant, I jumped ashore and crossed marshy land heavy with rushes and then on into a field. Some peasants were working there, harvesting wheat. But not many because of the damage to the crop. I kept going until I reached a cluster of huts: the centre of a village.

Half were knocked down, the rest were being rebuilt.

This was where I'd grown up, where I'd lost my mother to the plague, my father to a better life and my sister to a soldier.

An old man watched me approach and left the hut he was thatching. He bowed his head as I neared.

"My lord, you honour us," he said in his uncivilized, harsh country accent.

I gave the name of the matriarch of the village and he shook his head.

"Dead long ago," he said, and then he studied me long and hard. "Do I know you, my lord?"

"I don't think so," I said. "What is your name?"

"Nabetu, my lord."

I almost choked but managed to mask my shock. This was my cousin; the older boy who had never been nice to me. He couldn't have been more than thirty and yet looked ancient. Deep worry lines scarred his face.

He waited, wondering what I was doing there, I suppose.

"What happened?" I asked. "The crops, the village...?"

"Soldiers. They swept through here a few days ago." He took a long breath. "Most of us hid from them. We'd heard they were coming and took to the hills. Most of those who stayed were mown down." I knew he would have seen a lot of hardship in his life, a lot of death, but this seemed to have shocked him to the core.

"Why?"

He shook his head. "Perhaps we are the new Ibru. Perhaps Pharaoh thinks we are vermin to be eradicated."

I shook my head. "That cannot be true. You have Egyptian blood. You are his people."

"Then how do you explain this?" Nabetu swept his hand around, illustrating the ruined land. "We have little to harvest now, and within a few weeks we will have nothing. How can we survive?"

I looked around. The hut where Laret and I had slept was gone. I could barely remember the hardship and hunger. This was literally a different life.

My cousin was studying me. Despite his troubles he said, "Can I get you food or water, my lord?"

I smiled at his generosity. "That's kind," I said, "But I have this for you." I removed a silver bracelet and handed it to him. It wasn't worth a great deal to me. However, it could probably feed a man and his family for a week. I hadn't talked to Nefer-bithia about how much I would spend while away. I could give the villagers more later. After all, the Nomarch of Elephantine had promised great wealth and I was certain my wife would understand.

I left Nabetu then, bewildered but grateful. He was downtrodden, and I was sure that my gesture had lightened my heart in the eyes of the gods.

The pilot was relieved to see me return so soon, and we moored at Heirakonpolis before evening prayers.

Again I left the boat, but this time Paneb and Sadhu came with me. I visited the temple of Horus and prayed for all the villagers before we found an inn and ate a hearty meal.

I made sure that Sadhu drank only one cup of beer, although Paneb drank more than enough for all three of us, saying that he needed to forget the boat and the fact we would be boarding again in the morning.

I hadn't realized that he hated sailing so much, and within a short time of setting sail he was leaning over the side emptying his stomach of our evening's meal. I suspect it was the beer but he insisted the sickness was due to the unnatural motion of the boat.

The following morning, I had a pebble in my pocket and handed it to Sadhu.

"Throw it into the water," I instructed.

He tossed the stone and it plopped satisfyingly into the fast-flowing river.

"What does it mean?" I asked.

"Stones sink in water?" he wondered.

I tapped him on the side of the head.

"Ouch!"

"That's the same thing," I said.

He looked at me enquiringly, and I wondered if I'd looked so dumb when old Lord Khety had asked me the same thing.

I said, "Actions have consequences. Throwing the stone in the river causes a splash."

"And the action of hitting me hurts," he said, getting why I'd tapped him on the head.

"Or makes you think," I said. "But, yes, it's another consequence of an action. It's the law of nature—*ma-at*."

He nodded.

"Decisions," I said, "also have consequences. And therein lies the similarity between the laws of Ra and Ma-at. You can decide whether to throw the stone or not. Judgements we make are the same. It is therefore a great responsibility being a magistrate. Our judgements have consequences."

"Like what punishment a man should have."

"A guilty man, yes. But I was thinking more long term. You show people, through your judgements, what is fair and just and they will understand how to live their lives in the way the gods intended."

He nodded again. "And this is how all magistrates work?"

"I'm afraid not," I said. "No, my boy, I'm afraid not."

He did exceptionally well reciting the philosophies I'd told him yesterday, and when he finished he said he had one more question.

"Do you always carry a pebble in your pocket, master?"

"Only when I'm teaching my pupil about actions and consequences," I said, smiling.

"Good," he said, "Because I thought it a little odd."

His words were strangely relevant, because the next place we moored was undoubtedly a little odd. We overnighted at Nebet, where people worshipped Seth. I didn't have a problem with this, but one poor man on our boat almost had a fit, he was so afraid of the God of Chaos.

FOURTEEN

I'd been gone for more than a day when a man knocked on the courtyard door of my home in Akhmin. Of course, I wasn't there, and it wasn't until later that I found out about the visitor.

The lower noble was the man I'd sent away before revisiting the dream temple. I'd assumed he was from the Nomarch of Elephantine, but he wasn't connected in any way to that earlier messenger.

Nefer-bithia invited him into the courtyard and apologized for my absence. When the man became distressed, she offered him a seat and wine.

"If you leave your scroll with me," she said concerned, "I will ensure my husband reads it as soon as he returns."

The man took a long breath before speaking. "There is no scroll," he said. "What I have to pass on cannot be written down."

"Really?" my wife said, finding it hard to believe. "You make it sound mysterious."

"Not mysterious," he said. He gulped at his wine and cleared his throat. "A matter of life and death."

"Then tell me."

"I cannot."

Now she shook her head. "This doesn't make sense."

"I'm sorry, my lady, but I am under strict orders…"

"From…?"

"I cannot say." He leaned forward, more earnest now. "Tell me where he is so that I might get the message to him."

Again Bith shook her head. "You need give me good reason. For all I know, you could be someone my husband would not speak with. You need to convince me otherwise."

"It's a secret," he said.

"I gathered that. If that's the best—"

"Your husband may be who we are looking for."

My wife stood. "I think it's best that you leave. You are talking in circles and wasting my time."

The man didn't move, but raised his eyes to the heavens and then back. "Did Lord Khety tell you about an incident in the square—an incident in which a man was killed?"

Now she was interested. "Yes, he did."

"That man was looking for someone. In fact he wasn't the only man who has been searching for your husband."

"But my husband has been here in Akhmin. He's not been hiding. It's been no secret."

"Yes, but you see, we didn't know we were looking for him." He raised a hand to stop her saying he was talking in circles again. "We were looking for someone and believe your husband is that person."

She said, "The man who died in the square—the man from the group of players—was trying to attack my husband."

"No, my lady, he was trying to speak with him."

She shook her head.

"Perhaps this will persuade you?" The visitor pulled something from his tunic and held it in his closed fist until he seemed satisfied that no one else was looking.

In his palm was a ring.

She took it, turned it around and handed it back.

He hid it within his tunic and said, "I could only show this as a last resort. You understand?"

"I do." Her voice was quiet, lost in her throat.

"You know now why I cannot say too much. This is too sensitive."

"I think I understand."

"Then please tell me where I can find him. We need to know if he is the boy."

"Elephantine," she said. "You'll find him with the Nomarch of Elephantine."

FIFTEEN

When I'd been to Elephantine before as Lord Khety's assistant, we'd been on the northern border. I'd not seen the incredible city and religious centre that spread from the west to east bank, covering a myriad of islands.

We moored at the public quay with more ships than I'd seen here before. This was a major port, and the pilot explained that it was both a destination and transfer point. Just south of us were the hills through which the Great River cut. However, it was choked with boulders and a cataract and no boat could travel further.

Merchants transferred goods by caravan onto the road and to ships waiting at the port on the far side of the cataract. Of course, goods came back the other way and Elephantine had been strongly influenced by trade from foreign lands. Kush lay to the south, and I'd heard that a river ran to the Sea of Reeds to the east and brought goods from Punt.

After we'd settled the remainder of our fare, I followed the nomarch's messenger through the crowded, vibrant streets. Paneb walked one step behind on my right shoulder, Sadhu on my left.

The palace backed onto the river. A high-walled building at least three times the size of the administrative centre in Akhmin. There was a central tower, colourful flags, and I suspected the view over the Great River and the islands was spectacular.

We entered through impressive wooden doors and I found myself in a courtyard with a fountain that created a scattering of coloured light in the sunshine.

Sadhu seemed mesmerized by it, and I had to call him away. I was taken inside and through a hypostyle hall fronting the main building. Once inside this, I was told there was the Great Hall followed by offices ahead. Above were private rooms and accommodation.

There was a room to the left and we were shown into it and left alone. After waiting for an interminable time in an uncomfortably hot room, a lower official arrived and bowed low. Overly obsequious, he wrung his hands and apologized that the nomarch was too busy today. He ushered in drinks and food, and repeated his apology before scurrying away.

"What now?" Paneb asked me.

"We wait, but not here," I said. "It's airless and I'll not last another hour." So my men gathered food into a couple of bags and we marched out.

I said, "We look for lodgings." It was something we always did when we arrived in a new town and expected to stay over. First priority: find somewhere to sleep tonight. If we left it too late we might find ourselves on the street without a roof, and in a strange place I dreaded to think what might happen.

However, we were barely twenty paces through the hypostyle hall when the grovelling official was racing after us.

"My lord!" he called effeminately.

Paneb spat air. "If he complains about us taking the food, I'll run him through!"

But he wasn't complaining. He was overly apologetic again. "My lord, please, please, please come with me. I will show you to your rooms."

"Now that's more like it!" my slave muttered under his breath.

He looked down his nose at Paneb and Sadhu, and they realized they'd have to find accommodation elsewhere.

I left them in the hall and instructed them to meet me later. Then I was taken to a small block of rooms that were the guest quarters. From their position, I guessed these were far from the best, but when I saw the rooms, I knew that they were more sumptuous than any I'd slept in before.

The walls had gaily painted murals and hanging tapestries depicting strange lands and animals. The bed was wider than any I'd lain on in my life, and I was delighted that the pillows seemed to be fluffed up with goose down. I think I may have giggled, and I was relieved that there was no one there to witness my childish excitement.

After washing and changing, I lay on the bed and it moulded to my body. I closed my eyes, grinning. A knock at my door made me leap up, heart racing as though I'd done something wrong.

The young official at my door said, "My lord, Mayor Renseneb would be honoured by your presence if you can spare the time."

Of course, I had plenty of time since the nomarch wasn't available, so I followed the young man and we were soon in the administrative sector. However, I saw the mayor's office and we walked straight past it.

"Where are we going?" I asked.

"Mayor Renseneb's home, my lord. It's not much further."

The mayor's house was a fraction of the size of the palace but it was still four times bigger than my own in Akhmin.

Servants fussed around me and my feet were washed despite being clean, then I was shown to a section with a table, casual benches and shade from an arbour.

Before I took a seat, a voice boomed from behind me. "Lord Yan-Khety, my dear fellow. What a pleasure."

I turned to face a portly man with a red face and small eyes. From his stomach, I assessed that he liked the finer things in life. From his jewellery I could see he had considerable wealth.

For a moment I thought he looked familiar and then decided he had that kind of face, especially for a successful administrator.

"Mayor Renseneb," I said, bowing. "Your reputation comes before you." This wasn't true. I didn't know the man but saw that he was flattered by my greeting.

Servants brought meat, bread and wine and laid them on the table. A smart woman fussed behind them and then shooed the servants away.

"The Mistress of the House," the mayor said, which was a term for the wife of a high-class noble. I might have guessed she was his sister rather than his wife, they were so similar: the same height, same roundness and dripping with excessive jewellery. My eyes were particularly drawn to a silver necklace with jewels that rested on her ample bosom.

I bowed and she returned the gesture before leaving us alone.

Renseneb asked me to sit and eat, then he said, "Do you know why you are here?"

"At the request of the nomarch," I said. "He sent a message about a legal case that requires my skills."

"It will be a high court case. You will be the third judge with me and Nomarch Userhat. Have you served at high court before?"

"Never."

"Ever been present?"

"No, my lord."

"Ah," he said and smiled. "Interesting."

"May I enquire about the case?"

I saw the flicker of a frown before he smiled again. "That, my young man, will be for us to learn on the day of the case. It seems that my learned friend Userhat is keeping it hidden."

"You found good rooms?" I asked Paneb when I met him with Sadhu later.

"One room," my slave grumbled. "We have to share."

"But it's clean," Sadhu said, clearly less disappointed than Paneb.

We walked and soaked up the atmosphere of the town. I'd never been further south and suspected the border towns beyond, such as Buhen and Mehku, were strange indeed.

Unsure of how long we would be here, I purchased a gift for Nefer-bithia from a market—an unusual shiny vase that looked like it was made from broken water—before we found ourselves at the southern end of the town. The quay where we'd disembarked was close by and I spied a wide stone ramp that ran into the water.

I asked the quay master and was told this was where boats came out of the river. I thought he was joking but he was sincere.

"The royal barges," he explained. "When royalty want to travel up river from here, they get their whole flotilla picked up and carried to the far side."

Incredible. I figured that the pharaoh would travel to the edge of the Two Lands but couldn't imagine his great boats being picked up and carried for miles beyond the cataract.

We turned back and found different streets and different experiences. I noticed more soldiers around than I would have expected.

"Did you notice all the military when we sailed past Waset and the City of a Thousand Gates?" I asked my slave as we strolled.

"No, my lord," he said with a frown.

"It struck me as odd. Why so many soldiers there... and here?"

"Trouble?"

"Hopefully not. I've had enough experience of the army to last me a lifetime."

We kept walking, and when we stopped for a drink, Paneb said, "You haven't mentioned the last time we were here."

"Should I have?"

"We passed the ferry operation just before this town. It was the case you argued about with Lord Khety. And the time you said you'd leave."

"I've given it no thought," I lied. Over the years it had troubled me greatly. An unresolved case as far as I was concerned. However, at that moment I was more worried about the soldiers. Something was definitely going on, and I was sure that the destroyed villages were somehow linked.

Later, I'd forgotten about the soldiers and got caught up in the exotic atmosphere of Elephantine. And now I was thinking about my wife. Her smooth skin, her warmth. I felt her cool fingers caress my chest. And then I remembered where I was: in the guest rooms at the nomarch's palace!

I sat bolt upright then dashed to the drapes and pulled them aside.

The moonlight showed a girl sitting on my bed.

"Who in sweet Horus's name are you?"

"My lord," she said, smiling so that her teeth flashed in the pale light, "I am here for your pleasure."

I took a step towards her and found my eyes drifting down to her perfect small breasts. Apart from a skimpy skirt, she had nothing on except for a thin golden chain around her waist.

She tapped the bed. "I am sorry for alarming you, sir. Come back to bed and let me massage your back."

I shook my head. "I'm married."

She smiled, so I added, "I love my wife and have my first child on the way."

When she did not move, I clarified: "I would like you to leave now."

Her smile vanished, and when she spoke I heard the croak of sadness in her voice. "Do you not like me, sir?"

"That's not the point."

"I could arrange for a younger girl, a Nubian or perhaps a dwarf from Punt if that is your preference?"

"No," I said firmly.

"I'm sorry," she said, and now she sounded on the verge of tears. "I have failed."

"Failed?"

"I am here for your pleasure. My master will be annoyed if I cannot make his guest happy."

I sighed then edged back towards the bed. "You may stay, but you may talk to me until I fall asleep. Then you will retire to the bench and sleep on there."

Now the smile returned. "I can do that, my lord."

I climbed back into bed and indicated that she sit on the edge rather than lie beside me.

She said, "What shall I talk about?"

"Anything."

She spoke softly for a while and I learned she was in her early twenties and one of eighteen girls in the nomarch's harem, and she had been since the age of twelve. Her name was Tihepet, and I had to admit she was highly desirable. Had I been a single man I would surely have sampled her delights.

"What do you know about the mayor?" I asked.

"He visits from time to time."

"What's he like?"

"Young girls." She laughed mirthlessly. "I'm too old these days."

"I meant his personality," I clarified.

"Ah, well a bit mean-spirited. Very serious, a bit like you."

I felt like arguing about my own seriousness and telling her that I could enjoy myself, but I bit my tongue.

"Tell me about my host," I said.

"The nomarch... he doesn't visit us quite so often as he used to. He's... er... overweight with gout.

Grumpy, yes, that's what I'd say about his personality. And he has three sons."

"Oh?" I prompted, assuming she wanted to tell me about them, having raised the subject.

"The oldest had a mean streak. Could be rough with the girls."

"Had?"

"He's now in the army, a first officer in the Blacks."

I nodded. I'd been in the Black army—a period of my life that I'd rather forget, although I was a scribe, and as a first officer, the nomarch's son would be leading men into battle rather than translating and decoding enemy papers.

"The second son?"

"They say he is destined for the priesthood." She laughed with irony. "He may not have his brother's vicious streak but he likes two girls at a time."

"Two girls?" I said, genuinely surprised. "What can a man do with two girls?"

She looked at me like I was joking and then gave me a pitying look.

"Never mind," I said, feeling surprisingly embarrassed at my naivety. "What about the third son?"

"Wesperen? I don't know what he's destined for." She gave me a conspiratorial glance. "But he's weaker than his brothers. He doesn't come often. I think he prefers his beasts."

"His beasts?"

"A cheetah and lion cub. He has them on leads like they're a pair of dogs. He regularly visits Kush and comes back with unusual things."

"You don't like any of them," I said.

"Is it that obvious? But I have a job and it's a good life." She reached over, and I didn't recoil when she touched my arm. "You, on the other hand, are a nice man—an honourable man. What a shame you don't want to…" There was a question in her voice.

"I don't," I confirmed.

"But you don't sleep well, sir, do you?"

"Not often."

"Let me rub your back, and I promise that I will do nothing else."

I thought about it for a few beats before rolling over onto my front. My back did ache from sitting on an uncomfortable boat for three days and one bad night on board at Nebet.

I suppose I fell asleep quickly because I don't remember much of the massage. Perhaps it was being back in Elephantine, or more specifically my conversation with my slave about the ferry case, but very soon I began to dream.

SIXTEEN

The first time I had the dream was after my first day at Lord Khety's home. Paneb—although I had to call him by his proper name Hapuseneb in those days—had given me hand and back-aching work and I guess I had the same dream now because of my aches.

I dreamed I was a magistrate. I wore the gown of office pulled tightly around my shoulders and stood before a circle of spectators who screamed for justice.

In the centre stood the captain of the guard, the one who had taken and killed Laret. Anubis was there. The crowd stopped shouting and Anubis read the list of crimes the captain had committed, telling of how he had taken a young maiden on the pretence of taking her to be trained as a royal dancer. How he had abused her and disrespected her. How he had taken her life with a short sword and had her body thrown into the Nile.

The captain said nothing as the charges were read out, his granite face impassive. But his face was different because the gouge from Laret's hook had badly scarred him and the livid mark ran over an eye and twitched with guilt.

When Anubis finished, the crowd began to shout once more. Then they were no longer just people, but demons: the devourer, the bone-crusher, the serpent, the ba-eater, the beheader and the water-demon. They were all there, a morass of terrible creatures all eager for death.

I raised a hand and they fell silent. Then I invited the captain to speak, and as he defended himself, denying each charge, I shouted, "Liar!"

The defendant finished, to the derision of the baying demons.

I pronounced the death sentence and watched as the demons destroyed the guilty captain the way a hungry child might tear at a chicken carcass.

Although I was relieved that he had been punished but felt guilty myself for condemning him.

And then I was north of Elephantine about three years later.

The old Lord Khety was there and I felt guilty towards him now. I'd abandoned him and we'd argued. I hadn't been there when he'd died. I hadn't supported him in his final years.

I could see the damaged ferry-raft tethered at the water's edge. The Overseer of the Waterways waited for us to approach before stepping from beneath his sun shade and bowing a greeting.

The magistrate said quietly, "Is this the ferry?"

"It is, My Lord Khety. It is of basic construction, operated by a ferryman and his junior, who pull the raft across using a rope strung from bank to bank. As you can see, the ferry can comfortably take ten people, but on the day of the accident there were at least sixteen people on board."

"How many died?"

"Four passengers and the junior ferryman."

"How many bodies were retrieved?"

"Just one. The others are unaccounted for, swallowed by the torrent of the Great River—or worse…"

I said, "My lord, we should examine the ferry."

The magistrate looked disapprovingly at me for the interruption, but he just waved his hand to indicate we should go and see the raft. When we reached it, he stood on the bank and I climbed on board. I paced out the size and checked the construction.

The magistrate asked, "Are there other crossings close by?"

"This is the only raft ferry," the official said. "There are a number of small boats that operate along the bank here."

"And their prices?"

The overseer looked perplexed. "I do not think that is relevant. The ferryman is guilty of overfilling his craft. The guide rope was old and could not take the strain of the heavy raft in the fast-flowing waters. Please forgive my rudeness, My Lord Khety, but the case is straightforward, the ferryman is responsible and should be sentenced."

"Are you a judge now?" the magistrate bellowed, and I saw him wince afterwards with regret at the pain caused by the effort.

"No. I just thought—"

"Then don't think!"

I whispered, "My lord, we should see the guide rope."

The magistrate instructed the overseer to show us the rope that had once strung across the river.

"It is not here," the official responded.

The magistrate established that the rope had been taken away and disposed of. He insisted that a runner be sent to locate it and, while we waited in the shade erected by Paneb, the magistrate removed his wig and used a damp cloth to wipe cool his shaved head and neck.

"What do you think, Yani?" It was the first time the old man had called me by my familiar name.

"My lord?" I said, and my voice caught with emotion.

"What's going on here? I would like your opinion."

"I do not like the fact that the rope has been taken away. It is important in this case. And the overseer has not filled me with trust."

"Is that your prejudice talking or your logic?"

I thought for a moment and glanced over at the Overseer of the Waterways. The man looked worried. "My logic, I think. For the trial, I know it is not planned, but I suggest you ask the overseer to speak as well as the ferryman."

Before the magistrate commented, he pointed towards two sweating boys as they returned with the heavy coiled rope over their shoulders.

When it was laid before the magistrate, we examined it and found both ends cut through.

The magistrate called for the overseer to account for the cuts.

The official said, "To remove the rope we had to cut it free."

"But to see evidence that the rope snapped, I would need to see the frayed end."

The official spoke urgently to an assistant, who in turn spoke to others before returning and spoke to the overseer.

"We do not know where the frayed end is."

The magistrate shook his head. "That was key evidence and there is no explanation for cutting the end that was frayed if the rope was to be destroyed. Without this evidence I will not try this case." He waved to Paneb, who started to dismantle the sunshade.

"But..." the official said as he scurried after the magistrate who had begun to walk back to the town. "People died and their relatives need someone to atone for the murders!"

The magistrate stopped and, with his face close, gave the official a withering stare. He whispered, "Do not press me, for you may regret the outcome of further investigation."

The overseer stepped back, bowed and stood still as the magistrate and his entourage returned to the town.

"Tell me what you think happened here," the magistrate said to me as we packed to return home.

"I don't think there was ever a frayed end to that rope. I think it was deliberately cut and then removed so we wouldn't see it."

"Why?"

"I don't know, but a deliberate cut would mean someone intended for an incident and perhaps for the ferryman to be convicted. I would like to have asked the overseer if he was taking bribes. Perhaps the ferryman did not pay up?"

"I have no doubt the overseer is charging the operator—what I will call—a commission, but to challenge him in public without any evidence would have been a serious and unacceptable affront to his position. Of course, it could be one of the other operators..."

"Or the junior ferryman who had opportunity and whose motive may have been to take over the business."

"And yet he died."

"There is no evidence that he died, his body was not found."

"Interesting." The magistrate nodded and was deep in thought for the rest of the walk to the temporary accommodation.

"May I ask what you will pronounce, my lord? Will you say it was an accident and that the ferryman has no case to answer for?"

The magistrate studied me. "That depends on you—whether you are still intending to leave."

"My lord? I don't understand."

"I could keep the case open. If you stay with me, I will let you investigate further. You learned the Wisdom Texts by rote and you write as well as any scribe of your age. You have a natural talent and eye for justice, albeit naive at times, and to have you die by a spear in some foreign field would be a travesty."

"Are you saying I could be a magistrate one day? But I am low-born, my lord, I know I would never be accepted by society."

"I have thought about that. My plan is to either adopt you as a son or approve your marriage to my daughter, Nefer-bithia. Don't think I haven't seen the way you two look at one another!"

Never in my wildest imaginings did I see myself accepted into a higher class. After I caught my breath, I said, "You are too generous, my lord."

"No, I am a selfish old man who needs you. I need to pronounce my judgement now, so what is your answer. Will you stay?"

I bowed and raised my hands from my knees to show extreme respect. "Master, I have made up my mind and know my destiny lies in another direction." When I looked up, the magistrate had a tear in his eye.

"So you are bent upon revenge against this soldier. Is he still at the garrison in Waset?"

"Two years ago he left. A promotion, I heard, to head the fortress at the border town of Gaza. That is where I will go."

"You should learn to fight before you confront this man. Do not go to a common garrison; you are a good-looking boy and you know how soldiers can be!" Anyway, if you are to have any chance of survival in battle, you should go to the military academy in Memphis."

"But, master, that is for officers, and they will not take someone without good provenance."

"Is there nothing I can say to change your mind?"

I shook my head.

"Somehow I suspected not. Take this document to the military academy." The magistrate handed me a scroll, sealed with the mark of the chief magistrate of the Land of the Arch, the first nome. "With my word they will have no choice but to enrol you."

"Master." I repeated my bow, but the magistrate quickly strode from the courtyard and past Paneb, who now stood like a statue by the gate. He watched as I finished packing his shoulder bag.

"That is a bad omen, that is!" the slave said.

A cluster of sparrows fluttered frantically and inexplicably in one corner.

I stepped towards the gate. "I don't believe in omens."

"We have never seen eye to eye, young Yanhamu. You were born a village peasant. You are not noble or even of artisan stock. However, I have accepted your elevation above me without protest and I recognize that his lordship has seen you have a good heart. Be safe on your life journey. Remember his lordship and, when you have tired of the army, if you are still alive, come back and check on him. Will you do that?"

"I will."

The slave moved aside and let me step into the street.

"Boy!" he called, as I started to walk away, and he ran up beside me. "You may not believe in bad omens, but I do and you'll need something to ward them off." He pulled something from his tunic and held it out, closed inside his fist. He placed a small bag into my hand and for a moment held it there.

"I believe this belongs to an honest man," he said.

I opened the bag. Inside gleamed the unusual silver amulet: an eye inside a circle.

SEVENTEEN

When I stirred, the girl called Tihepet was still there, lying on the cushioned bench beyond the end of my bed.

"Don't be startled," she said.

"I forgot you were here. We didn't...?"

"No, sir, we didn't do anything. Thank you for not throwing me out."

I wrapped the sheet around me and got up. "You're welcome."

"Can I come again tonight?"

"I don't think that's sensible."

"But you slept well with me here. You dreamed, didn't you?"

I nodded although the dreams were now muddled in my mind, not like the dreams at the temple.

As though she were reading my thoughts, she said, "I can help your dreams and maybe then you can get them out of your system."

"What do you mean?"

"The older ladies use the white powder. I can bring you some tonight."

I thought about it. And when she said that her master would be cross if she didn't comfort me each night, then I agreed. Providing she accepted that nothing else would happen between us and that she covered her breasts.

After the girl had left, I went in search of my host. However before I could reach the Great Hall, I was intercepted by a junior official.

"The nomarch isn't available," he said. "I can call a breakfast for you, my lord. Is that your wish?"

"Is the mayor available?" I asked.

"I don't know," he said, but before he could say more, I turned on my heel and marched out. Outside the palace gates I found my slave and the boy waiting. If they were going to say something, they didn't. I must have had a frightful countenance as I marched past them.

They scurried behind me as I kept going all the way to the mayor's office.

"Where is the mayor?" I demanded.

"My lord…"

I stood with my hands on my hips, clenching and unclenching my teeth. What was going on? Why was I here? I'd been told this was urgent and yet it seemed anything but.

Then the effeminate official who had met us yesterday appeared.

"A thousand apologies, my lord," he said. "It seems matters have been delayed. Please…" He waved an arm indicating I should follow and then went through a door.

I hoped to see the mayor on the other side, but again I was met by a table of food.

"Please," the official whined, "enjoy the mayor's hospitality."

I could see the look on Paneb's face and guessed he hadn't eaten yet. The sight of the food also made my stomach rumble.

I closed my eyes and nodded and my slave and Sadhu took some bread and figs. I sat and poured a glass of goat's milk.

"Talk to me," I said to the official. "Why am I here and what's going on?"

The man, relieved at my relaxation, took a breath and half smiled.

"My lord, Nomarch Userhat requires you for a high court case."—I pretended this was news to me—"It's of severe importance and it will commence as soon as possible. However the mayor and nomarch have been called away on important business."

"And I'm expected to just keep on waiting?"

"I believe the case will commence tomorrow morning, my lord."

Although I had now calmed down, I still said, "Make sure it does, otherwise I will have to return home. And that would be a shame."

"I will pass the message on to the mayor," he said with a bow.

"What are we going to do, my lord?" Paneb asked me after the effeminate official had left us.

"Kill some more time."

"Another trinket for your wife?"

"She has enough trinkets," I said, realizing he was referring to the vase I had purchased. "No, we will travel down to where the ferry accident occurred. I was never content with the outcome."

Paneb rented a donkey for me and carried a shade to protect me from the sun.

"I heard that guests of the nomarch can expect young ladies," Paneb said quietly so that Sadhu couldn't overhear. Maybe he thought his conspiratorial tone would prompt a confession from me.

"No such luck," I said, not meeting his eye. "Who told you that?"

"I met a palace harem eunuch," he said. "In fact, he gave me an idea."

"An idea, Paneb?"

"An alternative job should a certain magistrate no longer require my services."

I laughed. "But you aren't a eunuch."

"Although I could be!" Now he chuckled. "Did you know that you still have the er... desire if you are castrated later in life? Not all eunuchs were snipped as children." He laughed again. "Know where I'm going with this?"

"No," I said, because I was, at that moment, distracted by the land on the west bank of the river. I saw beehives. Hundreds of them.

Paneb was still talking. "Well, with the desire, you can still do it. And it makes the girls happy."

"What?" I said, refocusing on my slave's mutterings.

He said, "It's a great job. The girls don't confess and the eunuchs certainly don't tell."

"And yet a eunuch told you!" I said, cocking my eyebrow at him.

He shrugged. "Well I believed him. He was too old now and had too much beer, so, yes I believed him, and all you need do is release me as your slave—"

"I'll tell you what," I said, "I'll go further. I'll even cut your balls off to help you on your way."

"I'll consider it," he said, as though I was being serious. "After all, there are few benefits working for you."

We stopped at the small town where the ferries ran to the east and found somewhere to rest.

At a bar serving fresh water, I watched people queuing and being transported to the other side. Fewer travellers came back the other way.

"One thing I didn't ask when we were here all those years ago," I said, "was where these people are going."

"To the villages and the honey farm over there?" Paneb suggested.

"No," I said, and waved the owner of the bar over. When I asked, he explained that the northern necropolis for the first nome was over there—a few miles walk through desert in the opposite direction to the honey farm.

I asked, "Do you remember the accident a few years ago?"

"Of course," the man said. "I was a boy at the time and my uncle died in that accident."

"I'm sorry," I said.

He must have seen something in my face because he asked, "How do you know?"

"I was the magistrate's assistant," I said. "The case has troubled me ever since."

"Troubled you?" the man said leaning forward.

I wondered what to say before asking, "Do you think it was an accident?"

"It's not my place to judge, my lord."

"Imagine it is," I said. "I give you the power, just here and now, to say it as you saw it." I waved my slave and Sadhu away so that they couldn't overhear.

"It was deliberate," he said quickly and quietly.

I nodded. "The ropes were cut."

"Yes."

"Why?"

The man looked uncomfortable.

"You're only telling me," I said. "Speak."

"I will not be punished?"

"No!"

He swallowed. "I believe the ferryman did not pay the price."

"The price?"

"Unofficial tax is the polite expression. I believe the correct word is extortion. There is much demand for ferry services and they're controlled by one man."

"The Overseer of the Waterways," I said.

"He was the man. I heard him tell a slave to cut the ropes because the ferryman wouldn't pay."

EIGHTEEN

That night the girl, Tihepet, came to my room. This time she wore material covering her breasts, and I was relieved. However, the gold chain dangling around her middle drew my eye downwards.

She'd brought the white powder and a bowl of goat's milk.

"How much?" I said, tipping the powder in.

"I don't know, my lord. All of it?"

"When I fall asleep, you will retire to the bench again."

"Of course, my lord."

I remember rolling over and feeling her massage my aching neck and shoulders, but then I transported to another time and place, just before the ferry case.

"They choose to live beside a field of bees," Lord Khety was saying to me. "How can they complain about that? And there can be no justification for theft or destruction of anything!"

I tried to argue that there had been no evidence of wrongdoing, but we didn't know the whole story. I said, "Perhaps there has been theft, but it does not mean these people are the guilty ones. Perhaps in the past there has been damage to beehives, but it could have been the wind. Perhaps bees have disappeared, but they are as likely to have been eaten by the birds."

"Perhaps. Perhaps. Perhaps! Have I taught you nothing about the Law of the Two Lands?"

"Yes, my lord, you have taught me that it is unfair." He scowled at me so I shut up. Then I couldn't help myself. "The law talks of harmony and justice and yet it seems to me that this justice is unbalanced, unequal."

Paneb coughed and I knew he was reminding me of my status. Despite my anger at the inequality of the law, I stopped talking.

The magistrate eyed me and gulped down some more beer. "Oh don't stop now, boy. Let's hear your wise judgement."

I swallowed and took a sip from my own cup of bitter southern beer. "The peasants should have the same rights as the beekeeper. Well, in fact, the beekeeper is merely a representation of the city and state. The overseer and the land registry clerk were not impartial witnesses because they are part of the state."

"Rubbish!"

"We both saw that the stakes had been moved over time. The area of the bee fields remains the same, but the beekeeper has undoubtedly moved them gradually over time as the desert has claimed the area to the north-west."

"The land registry does not deny the beekeeper this right."

"I do not deny that the beekeeper has rights— according to the land registry, but why should the peasants' houses not be counted. Why can't they have land rights?"

Paneb came to the table, apparently to clear away dishes, and glared at me.

"More beer, Paneb!" the magistrate ordered from the slave and nudged him aside.

I continued: "I would have judged that the beekeeper should move his stakes and hives one hundred cubits back and create an area between that the peasants must not encroach upon. The beekeeper can maintain his land by expanding elsewhere."

"You are a fool, boy!"

"Perhaps…"

"Ha! Perhaps. Perhaps. Perhaps!"

He quaffed another beer and yelled at Paneb again.

I felt tears prickle my eyes. I had not intended it to end this way, but I could hold back no longer. "I'm leaving," I said.

"No you are not. I need you." There was a subterranean growl full of menace in the magistrate's voice.

"You need me because you are going blind, old man." I stood with my hands clenched in frustration. Immediately, I felt my arms pinned by the slave's strong grip.

The magistrate slapped the table. "Sit down. I have not finished. And never show me such disrespect again!"

I was forced to sit, and although released, I knew Paneb stood behind me ready for whatever happened next.

For a long time, the magistrate looked into his drink. When he looked up, the anger had dissipated and a sadness was reflected in his eyes like dull cataracts. "Yes, I need you to be my eyes. Even when you first boldly spoke to me, I knew my power to see the truth was fading, and over the past three years it has become so bad that I can no longer make out a man's features when he is more than two paces away. Without your ability, I am finished.

"Have I not fed you? Have I not taught you to read and write? Have I not pretended you are not from the gutter? Have I not let you live amongst the high class and shown you a life you would never have lived?"

I felt like saying that his motivation had been selfish, but used a calming trick the magistrate himself frequently used; I counted to three before saying, "That is true."

"And where will you go? Back to your stinking village?"

"I will join the Medjay."

The magistrate laughed loudly as though I'd told him a great joke. "Egypt's best fighting force of Nubians. Well good luck with that!" He stopped laughing and stared, the animal growl returning to his voice. "If you leave, you leave with nothing. You are but a boy who does not know how to fight. You will be the lowliest and the weakest and just padding for His Majesty's front line against the Hittites. You will be dead before a year is out."

"That may be, but I must at least try to learn to fight. I am a man now and I have my honour."

"What on earth are you talking about?"

I stood slowly and bowed. "Because, my lord, I have learned that the law cannot bring me justice. There is a man who must pay for the death of my sister."

NINETEEN

Why was I dreaming about the bees? The trip to the site of the ferry disaster had brought back the old memories and triggered the dream. The honey farm case was two days before the ferry case, which had been the day I left Lord Khety. Paneb had been right to be cross with me. I'd been disrespectful to his lordship and he had returned my betrayal by giving me papers of adoption.

I must have started to wake, because I was aware of being back in my own time and thinking that the flower fields for the bees were much bigger than before. And there was no sign of the villagers who had been forced back. I suppose they'd been moved and moved again over the years.

Taking the dream powder outside of the temple was different. Yes, I felt like I was transported back through time, but I couldn't direct my dream as I had before.

I didn't want to dream of bees or ferries. I needed retribution for the death of my sister.

And suddenly the light changed and I could smell dung. I was in a tent with my friend and colleague Thayjem. The army was on the outskirts of Ugarit and had been pressing north, driving the enemy back.

But we were translators, and in front of me was a Hittite document that appeared to be a list of supplies.

Thayjem was grumbling about the smell and the flies and that he'd joined the army to fight. He was always moaning, and I'd learned to tune him out and focus on my translation.

Something was amiss. Every now and again I found written words that appeared out of place. I doubted my translation skills were to blame and these place names and numbers troubled me.

And then realization struck me. "Oh, Ra protect us!"

"Hey, you're supposed to pray to Seth!" Thayjem laughed. "We're in the Black army, remember?"

And then time seemed to jump. The light was fading and braziers had been lit when a chariot pulled up outside our tent and a mid-ranking officer charged in. He looked us up and down disparagingly.

"Which of you girls is responsible for the message to the Fourteenth this afternoon?"

I stood to attention, a hand on each thigh. "It was me, sir."

"And you ordered a retreat?"

Thayjem gasped.

The mid-ranking officer continued: "You are to come with me immediately. The commander wants to see you." He turned, marched to his chariot and pulled himself athletically beside a driver. I slung my scribe's satchel over my shoulder and squeezed beside the officer on the footplate.

The charioteer lashed at his horse and it jolted into a gallop. Clinging to the rail, we were driven at speed along the dusty track, leaving the tents in the supply section and heading for the Seth commander's encampment nearer the front line.

During the twenty-minute journey, I shivered. The evening air had a chill, but I realized it was more than the drop in temperature that cooled my skin. As we neared, I could see the long flowing black pennants against the dying embers of the sky and I thought of serpent's tongues tasting the air and judging my fear.

When the chariot pulled up at the massive tent, bigger than most noble's houses, we jumped off. Beside two giant Nubian guards, with faces blacker than river mud, the mid-ranking officer told me to wait until I was called.

I wiped dust from my tunic and shoes and, taking a damp cloth from a slave, cleaned dirt from my face.

The wait was so long that I became thirsty and wondered whether I'd been forgotten. Finally, an attractive boy wearing kohl around his eyes stepped between the guards and said I should follow.

I was led into a section of the tent and I knew immediately that this was Apephotep, a large man with a charisma that seemed to fill the air like an invisible cloak. I thought the air shimmered, although this could have been the effect of the fading light and torches around the tent. To his side stood a scribe and behind the commander were six slaves with the markings of deaf mutes who encouraged the air to circulate by moving their ostrich feather fans like the rhythm of a gentle sea.

I stepped forward, eyes down and bowed, lowering my hands to my knees and out.

Apephotep growled, "So you are the imbecile who ordered the retreat."

"Sir, I found something that suggested our intelligence was false. I did not mean to order a retreat, merely to prevent an attack that would have left our men exposed. I believe we were the victims of misinformation."

"Look at me!" The big man slammed his fist on the table. "Do you realize the punishment for such a loss of face? The Blacks are the most fearless of Horemheb's armies. We do not retreat!" He calmed but continued to glare. "Your job is to use your head, is it not? How would your clever head feel if it was separated from that pretty neck?"

I did not answer.

"But you were lucky. The message got to the Seth Fourteen just in time. There was a fight and we were victorious." The officer studied me for a while as though deciding my fate, before he said, "Glory to Pharaoh, the living god, he who unites the Two Lands."

"May he live for eternity in the palace of Ra," I recited.

"Glory to Horemheb, our beloved general who will make our great nation powerful once more and drive the usurper from our beloved land, the land of the true gods."

I was unsure how to respond. Men whispered ill feelings towards the pharaoh and said terrible things in the stupor of their beer, but I had never heard Pharaoh Ay referred to as the usurper before. It was tantamount to treason.

Apephotep watched my reaction and then said, "What are your politics?"

I shook my head. "I have no politics, sir."

"Is Horemheb your leader, no matter what? Would you lay down your life for him?"

"In this foreign field, My Lord Horemheb is Egypt." I kept my face straight. I knew there was only one answer I could give and prayed I could mask my feelings as well as I could read others. "Of course, sir," I said. "Without question."

Apephotep nodded thoughtfully and let me sweat before saying, "Your life shall be spared, although I must tell you my decision was a close one. If you had realized the subterfuge before, the leader of the Fourteenth would not be wounded and now lying in the care of the priests of Bast."

Apephotep beckoned me forward and the scribe indicated I should kneel. To my surprise, the commander reached forward and, over my head, placed a collar of office with gold embroidery and trim and lapis lazuli beads. "You are to report to Serq, the leader of the Fourteenth, as his personal strategist and officer second class. You will be responsible for his personal safety and you will take a blade in his place if the time comes."

As I stood, I noticed a few specks of dried blood on the collar and couldn't help myself.

"What happened to his last one?"

"He asked too many fucking questions!" Apephotep guffawed. "Now, the captain's boy is here and will take you to the temple."

A temporary temple of Bast had been created. Torches burned brightly around a space the size of my courtyard at home. Bundles of papyrus flowers represented the walls and three foot statues of the cat goddess were guarding each corner. An awning overhead was heavy with smoke from the torches and incense that smouldered in bowls.

Thirty or forty wounded men lay or sat on the ground and priests walked between them chanting and rattling their sistra. All the wounded would have

121

Egyptian blood and none was lower class. The gods of health, it seemed, were for the higher classes only.

I knew of the commander of Seth Fourteen by reputation. One story was that he had gained the name Serq because of the speed of his aggression, like the strike of a scorpion. Others said it was just because a scorpion had stung him in childhood, leaving its mark on his face.

The boy, who had led the way from the Seth encampment, pointed to a chair at the rear of the yard. I walked over and bowed my head to avert my eyes and stopped just short of the captain's chair.

"My new strategist," Serq said in a voice that was rough but slightly higher pitched than I had anticipated. "What's your name?"

"Yan-Khety, sir."

"I knew of a Khety once. A magistrate from Waset. Are you related?"

I hesitated. When I enrolled at the military academy in Memphis I had been surprised at the magistrate's letter. Instead of an introduction, it was a statement of my heritage. My acceptance had been guaranteed and the enrolling officer had noted the name.

I said, "I am his son, sir."

"Gods protect me, a strategist and a judge!" He laughed mirthlessly. "Let me see your face."

I looked up and choked. The light was poor, but the evidence was clear: the man in the chair had a hard face with a small scar on his left cheek that looked like his namesake—Serq, the Scorpion.

My legs buckled. I grabbed the chair for balance. After more than two years in the army, I had finally come face-to-face with Captain Ani, the man who had taken my sister.

A priest started banging a drum. Then louder, in an unreligious fashion. Maybe a soldier then? I looked around, wondering who could be so crass. Again and again he banged. Louder and louder. And then I was back in my room at the palace. The girl wasn't there, and I could hear Paneb shouting my name.

TWENTY

My head was light but my legs felt heavy as I staggered to the door. "Enough of the banging!" I shouted.

Paneb stood on the other side, and I'd never seen him in such a flap.

"It's very late, master," he said, entering.

"Late?"

"The hour is late," he explained slowly. "You have overslept and everyone is waiting."

"Everyone?" I said, my brain still slow to catch up.

He held up my formal robes and nodded. "The court is waiting for you."

With my slave's assistance, I was ready and downstairs within minutes. Sadhu was there, all wide-eyed and with a hundred questions. I ignored him and was given fruit and water as I waited in an entrance hall.

Finally, I was taken alone through a series of corridors and into an office. Nomarch Userhat was at a desk, reading as I entered. A frown didn't sit well on his big face, which was red and too widespread to be rouge. When he levered himself out of the seat I saw that his body was even more enlarged, larger than the mayor's. He was probably in his late forties and appeared healthy with the exception of his weight and a limp. This must be the gout that the girl Tihepet told me about.

I nodded a greeting, momentarily unsure what to say.

He just glared at me for a moment before speaking. "What sort of disrespectful behaviour do you call this?"

"My lord—" I started.

"I am a busy man, Magistrate Yan-Khety. Do you think I have time to sit around waiting for you to wake up?"

I raised both hands in apology. "I wasn't informed that the court would be heard this morning."

The nomarch tutted like I had spoken nonsense, and yet it was the truth. However, had I been up with the sun, I would have surely discovered the plans.

He took a step towards me and held out a chubby hand. "Let this not happen again. Understood? I expect—and deserve—respect."

I held his hand briefly and bowed.

The nomarch's grumpy countenance faded. "I met your father once. A worthy man."

"He was, my lord."

"And yet he never told me he had a son."

I smiled. "Perhaps *I* wasn't worthy."

The nomarch smiled at my joke. "How are you enjoying my hospitality?"

"You are most kind."

"Excellent. This case is likely to take a few more days, so you can continue to enjoy it."

"Thank you."

"I don't ask for recompense, of course, you understand that?"

I had taken it for granted, but his question made me doubt it. Again I thanked him for his hospitality and the chance to officiate at a high court case.

"You haven't served at high court before, have you?"

"No, my lord."

"Well, the first rule, Yan-Khety, is to stop referring to me as 'my lord'. In this court, you, the mayor and I are equals in the eyes of the law. Understood?"

"Yes."

"We will hear the accusations and then ask questions of the accused and witnesses before pronouncing judgement."

"What if we disagree?"

He looked at me as though I was joking, then shook his head. "We won't disagree. Now, let's get to the Great Hall shall we?"

"I have my men," I said.

"Your men?"

"My protector and my scribe."

"The slave and the boy? You won't be needing them. We have the court's guards and official scribes. It wouldn't do to have another scribe recording something different now, would it?"

"The boy is my assistant and in training. I ask permission for him to attend."

I could see the nomarch pondering my request and so I quickly followed up with: "And I promise that he won't write anything down."

The nomarch sighed and nodded. "All right—for now, but anything untoward and he's out. Understood?"

"Accepted," I said, and even as I uttered the words he was instructing a man at the door to fetch the mayor.

He led the way back into the labyrinth of corridors, favouring his left leg. Despite a walking staff, his plump body swayed and lurched as he walked.

Hovering outside the doors to the hall were my slave and assistant. In front of them were two burly guards. The soldiers parted to let us through and my aides started to follow.

"Just Sadhu," I said, and Paneb accepted with a curt nod. I knew he would wait outside, listening in case I needed him.

Through the doorway, we walked into the Great Hall, which was as wide as it was long. I think it could have held maybe a hundred people. Instead, there were three empty thrones to the right, two scribes straight ahead with pedestals and a bench to the left. The thrones were set in an arc, spaced about two paces apart. The nomarch pointed to the first and I took the seat.

"Stand behind, keep out of the way and say nothing," he said to my assistant. Then he waddled to the middle throne and plopped himself down. Immediately, a young man scurried up and placed a footstool under his right leg before hurrying away.

I'm not usually guilty of nerves, but in that instant I felt a shiver. This was my first high court case. I had no real idea of protocol and here was the most important man of the Land of the Arch, the first nome. He was sitting within touching distance, for Horus's sake!

Next to arrive were a chattering group of officials. I spotted a couple that I'd seen before, including the effeminate one, but the others were unfamiliar.

Based on the size of the nomarch and mayor, high office in these parts meant good living. However, I registered that none of the officials on the benches looked overweight. They had yet to make it in their careers, I guessed.

They quickly settled and fell into a hush. A moment later I saw Mayor Renseneb march through the entrance. He nodded towards me as he passed. Then I saw him meet Nomarch Userhat's gaze. I pride myself at being able to read people but I could not tell what that look meant. It appeared friendly and yet challenging.

The mayor took the third throne.

I expected the tribunal to commence then but Userhat raised his hand and a servant brought him a drink. He knocked it back before belching.

A door behind me creaked open and shut and then an official in a formal white and crimson gown knelt before the nomarch. In his outstretched hands was a golden judge's rod similar to one that I had for my local tribunals.

The nomarch took it and said, "Now then, let's commence, shall we?"

A man dressed as an administrator appeared from behind me and I wondered whether there were more back there. The itch to turn and check was strong but I felt it inappropriate, and then the moment was past because the man started speaking.

"This is the Set-Ma-at," he said, facing the nomarch but really directing his speech at the scribes. "It is the court of the first nome presided over by the governor, Nomarch Userhat, in this the first month of the harvest in the sixth regnal year of Pharaoh Horemheb's reign." He went on to list the pharaoh's many titles before returning to the nomarch and praising him with titles, such as Keeper of the Gate to the South, but then others which hardly seemed likely or appropriate for the fat man. Userhat looked like he'd never done anything in his life except enjoy himself mainly with food and drink.

The nomarch nodded in recognition and then tilted his head towards the mayor.

The speaker immediately addressed Mayor Renseneb, recognizing his presence at the court and his various meaningless titles.

Throughout, I watched them both and couldn't help think they were cut from the same linen. Userhat looked perhaps ten years older than the mayor.

The mayor smiled at the expansive words of the administrator and nodded to the nomarch, probably in gratitude. I figured that the words had been dictated by Userhat in advance of the court.

I was intrigued to hear what he had to say about me and felt that frisson of nerves again as the administrator turned in my direction.

"Also in attendance is Lord Khety, magistrate of Akhmin, son of Lord Khety, the highly respected law giver—" He went on to speak of my adopted father rather than me, and I could swear that the mayor found it amusing. The way he smiled then reminded me again that he seemed familiar.

The nomarch let proceedings pause as he waited for the scribes to stop scribbling and then he banged his staff on the ground three times.

The real action was about to begin.

TWENTY-ONE

The city Chief of Police was introduced and the man marched confidently into the space vacated by the previous speaker.

"My lords," he began, "I bring before you a terrible case of robbery, one so terrible as to be an affront to our forebears, one so blasphemous to be an affront to the gods themselves." He stopped, his face suddenly grave, as though he himself had just discovered how shocking it was, although I could see it was an act.

The look on Mayor Renseneb's face, however, showed intrigue, and I decided that he really didn't know the details of this case. When we'd met, he'd said the nomarch had kept the case secret. At the time I wondered if he was just keeping me in the dark.

I took a furtive glance at the nomarch and thought he may have had a smug look on his face.

After the dramatic pause, the Chief of Police continued: "This is the sad news that a necropolis has been disturbed." Again he paused, and I saw Renseneb inch forward in expectation.

"And not the tombs of mere citizens, my lords, but the tombs of nobles," the chief announced to a collective gasp.

He continued to describe the location of the tombs, which were in the rocks of the western back, just north of Great Elephantine Island. I was certain that everyone except me knew the tombs and that this was more showmanship from the policeman.

Finally, he moved on to say: "So far we have discovered three tombs to have been disturbed. I say 'so far' because it could be that others have been raided and the crimes covered up. It has only been by knowledge of the tombs that we appreciated the disturbance of the three, since the criminals tried to mask the break-ins." Again, he spent many times longer with the self-praise at the discovery rather than getting on with the detail.

I wanted to interrupt and ask him to progress. In my own court I wouldn't have accepted such grandstanding, but here I sensed it was acceptable and, in any case, it was really the nomarch's court and therefore his place to encourage a faster delivery.

Eventually, the police chief said that the head guard of the necropolis would tell us more, and we were introduced to a man who showed his nervousness by repeatedly running his tongue over his front teeth.

This man gave us the names of the three nobles who had had their tombs disturbed. When he went on to use the more direct expression "broken into and desecrated", it brought another gasp from the officials on the benches.

Unfortunately, this junior officer also had a long-winded way of telling us the story. We got a detailed description of the nobles, their past offices and achievements and then the precise location of the tombs as well as a description of their appearance.

When he started to repeat himself, the nomarch waved his rod of judgement towards the chief who then stepped forward, replacing the guard.

"My lords," the Chief of Police said, "this is a crime so terrible—" He must have read the look on Userhat's face because he hesitated and changed his speech. "My lords, we have arrested the two criminals responsible for this heinous crime. Unfortunately, we have not recovered the stolen items because they have already disposed of them. The men were known to us and I will bring them before you to admit their guilt. I will also provide a witness who will confirm their stories."

Although I remained silent, I thought, *Why do you need a witness if the guilty men have confessed?*

Userhat glanced at the mayor and then back at the policeman. "Excellent," he said. "And who are these guilty men?"

"Passer, the coppersmith, and Neni, the stonemason, my lord," the policeman replied. He may have been about to provide a more lengthy introduction to the felons but quickly fell silent.

"Excellent," Userhat said. "Now we will adjourn for luncheon."

I was shown to an antechamber with food and wine on the table. I thought the other judges would join me, but after a long wait I decided to sit and eat a little. I also let Sadhu take some food, although with water rather than the sweet wine.

After a few mouthfuls, my assistant said, "At the opening of court, the administrator said that this was Set-Ma-at. What did he mean, my lord?"

"The Place of Truth," I said. "It's an old expression only used at high court."

"I prefer your courts."

I nodded. My cases were short and to the point. This was long-winded and painful at times. However, I had to remind myself that I was a guest here and being paid a lot for my trouble.

Sadhu said, "If the two men have confessed, then why is this taking so long? Surely you could just hear their confessions and pronounce judgement."

"Due process," I said, guessing, since this was new to me as well. "High court cases are carefully documented and reported to the vizier. In this case it will go to Paramese, vizier of the south. I suspect the report needs to be in great detail so that there can be no misunderstanding. It also demonstrates that the judgement considered everything and was fair."

"And just."

I patted him on the head. "Good lad."

"I was watching them—the mayor and nomarch." He whispered conspiratorially as though afraid someone might overhear.

I waited for him to continue.

"Did you see how they exchanged looks? It's as though this is some kind of game."

I shook my head vigorously. "The law isn't a game, Sadhu. I thought you..." I stopped suddenly as the nomarch appeared at the door and waived my assistant away.

Once Sadhu had left, the nomarch used his staff and limped over to me.

I bowed.

"How are you finding it so far, young Yan-Khety?"

I wanted to say *slow* but instead responded, "Interesting."

"Good. Very good. If you need guidance do let me know. However, I think you will do just fine. You are an intelligent man and all you need to do is listen carefully to the facts."

"Yes, my lord."

He waggled a finger. "All equals, remember?"

I nodded.

"Oh, and remember that you don't owe anyone any favours. Not me. Not Renseneb." He smiled. "I don't wish to malign my esteemed friend, but sometimes..." He leaned over and whispered in my ear just like my assistant had. "Well it would be ungracious of me to say more, but just watch out. That's all I'm saying." Then he surprised me with a thump on my back. "Now, let's get back in there and hear this case."

TWENTY-TWO

I felt a little disorientated when I retook my seat. What had the nomarch been implying about the mayor? I glanced at them both and they appeared equally earnest and ready for the confessions.

However, the guilty men were not called into the hall. Instead, we were introduced to a clerk of records who said he would list the stolen items.

After spending an inordinate amount of time describing the first tomb in the same way as we'd been told by the head guard, he started on the list of missing items: statues, gold, silver and copper items.

"The coffin lid had been removed and a golden dagger prised from the hands of the deceased," he said.

The mayor's eyes bulged, possibly at the audacity of the crime.

"How do you know?" I said, suddenly voicing a doubt. "How do you know it was prised?"

The clerk looked at me with wide eyes.

The nomarch said, "It's Lord Khety's first time. Strike the question from the records." This second sentence was aimed at the scribes, who didn't even look up from their work.

The nomarch said, "Take the rod and then speak."

He handed the rod of office to the servant with the white and crimson robe who then handed it to me.

The nomarch smiled, "Now ask your question."

I took a breath. "How did you know the dagger was prised from his hands?"

"I er..."—he looked at the nomarch—"it was just an expression, my lord."

"Please stick to the facts," I said. When he nodded, I continued: "You described the stolen items. I'm just curious to know how you found out about what was missing. Surely only the family and priests might know what was inside the tomb."

The wide-eyed look had been replaced by composure when the clerk spoke. "A family member was contacted."

"And you are sure they told the truth?"

"That is not the point," the mayor said quietly but loud enough for me to hear. I detected annoyance in his voice although he tried to mask it. "The clerk of records' veracity is not in question here."

The rod of office was taken from me and returned to the nomarch.

"Please continue," Nomarch Userhat said, and the clerk resumed his planned speech.

The items stolen from the second tomb included alabaster and linen as well as precious metals. Again, I wanted to question the source of his knowledge, but the mayor's narrowed eyes warned me against it.

More descriptions were provided before the clerk moved on to the third tomb. After verbally painting the image of the tomb—much grander and larger than the other two—he proceeded to tell us about the stolen objects. This one included a golden statue of Isis taken from the wife's casket.

I signalled for the rod and received it.

"Wife's casket you say? Were there two caskets?"

"Yes, my lord, the old governor's and his wife's."

"And how were they disturbed?"

"Their lids had been lifted."

"And replaced?"

"Yes."

I wanted to challenge him with, *how do you know?* again, but resisted the urge. Instead, I asked, "Did you inspect them?"

"Yes."

"Were they next to one another—the caskets?"

"Yes," the clerk replied after a moment's hesitation.

Renseneb snapped, "Where is this going?"

"No more questions." As I handed the rod back, I could swear I saw the faintest smile in the nomarch's eyes.

The Chief of Police returned and unnecessarily dictated the crimes of the two accused being the disturbance of the three tombs and the theft of the specific items.

I stifled a yawn at the slow pace of this trial and was rewarded by the calling of the first criminal. He wasn't *the accused* at this point. He was already labelled as guilty.

The man was brought in by two guards, one holding each arm. He was pushed into a chair that had been brought forward. It had a raised platform that went under the calves and pushed out his feet. As soon as he sat, straps were tightened around his legs, binding him to the chair.

Another man, calling himself Officer of the Guilty, took the floor and introduced the man in the chair as Passer the coppersmith, once of a temple in Nebet and until recently living in a village outside Elephantine.

When asked, Passer confirmed his name. He looked weak and scared, and his tunic was dirty and ripped. I suspected this had all happened since he'd been arrested.

The officer then asked the man to describe his crime.

Passer said, "We disturbed the tombs."

"Which tombs?"

"I don't remember."

The officer then gave the names of the three tombs that we'd heard had been broken into and robbed.

"Perhaps," the accused man said.

Immediately, one of the guards took a stick and thrashed Passer's right foot until blood was drawn. The man screamed and I clenched my teeth at the excessive beating. A glance at the mayor and nomarch told me they quite enjoyed the spectacle.

When he'd stopped crying, Passer was asked if it was the three tombs. He was given the names this time and repeated them one at a time.

"Let the record show that the criminal confirmed which tombs he disturbed," Mayor Renseneb said, and he nodded for the Officer of the Guilty to continue.

The officer then listed the stolen items and Passer confirmed them all, using specific names, such as the statue of Isis, when asked to repeat them.

Holding the rod of office, Userhat said, "The most valuable item appears to have been a golden dagger. Describe it in more detail."

The officer prompted Passer, who then said, "Gold. About this size"—he held his hands apart to illustrate a medium-sized knife—"with a red stone in the handle."

The mayor waved for the rod, his teeth clenched. I thought he would ask a specific question about the dagger but instead he said, "Have the man describe a break-in. What was it like?"

The officer asked the question and Passer started speaking. He was quiet at first and then gained more confidence.

"We knew the way in. We found the keystone and removed it. Once we had that we could lever the door open and get inside. There was rubble in the passageway and we had to dig through it. Once through, we came to the door to the burial chamber and chiselled through it. The valuables were in the burial chamber."

I took the rod and asked, "You said you knew the way in. How did you know that?"

I'd incorrectly directed the question at Passer, so the Officer of the Guilty repeated my question.

"We paid a worker at the necropolis, my lord."

The officer asked about the other two tombs and the explanation of the entry into each burial chamber was similar.

I took the rod again and could see that Userhat was happy for me to take it.

"Ask the man about the necklace."

The officer said, "Tell us about the necklace that you took from the wife's coffin in the tomb of the old governor."

I saw something in the prisoner's eyes then. Could it have been uncertainty? His hesitation brought a sharp rap to his exposed left foot.

"The necklace, yes. I took it from the woman's coffin. It was around her neck."

Userhat took the rod. "Have the man describe the necklace."

The officer asked the question and Passer said, "Beautiful."

"Ask him to describe it."

"Silver with sapphires and emeralds."

Renseneb made a funny small noise as I resumed the questioning. "Where was the coffin?" I asked, with a weird feeling that Passer was lying about something.

"In the tomb."

"In the same chamber or another?"

Mayor Renseneb stood. "Oh for Khnum's sake! Stupid questions. Give me the rod of office!"

The rod was taken from my grasp and hurried into the mayor's pudgy hand.

"Right. Now ask the prisoner if he is guilty."

"Are you guilty?" the officer asked.

"Yes."

The mayor cleared his throat. "It's late and I have administrative work to attend to. I propose that we reconvene in the morning."

Without waiting for the nomarch to agree, he strode behind the thrones and disappeared from my sight.

Userhat waved for everyone to depart. Sadhu went as well, and within seconds it was just the nomarch and me.

Userhat laughed. "Good fun, eh?"

I was bemused. "It's not what I expected."

"The mayor likes his cases nice and tied up. You got under his skin with all your questions." He laughed again and then looked serious. "Of course, there could be more to it."

"More to his annoyance? Like what?"

Userhat waved an arm. "Oh I don't know. Perhaps more will become clear. Perhaps you should spend time with old Renseneb. Now enjoy your afternoon and I'll see you in the morning. Early. Make sure you don't oversleep again, Khety."

He left through a private door and I collected Sadhu outside the hall. Paneb was there as well, and he looked excited. Like he was standing in a nest of snakes.

He beckoned me into a corner.

"Master," he said quietly, "remember the other man who came to your home? The one you thought was another messenger from the nomarch?"

To be honest, I'd forgotten all about the strange visitor.

Paneb continued: "Well, he's here in Elephantine and he's been looking for you."

"You met him?"

"Briefly, and he gave me this."

Paneb handed be a piece of folded linen. I unwrapped it and stared in astonishment. In my hand was the signet ring of the High Priest of Amun.

TWENTY-THREE

A shiver ran down my back. Why was I being given the ring of one of the most important men in the land, arguably second only to Pharaoh himself?

"What did he say?" I asked my slave.

"Nothing."

"What?" I dropped my voice to the tiniest whisper. "He gave you this and said nothing?"

"Well he didn't say *nothing*. I mean he said nothing about why he wants to speak with you, my lord."

I waited impatiently for Paneb to continue.

"He gave me an address where he will be at the third hour of night. You are to meet him there alone." My slave then whispered an address in the city, out on the far eastern extremity.

I said, "You've not repeated this to anyone?"

"Of course not, master."

I nodded. I hadn't needed to ask. Not really. I trusted my slave with my life and I trusted his discretion. "Sorry," I said, touching his arm. "I'm just disorientated with everything that is going on. I need fresh air."

I led the way out through the courtyard, past the fountain that cast the colourful arch and out into the city. I had a sense of the surreal, like the palace was in a different world. Maybe it was.

Without a plan, I stood for a moment and looked at the streets and the bustling city life.

"Master?" Paneb said, standing at my side.

I assumed he was questioning my indecision but he wasn't. He merely wanted to draw my attention to the man beside him—a young man dressed as a lower noble. His nose was lopsided, like it had been broken a long time ago.

"My lord," the man said with a bow. "You have many questions."

At first I blinked, and then I guessed he must have been in the Great Hall, must have heard me challenging the evidence.

After I nodded, he continued: "Perhaps you would like to visit the site... the tombs?"

Why was my mind not working properly? Of course that's what I wanted to do. That's why I was standing outside the palace looking mindlessly this way and that. I was waiting for my brain to register a subconscious thought: visit the scene of the crime. When I was unsure about a case, I often visited the location. That way I could get my bearings, get a better image of the criminal activity, get closer to the truth.

"Come then," he said, probably reading my face. "Let me show you."

I followed him around the palace wall until we reached the river and the nearest quay. All along the quays, there were small sailboats that would shuttle people to the islands or the eastern bank.

There wasn't a ferry like downriver because parts of the Great River flowed fast here with currents caused by the islands.

While my guide called to a boat, I noticed a military ship. It flew the flag of the Seth Army—unit Five.

I was still wondering why a unit would be deployed in the city when Paneb paid the boat's owner and we climbed aboard.

As the little craft surged away from the quay, my slave whispered in my ear. "The coffers are low, master."

I hadn't been worrying about costs and I saw now that Paneb had been. I reassured him with a smile. Once this case was over, I'd be a rich man. However, as I turned back and studied Elephantine Island's elaborate temples, I had a strange sense of foreboding, like I was missing something. Were the gods laughing at me?

As if in answer, the air filled with chanting. I'd heard it many times in the city already, but being so close made the hairs on my neck stand up. The gods weren't laughing. They were with me and urging me on. However bizarre this court case, I would find the truth.

TWENTY-FOUR

We rented four donkeys on the west bank and were led in a train. The challenging two-mile trek took us on a winding path through a rocky landscape. When we reached the necropolis a sleepy guard staggered out of his shelter and checked who we were. My guide with the broken nose had a document of authority and handed it over.

"Official," he explained to the guard, and they spoke briefly before the guard accompanied us into the enclosure.

Unlike common cemeteries, this necropolis of nobles appeared disorganized, and I figured it was a result of the ground. Most of the tombs were dug into rock rather than sand.

"How are the plots determined?" I asked as we walked under the baking sun, dust scuffing up under my sandals.

"City planning, my lord," the guard responded. He had a thick accent that I placed as far north, much further than Memphis and Heliopolis. "I'm afraid I don't know the detail but suspect it's a combination of wealth and status."

That made perfect sense. The tombs in the Great Field, where many pharaohs' bodies were interred, were chosen by each pharaoh and hidden so that only his successor and the high priest knew the location.

We were climbing a steep rise and the guard stopped by a tomb.

"This is the first," my guide said, and I could see where the entrance slab had been disturbed.

I noticed Sadhu studying the writing over the door and I reminded myself how he tried to improve at every opportunity.

I said, "What do you interpret, Sadhu?"

"It reads from right to left, my lord," he said. "An offering which the king presents to Anubis, Lord of the Sacred Land so that he may give... something..."

"A voice offering."

"A voice offering of bread, beer, oxen, oil..."

"Alabaster and linen."

"A voice offering of bread, beer, oxen, oil, alabaster and linen for the *ka* of the Baker of Divine Offerings Neferhotep... born of Bebi?"

"Yes, *born of Bebi*. Excellent," I said, truly proud of my young assistant. "So our first tomb belonged to a baker, but no humble baker. This man had reached high status overseeing the production of bread for the gods." I wondered if he'd ever actually kneaded dough in his life.

I realized the other three were looking at me, waiting.

The guide said, "Are we going inside?"

"No," I said. "This sacred place may have been disturbed but I feel no need for further desecration. Let's see the second."

My expectation had been that the three disturbed tombs would be close together. However they were not. The second was in a flatter area with a more simple entrance. Again, I could see where the door had been levered open but had been replaced.

I asked Sadhu to translate and he did well. This one had a similar bequest of Anubis and was for a Chanter of Khnum called Wadjhaw, son of Ami the Justified.

We moved on to the final tomb, larger and more elaborate. As Sadhu eventually translated, it had an offering to Osiris described as Lord Khentyimentu, Foremost of the Westerners, Lord of Djedu in all his places. This was the tomb of the governor, a past mayor called Mentu, Lord of Honour. There was also reference to his wife, Nefretiu, Mistress of the House.

I saw no evidence of a break-in here.

"Has this not been disturbed?" I asked the necropolis guard.

"They tunnelled in, my lord," he said.

"Show me."

We went higher still and found a hole in the ground. There was a natural fissure between a rock wall and flat ground that had been widened. Sadhu was slim and could have entered, just about, but Paneb and I would have become stuck.

The guard said, "I assume you won't be going down, my lord."

The guide was looking down into the darkness.

I shook my head. "This should be resealed."

"I'm sure it will be," the guide said.

I sighed. "Terrible. Let's go."

The guide was still peering into the darkness and the guard didn't move. He said, "This is where the desecration occurred."

I remembered the expression being used by the Chief of Police at the start of the case and realized it hadn't been explained.

"What happened?" I asked.

"They were celebrating, my lord. Drink or something else that made them merry, I don't know."

"Were you here? Were you on duty?"

"They say the crimes took many nights, my lord, but I was here the night of the… er… celebrations. I was… er… confused."

"Confused?"

"I am just a humble servant," he said. "I am not a learned man and so I thought it was the gods visiting the dead. I was… I was afraid."

"The gods?"

"Well I saw just one. The god Maahes. I fell to my knees and prayed. I am sorry, my lord. I neglected my duties because I thought it was a god."

"What's your name?" I asked.

"Nakht, my lord."

"And you haven't told anyone else about this, Nakht?"

"No, I have been too embarrassed. Now I think that I was fooled. Why would Maahes be here in the necropolis? And it happened on the same night as the break-in."

Before we left the necropolis, I saw a vulture circling out to the west. Many birds would mean a carcass, but one on its own was considered a propitious sign.

When we arrived back at the public quay I spotted Mayor Renseneb talking to another man. He nodded to me, finished his conversation and then waved me over.

"Enjoying the evening air, Lord Khety?" He seemed in better spirits than earlier, and before I could respond, he continued with: "What an interesting high court case, eh?"

"I didn't mean to offend you," I said.

He indicated that we should walk, and we strolled along the quay before turning towards the artisan sector of the town.

"Oh no, my dear fellow," he chuckled. "It wasn't your fault. I was simply distracted by the evidence."

I thought this odd. Surely it should have been the opposite.

"The necklace," Renseneb said almost casually.

"In the case?"

"You must have recognized... I thought it sounded similar to the one my wife was wearing when we first met."

I had but had filed the image away and thought nothing more of it.

We stopped walking and were outside a jewellery workshop.

"This is where we have all of our jewellery custom made," he said, then called a name. Immediately, an artisan scurried from the workshop and bowed deeply.

"My lord does me great honour by his presence!"

Renseneb puffed out his chest. "You lied to me."

"Sir?" The man hung his head. "I don't know—"

"When I have something made I expect it to be unique."

"Yes, my lord."

"But the necklace you made for my wife just two weeks ago—silver with emeralds and sapphires—wasn't, was it?"

The man tried to speak, his eyes imploring the mayor.

Renseneb shouted, "It was a copy!"

"I—"

"The old governor Mentu's wife had one just like it!"

"I... I didn't know." The poor man sank to his knees in supplication. "An honest mistake, my lord... I pro—"

The mayor struck the man with a stick. Then he raised his hand to do it again.

I caught his arm and Renseneb glared at me before his temper subsided.

"I apologize for stopping you, Lord Renseneb, but the man was telling the truth."

The mayor snorted, breathing, relaxing his chest. "The truth?"

The man on the floor nodded vigorously and the mayor waved him away and then nodded, indicating that we should walk again.

"The truth?" he said again. I'd thought it had been either rhetorical or directed at the jeweller. Instead, he was asking me.

"I have a gift," I said. "I am good at reading people—most of the time." I qualified this because I couldn't judge either the mayor or nomarch. Perhaps that was a consummate politician's skill. Whatever, I didn't need to. They weren't on trial.

"So you knew the necklace in the trial wasn't the same one as my wife's?"

"No, my lord, I mean I knew the jeweller was telling the truth. When he made your wife's he thought it was unique. Perhaps he once saw the other necklace, but his copy wasn't intentional."

The mayor gripped my arm before saying farewell when we returned to my men.

"I'm impressed with you, young... Yanhamu, isn't it?"

"Yes, my lord."

"Then let's look forward to tomorrow. Let's find out what's really going on in this high court case."

TWENTY-FIVE

I chose a temple for evening prayers and then strolled along the river afterwards. There were many priests here, offering a variety of services: blessings, fortune telling and medical treatments.

Sadhu hesitated beside one and implored me with his eyes.

"My lord, I would be eternally grateful."

I looked from him to the priest. The religious man was offering to identify the location of a client's father in the sky. The star that he had become.

Sadhu said, "I know he's watching me, but I've always wanted to know which one he is. Master?"

I nodded to Paneb and my slave handed the priest a piece of copper.

The spectacle fascinated me. First the priest purified himself and then Sadhu with water and oil. Then he seemed to read lines on the boy's face and hands and feet. All the time he chanted prayers and kept glancing up.

Finally a revelation came to the priest and he pointed to a faint dot about a hand's span above the Great River in the sky.

Sadhu was crying when he stood up.

I was so taken by the experience that I stepped forward ready for my own reading. I couldn't remember my father's face nor did I know whether he was alive or dead. Still, I found myself sitting before this priest of the heavens waiting to be told where my father was.

The same ritual was performed: the purification, the chanting and the reading. It seemed to be taking longer than for the boy, and I thought I saw doubt on the priest's face.

"Is there a problem?"

He didn't answer and continued to look perplexed.

"Could it be that my father isn't dead?" I suggested.

He took a breath. "Yes, that'll be the explanation." Then he stood up and did something unexpected. He returned my payment.

I was going to protest but Paneb gave a subtle tug on my gown and I graciously accepted the refund.

We walked some more and I let my men lead the way because my head was elsewhere. The priest was lying when he agreed with my suggestion. I didn't think he was a fraud, I think he genuinely expected to find my father's star but couldn't for some reason. That failure and his sense of pride had resulted in the refund. If my father was dead, he was either eaten by the Devourer or in the heavens. If it was the former, then surely the priest would have said. If the latter, then why couldn't he find the star?

These thoughts spiralled around and around in my head until Paneb said, "We are close."

My focus returned and I realized we were in the area where we were supposed to meet. The hour was now close and I would find out why the stranger delivered the high priest's ring.

A pounding of feet on the stones made me turn, and a squad of soldiers ran down the street. We stepped out of the way just in time, and I had to stop my slave drawing his short sword.

"You show that and they'll kill you," I said.

"If you need defending—"

"I don't," I assured him. "Now where is this meeting place?"

"Here I think," Paneb said, and he led us down an alley and under an arch. Suddenly we were surrounded by soldiers and forced against a wall. Again I slapped my slave's arm to prevent him committing certain suicide.

"Black's forever!" I shouted, like I was leading a celebration.

The soldiers stopped pushing us and the closest ones stepped back to allow an officer through.

"You Seth Army?"

I puffed out my chest, feigning more confidence than I felt. "Second Officer, Seth Fourteen," I said. "Who are you?"

"First Officer Mehku, Seth Five, sir. I apologize." He saluted me and I returned the gesture. His men eased back, although I now realized there was someone on the floor at the back of the dark courtyard we'd entered. Three soldiers held him down.

"What's going on?"

"We have apprehended an enemy of the state, sir."

"Who is he?" As I asked, the man on the floor was being dragged to his feet and then across the stones towards the entrance arch.

"I can't say, sir."

"What's he done—?" Before I could say "wrong", my tongue lodged in my throat. The man being dragged glanced at me with recognition in his eyes. This was the stranger we'd come to meet, I was certain of it.

The officer was speaking, and I realized he'd just said something like he couldn't tell me anything about the man.

I nodded. "Good night, Officer Mehku, and the strength of Seth be with you."

"You also, sir," the soldier said, and within a few heartbeats, we were alone in the courtyard. My hands were shaking.

Sadhu bent double and evacuated his stomach. Paneb helped him back up and checked I was all right.

I said, "If they hadn't been Seth Army, I predict we'd have been interrogated along with that poor man they had."

Sadhu said, "I can't believe they'd have treated you, a noble, like that, my lord."

"Believe it," Paneb said, and I nodded confirmation.

We made our way out of the courtyard, out of the alley and back to the more open streets.

I said, "In the eyes of the law, status doesn't matter."

"But the army isn't the law," Sadhu said.

"Right, but they will have been acting on behalf of…" I trailed off, because no one would dare arrest an emissary of the High Priest of Amun. So the stranger wasn't acting on behalf of the high priest. He must have been a criminal. I kept telling myself that because the alternative just didn't make sense.

TWENTY-SIX

The girl, Tihepet, came to my rooms later than before, and she brought more white powder.

I said, "You can stay, but I mustn't take any more dream powder because I almost didn't wake up this morning."

"Have you completed your dream?" she asked.

I shook my head.

"Then I gave you too much. Take half this time and you'll be fine."

I felt my resolve slip away. "Will you wake me before sunrise?"

She promised and I let her give me the powder mixed with goat's milk. I thought I wouldn't sleep at all because of what had happened with the soldiers but at some point the dream found me.

Darkness gave way to the glow of many burning torches. I was back in the makeshift temple of Bast in Ugarit, surrounded by wounded officers and priests.

And the man before me was shouting.

"What's wrong with you? I hope you're not squeamish at the sight of blood!"

I tried to compose myself. The man I hated—the man who had spoiled and killed my sister—was here.

After leaving the academy I had requested a posting to Gaza, but the captain wasn't there, and after searching local records, I could find no proof Captain Ani had ever been there. Now I looked down into the face that had haunted my nightmares for the past eleven years. He was no longer known as Ani. Now he was Serq, the scorpion.

"I asked you what is wrong!" Serq shouted.

I covered my mouth and ran from the makeshift temple. Beyond the bales of papyrus flowers I bent double and vomited. A priest enquired if I needed a prayer but I waved the man away. Standing straight, I gulped in the air, trying to force myself to return. As I looked around, I watched the priest I had waved away.

The man occasionally placed a bowl beside a wounded man and encouraged him to drink from it. As I watched the priest collect another bowl and fill it with something white from a jug, an idea came to me. A scribe always carried the tools for writing, which included arsenic, the substance that rich women used to whiten their skin and doctors as part of a remedy. I also knew it could be used as a poison. I collected a bowl, and after first tasting the milky substance, I poured it into the bowl and then surreptitiously emptied my pot of arsenic paint into the liquid.

I carried it carefully to Serq, who eyed me suspiciously.

"A thousand apologies, sir." I bowed, averting my eyes and feeling better for it. "The incense—I think it was affecting me." Placing the bowl on a table beside Serq's chair, I said, "Sir, this is goat's milk, if you are feeling up to drinking it."

Serq looked disdainful. "I've only got a slight leg wound, Khety. I'm only here to ensure the goddess *favours me and prevents infection. Now tell me how you knew there was to be an ambush today."*

"I knew we had information about troop movements of the enemy that had been obtained from documents in the possession of a messenger. I was translating a tablet that seemed to be list—a food order—but I got suspicious. There seemed to be code. There were numbers and town names in the wrong places, sir. They were in the same places in the other document, which I recall had the same numbers which couldn't be explained."

"So you couldn't be sure it was a trap?"

"No, sir."

Serq thought for a moment, staring at one of the braziers. "Then it was very bold of you to send the message to my force. If you had been mistaken, the loss of face would have been unacceptable. And you know the punishment for that."

I nodded and noticed Serq still seemed to be deep in thought.

Eventually, the leader of the Fourteenth said what was on his mind: he began to talk through strategies and battles he had fought. I found myself only half listening. I kept staring at the bowl, wondering what would happen if Serq drank it; was there enough arsenic to kill? I had heard of men foaming at the mouth and writhing with terrible gut pain after being poisoned. I touched the electrum amulet I now wore around my left wrist and thought of my sister. She would be in the Field of Reeds, I was certain. I was also certain that Laret watched over me at night like she had as a child after our mother had died and father left. I smiled at the memory of her pretty face and generous heart. She was waiting for me but, if I murdered this man, there was no way I would be allowed through the Gates of Judgement. Ammut would destroy my ba and it would be an eternity of nothingness.

Serq picked up the bowl. He continued to talk about victories and the glory of war, especially under General Horemheb.

I stared at the white liquid as it swirled with the man's gestures. And then Serq placed it to his lips.

In that instant, I saw a priest behind shake his head. The man had a Bast mask and, as I looked closely at the cat's face, I saw my sister's eyes looking back, pleading with me.

"No!" I struck the bowl from Serq's hand.

The leader roared with fury and I fell to my knees. "Your pardon, sir! I saw an evil bug drop into the liquid." My voice trembled as much as my hands and I gripped the amulet and prayed for strength. I could not kill the man like this. My sister had given me a sign that this was not meant to be, but now I knew my life clung to my body like a spider dangles on a thread.

I waited, prostrate before my new leader.

Serq stood.

The whole temple became filled with chattering. The occasional moan, chanting and sound of the sistra was gone. I glanced up and realized Serq was looking west. Everyone who could stand did so. Everyone was looking west.

The night sky had a bright orange patch tinged with purple.

"It's Ra!" someone shouted. "Ra has returned from the underworld!" There were more shouts and chanting and bowing in supplication.

I stood and stared at the strange light. The purple edges looked like cloud, billowing, forcing its way up against the night's dark cloak.

And then the ground trembled—a weak shake at first, and then it was like being on the footplate of a chariot driven fast over rutted soil. Men cried out. The shrine to Bast tumbled. A fire started on the ground where a brazier had fallen and then caught a bale of papyrus.

I fell and pulled myself up next to Serq, who was holding onto his chair.

"That is not Ra," Serq said quietly and, as if in response, the air was filled with a terrible roar, like a thunderclap, only this didn't end.

A group of men, closest to the fire, pushed the burning bale away and stamped down the flames on the ground. The head priest composed himself and began to lead prayers. Like others, I knelt and extended my arms towards the light.

Serq knelt beside me and muttered again, "That is not Ra."

I braced myself for another reaction to Serq's heresy, but if anything the roar began to diminish.

We stayed like that for a long time, the priests lamenting and Serq occasionally grumbling his doubts. I noted the moon had travelled a full house— an eighth of the night sky—when I heard another far-off sound. At first it was a whisper in the air and then the sound of a million locusts heading towards us. The priests stopped and everyone stood and stared west again. The glow was still there, more faint and purple, as though the dark clouds were building and pushing the sun back into the underworld.

Then I saw it, a wall of water rushing into the valley, tearing up trees and ploughing through the earth like a river breaking a child's mud dam. Almost as soon as I spotted it and started to wonder what it was, the tidal wave crashed through the temple and swept everyone away.

It was two days later, and as the survivors reformed into the semblance of an army, I was assigned a unit of twenty. We marched north, and I needn't have worried about being in the front line because the enemy was routed.

The tsunami that reached us, ten miles inland, had swept the enemy away. Everywhere was destroyed; whole towns had been turned into fetid land covered in jetsam. By the time the horns sounded to signal the end, I was relieved that I hadn't drawn blood even once. I gathered my men in one of the main encampments and we celebrated long into the night with beer, singing and dancing. Animals were butchered and roasted, for there was certainty we would be returning home. And when my men were tired of talking about all the women they would make love to, they talked of how they would spend the gold they would earn as the heroes who defeated the Hittites.

In the morning, the leaders and high priests returned from a meeting with the general. They moved amongst the units and reported the news that the great victory had been in the name of Ra, who had spoken to Horemheb and told him it was time to return to the Two Lands and drive out the usurper of the crown. We were told we would also receive twice our allotment of gold. A ripple of cheers ran through the legions as they heard the news and then the whole army began to chant the name Horemheb.

I didn't see Serq after the wave struck us. He wasn't one of the surviving leaders nor was he mentioned. I prayed long and hard to Ra—or whomever had brought the tsunami—and thanked Him for destroying my enemy for me.

TWENTY-SEVEN

The girl shook me awake and I tried to return to the dream.

"Master, you insisted," she said, shaking me more. Finally she resorted to cold water, and I accepted the dream would have to wait until tonight.

I washed, dressed, prayed and then breakfasted. The whole time I disciplined myself to focus on the court case, and put all other distracting thoughts from my mind.

During the hour I had waiting for the rest of the high court to assemble, an idea struck me and I spoke to Paneb before returning to my throne.

The nomarch arrived before the mayor again.

"Ask lots of questions again, young man," he said after wishing me a good morning.

"I intend to, my lord," I said, and he responded with a self-satisfied smile.

I looked over the men on the benches expecting to see the guide from last night, but he wasn't there. Had he been there yesterday? I didn't know. If he hadn't then how did he know? I wished then that I'd asked him who he was working for.

Mayor Renseneb arrived last and looked like he hadn't slept well. He gave me a curt nod, as though our relationship had frozen. Which seemed at odds with our conversation last evening.

This sense was heightened when the mayor spoke to the court and announced that the judges would not ask questions until after all statements had been made.

I looked at the nomarch, who just raised an eyebrow. I thought there was a small smile on his lips too, but couldn't be sure.

First on the floor was the police chief again, and we received a recap of the case against the two men and a summary of Passer the coppersmith's confession.

Next, the Officer of the Guilty came in and the second accused was strapped into the chair. This man was also thin, dirty and had been beaten.

This was Neni the stonemason, and we heard him give the same confession to the crime of disturbing the three tombs. At one point his feet were beaten until he accepted the version dictated by the prison officer.

"We'll take a break," the mayor announced.

"With your indulgence, My Lord Renseneb," I said, "I would like to ask a question."

Renseneb glowered but Nomarch Userhat made sure I received the rod so that I could speak.

Careful so that I directed the question at the officer, I asked, "How did the prisoner enter the tomb of the old governor Mentu?"

The Officer of the Guilty directed the question at the prisoner, who didn't look at anyone when he replied, "Through a hole in the roof."

"Ask him if he could fit in the hole."

Uncertainty flashed on the prisoner's face before he responded. "Of course."

I remembered the doubt on the other prisoner's face when I'd asked about the interior of the third tomb, so I did the same again.

To the officer, I said, "Ask the man about the necklace in Lord Mentu's tomb."

In the corner of my eye, I saw Renseneb tense. Perhaps he thought I was going to question its provenance or somehow link it to the mayor's wife.

The officer said, "The necklace was in his wife's coffin wasn't it?"

"Yes."

"I want to hear the prisoner's words," I snapped, surprising myself with my annoyance.

Neither the officer nor the prisoner spoke. Both looked at me.

"Ask the prisoner to describe the wife's coffin."

After being prompted by the officer, prisoner Neni said the coffin was in the same chamber. "We took off the lid and removed the necklace. Afterwards we replaced the lid. Lord Mentu's coffin was next to hers and inside we found a golden dagger."

"Wait!" I said. "The golden dagger was from the first tomb."

Userhat indicated for the chief scribe to come before us and he read out the testimony from yesterday that clearly described the dagger. It had been stolen from the first tomb.

Afterwards, Userhat took the rod of office and challenged the prisoner.

Neni didn't look up. "A thousand apologies, I am nervous. Yes, the dagger came from the first tomb."

"Now we'll take that break," Mayor Renseneb said abruptly. "We'll resume with witness statements."

He got up and the court was adjourned.

The nomarch smiled and directed me to a side chamber where we were given water and hot towels.

"You are doing well," he said. "You are thinking more clearly today it seems."

"Yes, my lord." I waited until he eased his shoulders and took a relaxed pose, feet outstretched. His thick and discoloured right ankle poked out from beneath his gown.

"With your permission," I began, "I would like to recall the other prisoner."

"Why?"

"For clarity, my lord. In fact, could I have permission to call anyone?"

He smiled indulgently. "You have my permission."

"What about Lord Renseneb?"

Userhat almost choked. "You want to call him?"

"No. I mean, what if he objects?"

"I'll deal with it," Userhat said. "I'll deal with it."

TWENTY-EIGHT

Nomarch Userhat set the rules for the next session as court began again. He proclaimed, "Any judges in his wisdom may call any prisoner or witness to the stand."

Mayor Renseneb opened his mouth to complain but then shut it again. I realized that, like for this morning's session, when one senior judge makes an announcement, the others must accept.

I cleared my throat. "Please call for the Officer of the Guilty to bring Passer the coppersmith back into the court."

Renseneb fidgeted as we waited, and finally, the poor prisoner was dragged into the hall and strapped to the chair.

"Yesterday, the prisoner told us about breaking into Lord Mentu's wife's coffin and taking her necklace. Please ask the prisoner to confirm."

The prisoner was asked and answered, "Yes."

"Ask the prisoner how he got into Lord Mentu's tomb."

"Through the hole in the roof into the burial chamber."

"How big was the hole?"

The prisoner looked confused and received a blow to his feet for his silence. The officer repeated the question.

"I don't know, my lord." He looked at me, then away, then said, "I didn't measure the hole."

"Was it big enough to climb into?"

"Yes."

"So the prisoner went inside?"

"Yes."

"The roof was high, no?" I knew that tunnels were shallow but burial chambers of nobles were typically high, representing the heavens above.

"Yes, I had to drop down onto the floor," the prisoner responded to the repeated question.

"This morning we heard from Neni the stonemason who also entered the tomb. Is that correct?"

The officer said, "With respect, my lord, I don't think the prisoner can answer for the other prisoner."

"Strike the question," Mayor Renseneb instructed the scribes.

Userhat leaned over towards me. "Where are you going with this? It seems off the point."

"Indulge me, my lord."

He sighed. "Of course."

To the court, I said, "I call the chief scribe."

The chief scribe hurried before us and I asked him to read the other prisoner's statement concerning entering the tomb through the hole and taking the necklace.

"Now," I said once the scribe had returned to his position, "Officer of the Guilty, please ask Passer the stonemason how he got out of the tomb."

"Climbed out," the prisoner said.

"Wasn't the ceiling too high?"

"The other prisoner hoisted me up."

"Then how did he get out?"

"Again the question will be struck," Renseneb snapped. "A prisoner cannot answer for another prisoner. Now we will move on. I call the first witness."

The prisoner was removed and a boy of about six was brought in by a guard. He too was put into the chair and his bare feet exposed for a beating.

The boy told the court that he had overheard the two prisoners plotting to steal from the nobles' tombs. He was asked for detail and stuttered through a description of where he'd overheard them and also a description of the two men.

Despite receiving no beating, the poor boy was shaking as he was led from the Great Hall.

Another witness was brought forward and this man spoke more confidently. He was a city guard and said he'd seen the men in the early hours of the morning. They'd been carrying a large sack that contained metal.

Mayor Renseneb asked how he knew it was metal inside and the witness replied that he heard it clinking.

Userhat asked what the men did with the stolen items and the city guard said he didn't know.

We adjourned again, and after prayers, I was invited to join Mayor Renseneb.

He still seemed grumpy with me. "You can be difficult," he said between mouthfuls of duck.

I nodded. I felt like saying, *What changed between last night and today?* However, I simply said, "I appear to have offended you, my lord."

He studied me and ate. Again, I had the sense that I couldn't read this man at all. Then he said, "And I am sure you are a good magistrate. In fact, you have got me thinking."

"Yes?"

"This whole thing about the tomb and getting in and out. Something doesn't seem right. Maybe they didn't both go into the tomb, but then why lie?"

I said, "Your last question was a good one, my lord. Both of them are lying about something, although I can't tell what. I'm wondering if there was a third man."

"A third man? But the city guard said there were only two."

"Maybe he didn't travel back with them. A third man could have helped them both climb out of the tomb. But there is something else troubling me."

The mayor nodded thoughtfully. "How did they plan to dispose of precious items?"

"They couldn't just barter them."

"They could melt down the metal."

"Yes, but it would still be suspicious."

We sat ruminating on this for a few minutes and finished our food.

He said, "Shall we recall the head of the necropolis guard? I got the sense that he wasn't actually there."

"I'm sure he wasn't," I said.

"You have an idea?"

"Does the rule still apply? Can I still call any witness?"

He nodded. "Providing Lord Userhat doesn't change his pronouncement, then it still applies."

"Good," I said, and before we returned to the Great Hall, I went to find my slave.

TWENTY-NINE

"I call Nakht, the necropolis guard," I said after we resumed.

I had already planned this. In the morning I'd asked Paneb to find the man and then confirmed that the guard had been brought here.

His immediate appearance surprised my fellow judges, but neither commented as Nakht was placed into the chair with his feet strapped in. He'd been brought in by a master at arms and I saw fear in the man's face.

Mayor Renseneb pronounced the opening of the session and a new rule. The judges could speak directly to witnesses.

I nodded my thanks and took the rod.

"You are Nakht, originally from Taramu in the north and have been a necropolis guard here for three years."

"Yes, my lord."

"You are respected and trustworthy and honest."

"That is a requirement, my lord."

"You were the sole guard on duty on the night when the tombs were broken into."

This time, when he agreed, beads of sweat broke out on his forehead.

Userhat leaned towards me as if to whisper something, but I ignored him.

"In your own words, Nakht, tell us what happened. You will not be punished for the truth," I said reassuringly. "Provided, of course, that you had no involvement in the crime."

Nakht spoke in his thick northern accent. He spoke like an honest man, without too many words or unnecessary detail. He said that during the fifth hour of the night, he heard singing from the cemetery and went to investigate. There was no moon and it was hard to see, and at first he thought the men were just drunken revellers.

He'd drawn his sword and advanced but then saw that it wasn't three men as he'd thought but a god and two men.

"Did you think one god and two men at the time?"

He hesitated. "No, my lord. My immediate thought was three gods. Men would not dare commit debauchery in a sacred place."

"Why do you now think it was only one god?"

"Because two mortal men were arrested for the terrible crime."

I noticed the mayor watching closely. When I looked back thinking he wanted to speak, he gave a slight shake of his head. So I kept the rod and continued.

"Would you recognize the two criminals if you saw them again?"

"I don't think so, my lord. Like I say, it was very dark."

Then the mayor signalled for the rod.

He said, "But then why did you think the third man... thing... you saw was a god?"

Nakht said, "It looked like a god, my lord."

"Have you seen a god before?"

"Not in life, but everyone knows what the gods look like."

"Flying?"

"No..."

The far door creaked and I briefly saw my slave there before he was barred entry. It was long enough for me to see the look on his face. I'd asked him to find evidence and he'd found something.

Mayor Renseneb ignored the intrusion and continued: "You saw an animal then?"

The witness appeared confused, and I took the rod back.

"Nakht," I said, "at first you thought it was a man. So it looked like a man?"

"Yes and no, my lord."

After he didn't elaborate, I said, "Continue."

"He had the god's face."

"Which god, Nakht?"

He swallowed hard. "Maahes."

"Maahes," I repeated. "The lion god?"

He nodded as though unable to speak.

"You saw the head of a lion."

"Yes, my lord."

Userhat shifted in his throne.

I said, "You told me this yesterday and yet now you have been less forthcoming, why is that?"

When Nakht didn't speak, his bare feet received a beating.

"Stop!" I shouted, and the man's cries subsided.

When he was quiet, I said, "Nakht, tell me why you seem less sure now."

When the guard didn't answer, I yielded the rod to Nomarch Userhat.

He said, "You're afraid now that you realize you are guilty."

"My lord?"

"How did the criminals get past you?"

"I don't know, my lord."

"You were asleep!"

I signalled for the rod, but Userhat kept hold of it and repeated his challenge to the man in the chair.

I said, "Nomarch Userhat, I'd like to question the witness."

"He's now a prisoner, a criminal himself," Userhat hissed at me, and then publically: "Guards, take this wretch away!"

I said, "No, we haven't finished. Nakht, do you know a man who pretends to be a great cat?"

"Strike that!" Userhat shouted at the scribes. "Out of order."

Nakht was being escorted from the hall, and now I shouted: "Was the god holding a sword? Was that *god* actually someone well known acting as a lion?"

"Enough!" Userhat bellowed, his voice so loud that men took an involuntary step back. "This court is adjourned!"

But I wasn't done. I was out of my throne and snatching the rod. "I call the nomarch's third son to the court. I call Wesperen."

THIRTY

A servant came to my rooms in the palace and said that the nomarch requested my presence.

I had been bathing and made the man wait longer than I needed to. Then I followed him to the Userhat's private quarters, past ornate statues and brightly painted murals that were sectioned based on locations south and north of the Two Lands but also strange countries beyond.

"Gifts from our neighbours," the servant explained when I asked him.

"The nomarch is very wealthy," I said.

"Yes, my lord. Not as wealthy as a vizier, but certainly the richest nomarch in the land."

"But is he just?" I asked.

"That is not my place to say, my lord. He is a judge of the high court and what he pronounces is the law."

"Right," I said, and I knew I was talking for the sake of it. What I had done in court was unconscionable. I was effectively challenging the nomarch—my superior, and on his own turf.

When I entered Userhat's chambers, I heard my heart beating like a bass drum in my head.

"Ah, my good magistrate," Userhat said as he saw me.

"My lord," I said bowing. This was not the greeting I'd anticipated. I thought he would castigate me for my crassness in court.

He beckoned me over to a couch opposite where he lounged. When I sat a servant brought me wine and grapes.

Userhat smiled. "I apologize for my poor temper."

"No, my lord, it is I who should apologize. I forgot my place." Despite my words, I knew that in the eyes of the court we had been equal. I didn't need to show respect, although in his chambers, as his lesser, I thought it best to play a subservient role.

He smiled again and took another drink of wine. His eyes suggested he'd already had enough.

"It's been a difficult day," he said.

I thought he was talking about the case but he wasn't.

He leaned towards me. "Did you hear about last night?"

"Last night?"

"The trouble."

I shook my head, wondering what he was talking about.

"I probably shouldn't tell you…" He leaned back again as though he'd changed his mind. I wondered if he was playing with me and was reminded that I couldn't read him like most men.

"There is a conspiracy in the land, Yan-Khety. But I shouldn't talk about it."

"A conspiracy, my lord?" I prompted, unable to help myself.

He sighed. "People who want to overthrow the order of things, bring chaos to the Two Lands."

"Sand dwellers?" I asked, since throughout our history, the wild people to the west had troubled us. Not an army, not like the Hittites, but disorganized incursions and general troublemaking.

"Within," Userhat said in a whisper and cocked an eyebrow. "People within the state, not lawless infidels but men of high standing. It's abhorrent, quite sickening. They may be plotting to overthrow Pharaoh himself!"

"Outrageous!" I said.

I waited for the nomarch to say more, then prompted, "What happened last night?"

"The army have been hunting a man, a conspirator. And last night they found him in this very city. Our city, Ra save us!"

"Where?" I asked.

He gave me the name of a district I didn't know but then added, "It's a poor part, right over on the east."

I swallowed hard, recognizing the location. "Who was he?"

"None other than an emissary of the High Priest of Amun."

"The high priest?" My voice sounded squeaky as I said it. I took a gulp of wine to ease my throat. "Why would..."

"Look, I don't know for certain, but it seems Pharaoh Horemheb and the high priest have fallen out. There's talk of the high priest committing blasphemy, saying that Horemheb isn't of royal blood, isn't descended from Ahmose as he claims." Userhat shook his head. "You realize that I'm not agreeing with these ridiculous claims. I'm just telling you what I've heard."

"Why not arrest the high priest?"

"Would you arrest me?" He laughed. "Of course not. You can't just arrest the High Priest of Amun! But I understand there are better plans. The solution is to replace the high priest with another."

Or remove him in another way, I thought, but said nothing.

"So," I said, trying to piece it together, "why send an emissary to Elephantine?"

"I'm afraid there may be co-conspirators here, possibly even within the government. I don't know who I can trust."

I laughed nervously and took another drink. The man I'd failed to meet last night was surely this emissary. Why did he want to see me? Did he risk his life because he thought I could help? How could a lowly magistrate from the ninth nome do anything? I had no power.

We said nothing for a while and the silence made me feel awkward, second-guessing my host.

Finally, he pushed himself up and said, "Take a walk with me."

We went outside onto a balcony, a spectacular view of the largest island spread before us. From this vantage point I could see the main daily ritual in the temple of Khnum, the pouring of water from a tower down a chute into the river. The chanting reached a crescendo, and as the sound carried across the water I felt a religious tingle.

"Who is your patron god?" Userhat said beside me.

"Anhuris."

"Ah," he said, like I was unfortunate. He could have added, "Poor you". Instead, he waited a beat and said, "Do you pray to him?"

"Not as often as I should."

"But you pray to Ra?"

"Yes. Ra mainly, but others too."

"My son is a religious man," he said, and I realized he was talking about his third son, Wesperen. "He intends to become a priest, you know."

"An honourable profession."

And then he got to the point. "Do not tarnish his reputation with this case."

"If he is guilty—"

"Did Renseneb put you up to this?"

I turned and looked at the nomarch. "No, my lord. I found the necropolis guard myself and got him to talk. He told me about the incident and seeing Maahes. He specifically said Maahes rather than a female lion god like Tefnut or Sekhmet. The implication was clear. It was a young man."

"And you connected him to my son because of his pets?" Userhat didn't disguise his disdain.

"Initially, but then I had one of my men investigate. Your son not only has live big cats but also trophies. He keeps their heads."

"So in high court you would have asked if he had a lion mask?"

I said, "It is my belief that someone helped those two men disturb the nobles' tombs. Not only that but they had nothing when they were arrested. Where was the booty? Could they dispose of it so quickly? No, they had a senior person coordinate. That person would need access to the city plans—the necropolis plans. He knew where and how to target. He will have paid the men for breaking in and taking the items and then kept them for himself."

"Not my son."

"And my final proof would be a golden dagger taken from the first coffin."

"What, *the* golden dagger?"

"That's why I wanted him questioned. I believe he has the golden dagger. I believe he celebrated with it as Maahes that night and has kept it."

"He doesn't have the golden dagger," Userhat said scornfully. "You are so wrong about that. Mayor Renseneb likes fine things. In fact, now that I think about it, I wonder whether he has a similar dagger. His wife has a necklace—"

"It's a coincidence," I said. "I met the jeweller who made it."

"Ah." He looked distracted, or maybe it was the effect of the alcohol.

He went back inside, his limp more pronounced, and I followed. He looked distant and then suddenly focused.

"You are making a mistake." His voice was flat and harsh.

"I must be true to my heart."

"It's not much use if that heart is no longer inside your body."

My blood was suddenly full of thorns. The nomarch was threatening me. If I questioned his son, I would be killed.

Userhat looked into my eyes for a long time and I wondered what he was thinking. It was like he was trying to decide. Finally he shook his head. "I'm having fun with you, Yan-Khety."

Despite his humour I didn't believe him.

He continued: "I know in *my* heart that Wesperen is innocent." Userhat touched his own chest and I realized he was now pleading with me.

We went back inside and he gripped my arm. "Let us end this case quickly and get on with the more pressing, more serious concern of treachery." He paused, perhaps hoping for me to agree. I just returned his stare. Then he said, "There are senior people in our land, probably in my town, who are conspirators. Trust no one, Yan-Khety. Trust no one."

THIRTY-ONE

Tihepet wiped my brow with a cool towel. "You should relax," she said.

I kept thinking about two things: the emissary of the High Priest of Amun and what to do about Userhat's son. The truth was: I knew what had to be done about Wesperen. As I'd told my young assistant, the law applied equally no matter what a man's status in the world. It didn't matter if it was the nomarch himself, and it certainly didn't matter that Wesperen wanted to become a priest.

And that led to a second dilemma. Assuming that we found Wesperen guilty of these crimes, what would be the punishment? He'd not only desecrated tombs and stolen from the dead, he had acted like a god. I'd heard of men being put to death for pretending to be a god and so it seemed the likely outcome.

"Who is the magistrate of Elephantine?" I asked the girl.

"Lord Kheperure."

"Old Kheperure?" I laughed, the name immediately breaking my melancholy.

"Yes, master," she said uncertainly.

"He was the man... Never mind. I've known of him since I was assistant to the... to my father Lord Khety." Kheperure had been the witness to my adoption and my legal papers for the military academy. And then the obvious question struck me, one that I should have asked when I first arrived.

"Where is he?"

"I believe he went to Memphis, master."

"A court case there?"

"I don't know, master."

"But you do know him?"

She smiled. "He frequents the palace."

"What would he do?"

"Master?"

I couldn't tell her the case, nor would I expect to know what he would do, but I tried to imagine the old experienced Kheperure in my shoes. I suspected he would have handled it more subtly and would not have embarrassed the nomarch in the court.

"Generally, if he had a difficult case?"

"He would sleep on it," Tihepet said.

"What?"

"Lord Kheperure would tell you to sleep on whatever it is that is troubling you, master." She got up and poured the white powder into milk.

I accepted it without thinking and lay down. Like the first night, I let her rub my shoulders so that sleep would come quickly.

I was back in the city of Akhetaten, walking, rubble and crumbled walls all around. Purpose-built by Pharaoh Akhenaten, it was said to have once been the most beautiful city: towers and flags and awnings and open spaces like none other. No doubt there had been hanging gardens as well, although there was nothing but dust now.

Mercenaries had swept through the city killing everyone they had found, but this had not been the first attack.

After Akhenaten had died, the power base crumbled and returned to the twin locations: Waset, with the City of a Thousand Gates, and the administrative capital, Memphis. I didn't know the detail but I knew people in high office wanted to erase the memory of the pharaoh and his city.

Except for the swarms of flies feeding off decaying bodies, nothing stirred. I could smell the rotting flesh in the baking heat.

Thayjem came up beside me and said, "What are you thinking?"

"This is more terrible than war. Did these people really deserve this? They were Egyptians after all, and no man has the right to spill Egyptian blood."

"Well that's debatable—not that our blood isn't sacred, of course it is, but it is questionable whether these people were true Egyptians. Pharaoh has declared them outlaws, and their kind must be eradicated throughout the land if ma-at is to be restored, the gods satisfied and the Two Lands be the great power it once was."

"You sound like the political voice of the Administration rather than a human being."

Thayjem scoffed. "I just want to finish this stupid task and go home. What is it, twenty months since we had our victory parade in Memphis? And more than two years since Ra created the great wave that destroyed our enemies. We thought it was over then, but who could have known that we would march to Waset?"

I nodded, studying the architecture and trying to work out where the King's House ended and the Hall of Records began.

Thayjem continued: "I thought Ay would be declared the false pharaoh. I thought there would be a fight akin to the battle of Osiris and Seth." He laughed. "Did you notice the irony since we were in the Seth Army but on the side of the true pharaoh?" He stopped abruptly. "What are you doing?"

I wasn't listening as I dragged my hand along the damaged wall. "This city was the greatest in the world and now it is going to be systematically torn down, stone by stone." I patted Thayjem on the shoulder. "Take the men up to the royal tombs and get started. I'm just going to take a look at the records—if there are any still here. You know, for a while, not only the treasury records, but all written texts were brought here. It is said that Ra told Pharaoh Akhenaten to build a library for all the wisdom in the world."

Thayjem waved to the motley band of ten soldiers who squatted lazily in the shade. They reluctantly assembled themselves and led their horse and carriage back to the Royal Drive. Thayjem turned back and gripped my shoulder. "Don't be long and don't let the Medjay mistake you for an outlaw! If you get killed here, I'm not searching through the bodies to find you."

"Thanks!" I grinned. "And, if I find a Wisdom Text, I won't share it with you."

I watched the unit go and then returned to studying the walls, their murals and occasional hieroglyphs. I found a short flight of descending steps where the wall was damaged, and a hieroglyph appeared to have been chiselled out. At the bottom, I

185

heaved a wooden door aside and found a passage which led to an antechamber.

A noise surprised me and there was a light ahead.

"Is someone there?"

I walked through to a main chamber lit by lanterns and saw desks and hundreds of earthenware pots, from jug-size to the size of a small man, the sort used to store papyri and clay tablets. The room had been disturbed, tables knocked over and most of the pots broken. I moved shards of pottery aside and picked up a scroll. It was a record of food and animals transported from the Delta during a month. I picked out another: a schedule of activities of a tax collector and the payments due. Reading through another and another, I became disappointed by their mundane nature.

I sniffed the air and wondered if it had become more smoky and then jumped as I heard voices echo along the stone passageways. I drew my sword and headed towards the sound. The air became acrid with smoke. Passing through two small rooms I then ascended stairs, and I could now hear the voices clearly. It was an argument.

"Who's there?" I shouted.

There was a chamber lined with shelves, each with pigeonholes stuffed with papyri. A soldier appeared to have lit some of the scrolls, the fire of which spread rapidly. Another man was frantically trying to stop the destruction but had been struck to the ground.

The soldier looked across the chamber towards me at the same time as raising his sword arm to drive it into the man on the floor.

The soldier growled, "Piss off!"

"Stop!" I clashed my sword against metal and, through the smoke, took in more of the scene: the man on the ground was a noble, possibly by royal appointment; the soldier wore the blood-red cloak of a mercenary.

"I said, piss..." The mercenary turned towards me with the glower of a cornered jackal. "You!"

The shock made me drop my sword. "You... Captain Ani..." I stammered. "Serq, you're alive!"

THIRTY-TWO

The man on the ground rolled, but Serq slashed at him with his blade, splashing scarlet across the old man's white gown. He stepped and prepared again for a death blow, but all the time his eyes were fixed on me.

"Ani?" He laughed mirthlessly. "I haven't been called that for a long, long time. Do I know you from somewhere else?"

"You came to my village and took my sister."

Serq shook his head, uncomprehending. "It's the way of war. So you survived the great wave but stayed with the Seth. Good for you. I, on the other hand, recognized an opportunity and formed my own elite unit. Much more—"

"You took her to your garrison. You used her and you killed her."

A thought crossed Serq's hard face. The scorpion-like scar seemed to twitch with life and I was sure then that the man suddenly remembered who Laret had been.

Serq looked down and then up, attempting to mask his true thoughts. He said, "Look, you're a smart lad. You can join us. There's enough gold here to share. Once I despatch this old crone." He slashed down with his sword but struck wood as the old man diverted it. Serq tore his eyes from me and struck again, this time tearing through the old man's gown.

I bent and felt for my sword but grasped a metal rod instead. In a smooth movement I had it in my hand and was charging and screeching. "No...!"

The rod struck Serq in the chest but didn't stop. I drove forward with all the force I could muster.

Serq staggered backwards and then tripped over a bag on the floor. His eyes stared, glass-cold, and his mouth opened as if to shout, but only air rushed between his lips. His sword clattered to the ground and then he toppled.

I stood over Serq, my rod raised to strike again should the man rise. But he didn't. Instead, I checked for a pulse in Serq's neck, found none, and turned to the man on the floor.

The old man tried to lever himself up but then slumped. His gown was splashed with scarlet, his face pale, and when he spoke his voice trembled. "Pray, don't kill me."

"We've got to get out of here—now!"

I pulled the man to his feet and dragged him from the chamber of burning scrolls. The old man nodded and pointed in directions and we zigzagged through corridors into a small courtyard. Here, I carefully helped the old man sit and inspected his wounds. A deep slash to his left arm was causing most blood loss although a stab to the side concerned him more. I staunched the bleeding and gave him water.

The man said, "The records..."

"It's too late to save the scrolls," I said. "You saw how fast they were burning. What were you doing in there anyway?"

The man ignored the question and looked at his bloodied gown. "I need the apothecary. Please help me. I can show you where it is."

I helped him up and supported the old man as we went through the corridors of the King's House and out onto the street. We checked for mercenaries before I helped the man find the shop he was looking for. Inside, everything had been broken or knocked to the floor. While the old man searched through bottles and jars, I went through other shops until he found clothing. When I returned with a couple of gowns, the old man finished applying a poultice to his wounds and smiled.

"Yanhamu." I held out my hand. "Second officer and on a royal mission."

The old man studied me as he dressed. "My name is Meryra, also on a royal mission. Did you notice the sack in the records chamber? The mercenaries are stealing anything of worth. They are not collecting royal treasures for Pharaoh but for themselves."

I nodded. So that's what Serq and his mercenaries were up to: to appear to act for Horemheb but profit in the process.

Meryra interrupted my thoughts: "When you say royal mission, I presume this is also in the name of Horemheb?"

I pulled a scroll from my satchel bearing the mark of the Office of Pharaoh Horemheb. It was authority to collect the mummy of Akhenaten and treasures from the royal tombs and move them to the safety of the Valley of the Kings.

Meryra nodded. "I expected it would be so. While Horemheb tries to rid the country of the people he calls the outlaws, the Ibru—Akhenaten's and his queen's followers—he must also be seen to do the right thing by the priesthood and the gods. Each pharaoh has a duty to protect all pharaohs who have gone before." There was a deep sadness in Meryra's dark eyes as he added, "This is the same king who removed the guards from royal tombs. Even the tyrant Ay did not dare encourage the desecration of holy sites."

"And your mission?" I said sceptically, having registered the old man's criticism of Pharaoh.

"I will explain fully later. Clearly, you have been sent by the gods and we must move as quickly as we can. How are you to move the royal coffin?"

I told Meryra about the carriage and my small armed unit I had sent ahead. We would travel during the night and find cool places to leave the body during the daylight hours.

The old man said, "Excellent. Go to them and collect me when you return this evening. On the road by the Great River, the last building in the south has an animal enclosure. I will be in the hut behind it. Oh, and in Akhenaten's tomb you will find a coffin. It is empty but you should take it back as evidence. Do not bother looking for any mummies. They have gone."

Maybe it was the smoke and the heat, but I was suddenly dizzy. I thought I'd collapse, and yet a wave of satisfaction swept up through my body. I realized that the air was no longer choking and the daylight was night. And then I knew I wasn't in the past anymore, I was making love to my wife, my beautiful Nefer-bithia, sexy and lithe, and I'd been away too long without her caress. Been away... My mind was foggy, trying to comprehend. How had I got home?

I was back in the bedroom. The girl was there, on top of me.

I jolted with the shock and shouted "No!" at the same time.

The force of my words made her jump from the bed. She looked uncertain, her naked body fragile in the faint light.

"Don't you want me, sir?" She smiled encouragingly and moved forward.

I sat up and raised a hand. I saw that it was shaking. "I told you. I have a wife and I would never be unfaithful."

I got out of bed and pulled a robe around my nakedness.

She bowed her head. "Please forgive me, my lord."

THIRTY-THREE

I tried to focus on the court case as I ate breakfast but my mind was back in the room. How could I have been so foolish? I should have made the girl leave, not let her stay each night, probably not let her into my room at all. The need to revisit my past and take the dream powder had clouded my thinking.

When I arrived at the Great Hall, I found it empty except for Mayor Renseneb. He smiled at me encouragingly.

"You're going to do the right thing," he said.

"Which is what?"

"Call the nomarch's third son, Wesperen."

I hesitated and he scowled at me.

"Don't back down just because of who he is."

"I won't," I said.

"Good, because it would be a shame for your wife to find out about you-know-what now, wouldn't it."

My heart leapt into my throat. The girl had told me she was a gift from Renseneb. Did he just suspect inappropriate activity or did he orchestrate it?

I'm sure my face flushed, and before I could say anything, the mayor spoke again.

"Only joking," he said, suddenly friendly. "Let's finish this case and make sure the guilty pay for their crimes."

"My lords…" A voice disturbed us. It was an official from the nomarch's office, and he bowed in greeting us. "Lord Userhat requests a private audience with Lord Khety."

Renseneb's eyes flared. "Does he?"

No one spoke for a few beats, before the official said, "Lord Khety, would you accompany me please?"

As I moved away, Renseneb whispered, "Remember what I said."

My feet sounded loud against the flagstones, and I was led down corridor after corridor into a small room. I was left alone until Userhat appeared, looking like he hadn't slept.

Without preamble, he said, "What have you decided?"

"I would like to call your son to answer questions."

"I told you he isn't guilty."

"Then he has nothing to fear."

The nomarch laughed mirthlessly. "It takes two high court judges to draw a conclusion. I'm in a minority."

"Not necessarily."

"What has the mayor promised you?"

"Nothing."

"Payment for your cooperation?"

"The only payment for my services will come from you, my lord."

He scrutinized me for a moment. "He has something over you, doesn't he?"

"It would never force me to make an unfair bad judgement."

"I believe you, young man," he said. "But before you besmirch my son's name, I would like you to speak to him. Talk to him—man to man."

Before I could answer, the nomarch stepped out of the room and a young man came in. Wesperen, I guessed from his appearance, although he was taller and much slimmer than his father. He had all the arrogance of a privileged youth: a cocky smile and laughing eyes.

"So you are the magistrate from Akhmin." It sounded like an insult, like he was pointing out the lowly status of my town. Of course, he was right.

"In this room you are my superior," I said graciously. "However, in the high court you will not be."

The smile slowly faded.

"What do you want to know?"

I said, "Were you at the nobles' necropolis on the night in question?"

"No I was not." He answered confidently.

"Did you have two men break into the tombs and steel precious items?"

"I did not."

"Do you own a lion's head?"

"I do. There is no crime—"

"Have you ever pretended to be a god?"

"I would do no such thing," he said, but I thought it was untrue.

"I put it to you that on the night of the disturbance of the tombs, you danced and committed debauchery pretending to be the god Maahes."

"No!" he said firmly.

"Have you ever pretended to be the god Maahes?"

"No."

"Have you ever put the lion's head on yours?"

He hesitated. "Yes, but in fun. Not as a god."

"I ask again: were you involved in the crime?"

Nomarch Userhat stepped back into the room, behind his son. "He's already answered that."

I ignored the nomarch. "Tell me again that you are innocent of anything connected with the crime."

"I am innocent," Wesperen answered seriously.

"But not of pretending to be a god," I said quickly.

"Leave us," the nomarch barked at his son, and Wesperen scuttled away.

Userhat squared up to me, his eyes on mine. I could smell wine on his breath.

"So he prances around with a lion on his head. So what?"

"It's blasphemous," I said, maintaining his stare.

"But irrelevant to the case."

Neither of us blinked, until I finally nodded. "I won't call your son before the court. I think he's innocent of the crime at the necropolis."

Userhat's body sagged with relief. He closed his eyes. "Thank you."

"I just wanted the truth," I said. "I just wanted the truth."

The final court session commenced with a recap, and the coppersmith and stonemason were brought before us one at a time. They were challenged and beaten to obtain the name of the third man but none was forthcoming.

I felt the nomarch tried to implicate the necropolis guard, but neither of the guilty men named him, even under pressure. In the end, the two robbers were sentenced to death and the necropolis guard sentenced to a year in prison for neglecting his duty.

I played little part in the final interrogation and sentencing, and the mayor refused to look at me. However, when the court was closed, and he walked away, I had an odd sense about him. Despite failing to drag the nomarch's son before the court, he appeared strangely satisfied.

Userhat also appeared happy, and I wondered if it was simply a matter of the resolution of a case. It had been wrapped up and documented for the official records. Perhaps they saw it as a great pressure and the conclusion a relief. I myself was left with an uncomfortable feeling of dissatisfaction. We hadn't learned the whole story and I hoped the loose ends wouldn't trouble me. Of course, I knew they would.

An hour later, I was at the nomarch's office with Sadhu and Paneb. We were packed up, ready to return home.

"Lord Userhat won't see you," a junior official said after we'd knocked.

"Not convenient?" I said. "I can return."

The official shook his head. "Not later."

I smiled patiently. "I was commissioned to perform duties at the high court."

Sadhu handed the man the letter begging my attendance and offering a princely sum.

The official glanced down before returning it. "I'm afraid he's instructed me that you aren't to be paid."

"Pardon?" I'd heard the man but couldn't believe it. "We had an agreement."

He shook his head. "I'm sorry, my lord, but Lord Userhat told me that you wouldn't be paid because you failed in your duty. Personally, I don't understand"—he raised his hands in defence—"this is between the two of you, but all I know is that he has said you aren't to be paid by him."

I sensed Paneb move towards his sword and stopped his arm.

"Tell your master that we had an agreement," I said in a voice calmer than I felt. "Tell him that I—"

The man bowed his head. "May I suggest you speak to Mayor Renseneb?"

"Why?"

"As I understand it, my lord, the mayor was party to the agreement. He wanted you appointed as the third judge. It is the city mayor who pays state workers. And, of course, there is the other matter." He put his hands together in a way that suggested contrition. "I believe the mayor won."

"Won? What do you mean?"

But the official didn't respond. He just left me standing in the courtyard.

Annoyed and a little confused by the comment, I walked to the mayor's office. Once there, I waited a long time in the heat before Renseneb came out to see me. By his countenance I could tell he was in no mood to pay me.

"Your agreement was with the nomarch, was it not?" he said.

"But I did my job!"

He pursed his lips as though thinking, but then shook his head. "It's no concern of mine."

"The function is normally remunerated by the mayor."

"Not this time."

Although I didn't know what it meant, I then tried my final card: "I was told you'd won."

"What?" He looked surprised, but I thought there was a hint of a smile on his lips.

I waited for him to say more. He didn't.

I said, "I am out of pocket, my lord."

"A noble and a magistrate asking for a handout? I'm sure I must have misheard you. Good day, Lord Khety."

I walked out of the mayor's building, still annoyed and disorientated by the turn of events and conversations. It had never crossed my mind that I wouldn't be paid. I wasn't sure of the direction I was going in but my men tucked in behind and said nothing.

Then I heard running feet and turned to see a lower noble chasing after us. I recognized him straight away. He was the young man with the lopsided nose. The man who had accompanied us to the necropolis.

As he neared I spied a purse in his hand. It was clearly too small to contain the riches I'd been promised, but a purse nonetheless.

"My lord," he said. "Mayor Renseneb apologizes for any misunderstanding."

So this man worked for the mayor. It struck me then that the mayor must have wanted me to go to the necropolis. I'd been led by the nose. Which was ironic, looking at the man with a crooked face.

"The mayor would like you to have this—something to remember."

The purse was handed over, and as I opened it, the official walked swiftly away.

I glanced in, closed it, and stuffed the purse in my robes.

"Master?" Paneb said.

Inside the purse was a single item: a cheap body chain. The one that the harem girl, Tihepet, had worn.

THIRTY-FOUR

Besides my shame, I could not return to Nefer-bithia with a trinket when she anticipated riches. I'd been away for over a week and had nothing to show for my work.

"We don't have enough left for a boat home," Paneb said as we sat in the shade by the river.

"We could work our passage," Sadhu said, and I hoped he was joking. However, it made me realize something obvious. I was here because the main magistrate of Elephantine had been called away. While he was away, there must be tribunals to hear.

I stood up, feeling a renewed sense of purpose. Returning to the nomarch's palace, I pretended there was no ill-feeling about the lack of payment. Yet again I failed to speak directly to the nomarch. He was in the building but I communicated through an official. However, I got what I wanted and obtained permission to set up a street court in Elephantine.

Meanwhile, Paneb and Sadhu sold the girl's chain and in return bought an awning. Before the sun was more than two-thirds across the sky, we had set up the awning in the main square and pronounced that court would be open.

I stayed for another week and saved every precious deben that I could. At night I removed my robes of office and played a more humble man, staying in cheap accommodation and eating with the commoners.

I'm certain that Sadhu and Paneb found it hilarious, but they never showed their mirth and I was grateful for their sensitivity. Possibly because the bed was so uncomfortable, I slept badly. On the third evening I sent Paneb out to find me more dream powder but he came back empty-handed.

"They produce it from the red flowers on the western bank, master," he explained. "But it is not for sale"

"Everything is for sale," I said, annoyed that he'd failed.

"It's controlled by the state and most of it goes to the dream temples."

The embarrassment of needing the powder prevented me from asking the nomarch or mayor for it. As *the state* they surely had ready access to the stuff. So instead I spent restless nights with a runny nose and racing heart.

The dreams, when they came, were fragmented and disturbed. I had killed Serq. I had spilled Egyptian blood and my punishment should have been oblivion.

I was more awake than asleep when I remembered travelling with Meryra, the old man I'd found in the ruined city of Akhetaten, and what he'd told me.

"You did not spill his blood," Meryra had said. "It seems that blow to the chest stopped his heart, and anyway, I believe when Anubis weighs your heart, he will find it a good one. The gods are not stupid, my son. They know good from evil—and I can help you.

All you need to know is the language of the gods so you can speak the truth that they will understand."

I was amazed to learn that Meryra knew me. He'd met me as a boy—the man who had given me the silver amulet and told me about the Law of Ra. Although he was now dying, he spent his last days explaining it to me. He also told me that his secret mission was to ensure Pharaoh Tutankhamen reached the Field of Reeds. It was a promise he'd made, and after he'd told me the truth about the false pharaoh, Ay, I committed to completing that promise.

Meryra had told me how he'd hidden the truth as a code within clay tablets left at Akhetaten and how he'd gathered important items for Tutankhamen's tomb.

His words went around and around and I recalled snippets of conversation about why he had helped me on that day when I'd lost my sister. I'd railed against the gods and thought my life would end. I was nothing and he was a noble and yet he persuaded me that Laret had ascended to the afterlife and I would see her again.

What had he said when I asked why he'd helped? Something about me being a sign or a message from the gods to stay close to Ay and feign support.

He'd also given me the amulet, worth more than I'd ever known before. I asked him why.

Meryra had been in great pain, and when he answered, his speech came and went. But when he did talk, he said, "Perhaps it was my way of acknowledging Ra's message to me. Or perhaps I knew our destinies were entwined."

I sensed there was more to it but he died without telling me anything else.

At the end of the week in Elephantine my head was clearer, and at daybreak I decided it was time to go home. I could have stayed longer because there was a backlog of cases and still no sign of Elephantine's own magistrate, Kheperure. However, I missed my home and longed for the arms of my wife.

Despite—or maybe because of—the way it ate at my stomach, I knew I had to confess my infidelity to her.

THIRTY-FIVE

I earned a respectable sum during the week. Of course, it was nothing in comparison with what my wife would expect, but I would explain and she would understand.

Still saving as much as possible, I bought a donkey and cart for our journey to Akhmin and knew that I could recoup the money by selling it when we arrived home.

The journey took five days, and on numerous occasions I admonished myself for my stupidity. I could have worked another day in Elephantine and paid for a boat that would have done the journey in half the time. However, subconsciously I think I was deliberately delaying the meeting with my Nefer-bithia.

I whiled away the time teaching Sadhu about the law and writing my own notes. The dreams I'd had at the nomarch's palace needed to be documented, and it was cathartic to write them.

Sadhu had peered at my writing a few times and finally found the courage to ask.

"My lord, what language is that?"

I was writing in code, the way Meryra had hidden his secrets within mundane records. "One day perhaps I will tell you, Sadhu," I said. "But for now, continue with your lessons."

* * *

When we came to the villages south of Waset, I was shocked to see the peasants by the road. Normally they would have bread and water and pottery for sale. I'd bartered with travellers myself as a child. But these people weren't selling, they were begging.

Women with babies held their hands out, desperation on their gaunt faces. Children who would have run alongside us stood skinny and weak. I saw a young girl who was nothing but a sack of bones.

They were too exhausted to cry any more but we weren't. I didn't need to discuss it with my men. We readily handed out our provisions until we had nothing left but water. It broke my heart that I could give no more as we drove the donkey on through the last village.

By the time we reached Waset on the second night we were hungry, but it was a good pain. We weren't starving like those villagers and I gave thanks to the gods for our health. I also prayed long and hard for those wretches knowing that nothing short of a miracle would help them.

Giving away our food meant I had to spend even more for the rest of our journey and, despite my men knowing we should have gone by boat, neither made a comment.

We'd done most of our travelling when the sun was least fierce, but on that final day I wanted to push on and felt sick with the heat as we entered Akhmin.

There was great excitement among my servants when I entered my courtyard. Despite my dusty state

I rushed past their fussing hands and went up to find my wife.

It was only after I'd searched all the rooms, calling for her that I accepted she wasn't home. It was probably for the best since I desperately needed a wash and shave. So I returned to my servants and let them take over, looking after me, pampering me until I felt like a new man.

Now I felt ready to take Nefer-bithia in my arms and show her how much she'd been missed.

Darkness descended before my wife returned home. She came in quietly, and as I rushed to meet her, I knew something was wrong.

Her smile was forced, and when we hugged I felt her body tense.

"What is it, my love?" I asked, leading her into our private chamber.

She sat. Her eyes didn't have the usual lustre and her hands were clenched.

"Bith?" Concern rose from my stomach to my throat.

Eventually my wife sighed and spoke quietly. "I have been with a priestess of Hathor."

"Hathor…" I could barely speak. Hathor was the goddess of many things, especially femininity, and women would often consult a priestess of Hathor with their troubles. But I sensed this was something much bigger, although I couldn't voice it.

Nefer-bithia's eyes met mine. "I have lost the child."

I fell to my knees and hugged her legs. "Are you all right, my love?"

She sucked in air and I heard a tremble in her breath as she let it go.

"I have had pain," she said. "It's gone now though."

"Thanks be to Hathor."

She nodded, but her eyes were still cold and on me.

"What is it? Is there something else?" I asked.

"Tell me about your trip."

Her voice was matter-of-fact, and I put this down to her ordeal and the shock of losing our child. So I gave her a quick summary of the case and how it had all gone wrong with the mayor, cross that I hadn't called the nomarch's son.

Normally, my wife would have expressed opinions and asked questions, but she sat in silence and as still as death. Her hands had unclenched, and they rested on her thighs but remained tense.

Finally she said, "Anything else?"

"Well…" I swallowed. "It means that I haven't returned with riches, but I worked the city square tribunals and raised enough to make it worthwhile."

"And that's it?" she asked. "It's a good job I lost the baby then since we will not be rich."

It felt like a slap to my face, and I sat upright, letting go of her legs. "That's not fair," I said, able to keep my voice calm despite the sudden anger I felt. "I've done my best!"

"Really?"

I shook my head at her. Why was she being so unreasonable?

"What do you need to tell me?" Her voice was quiet but barbed.

And then it struck me. The excitement of seeing her and then the distress of hearing about the lost child had made me forget my guilt.

She knew. Somehow she knew.

I remembered seeing the vulture over the cemetery on the western bank of Elephantine. I'd seen it as a good omen. The sign of motherhood. But now I realized it was the opposite.

"You've been with another woman," she said without expression.

I pressed my palms together in contrition. "My body, not my heart, my darling."

A strange sound emanated from Bith's throat. I tried to give her comfort but she pushed my hands away.

"I lost the child because of you," she said, and now there were daggers in her tone. "The priestess told me that it was your fault."

I lowered my head. "Forgive me. I beg you. Forgive me."

But she refused. Her body stayed rigid throughout my expressions of love for her and my contrition. I told her exactly what happened, how I'd woken up and found the girl doing things to me.

"Have you finished?" she said when I finally fell silent, exhausted from my pleading.

I nodded and stood.

"Then you can go," she said. "And do not return."

THIRTY-SIX

I am weak. I left with nothing but my old servant, Sadhu and a heart so heavy that I could barely carry its weight.

By the time I had reached Akhmin I had overcome my desire for the white dream powder. The sweats and poor quality sleep had gone. However, after a bad night in the town without the love of my life, I was lost.

On that first morning I got up with a sense of purpose. First, I sent Sadhu home and told him to study and improve his writing. Then I told Paneb that I would visit the dream temple to escape this nightmare.

Paneb rarely questions my judgement despite knowing that he can, but he questioned me this morning.

"This is a mistake," he said as he carried my things along the temple road.

"You know nothing," I said unfairly.

"This is true, master. Usually. Today, however, I know that the dream temple is not the answer."

I ignored him and returned to my thoughts. The dreams of my sister and my revenge against Serq were done. I'd written them down and felt no need to revisit that world. Instead, when the priest asked me, I knew I wanted to travel back to the time when I'd learned the truth about Tutankhamen.

The cold morning air was filled with the smell of frankincense. Music from sistra was like a chorus of birds. As I approached the temple of Osiris I thought it looked mystical in the torchlight.

I was on the western bank opposite the City of a Thousand Gates, and the Great Field—the mountain on which Horus had been born and under which many pharaohs were buried—loomed in the mist behind the temple. I pulled an empty handcart, which was not unusual when collecting a coffin.

At the gate I could hear the incantations of priests, and then I saw the High Priest of Osiris in his leopard-skin. As I watched he placed the four symbols of protection for the afterlife on a mummy: the scarab, the djed, the Isis knot, and the ankh.

A temple bursar came over and asked if he could assist me. After introductions, I handed him a bag containing payment. He stared at the contents of the bag. Inside was a spectacular faience necklace from Tutankhamen's collection. It had been one of many incredible riches—the personal items of Tutankhamen—from Meryra's chest.

I was certain that the young pharaoh wouldn't mind the small price for Meryra's soul.

"This indeed covers the cost of the best materials," the bursar said. "Rather than a pottery coffin you can choose the finest tamarisk wooden one."

I bowed. "I am grateful, but no coffin is required, thank you."

As the mummy was placed on my cart, the priests looked surprised, but they made no comment at the lack of a coffin. They loaded the canopic chest and a shroud was used to cover them both. After the final sign, the high priest bade me a safe journey to the tombs of the nobles. But I had other plans.

The first rays of morning lit the mountain like the golden cap on the Great Pyramid.

Rather than take an obvious route, I circled around the area where the nobles were buried and took the track to the pharaoh's tombs.

As instructed, Thayjem and my men were waiting at the bend before the necropolis gates. Hidden from sight, two officers transferred Meryra's mummy and canopic chest from my cart to their carriage. When they were finished, the troop formed a formal guard around the carriage, I lead the way and Thayjem guided the pony.

"Papers!"

In the half-light of dawn it was possible the guard couldn't see my second officer insignia and I let the rudeness pass. I handed over the papers that I'd been given more than four months earlier. With authority I said, "By order of Pharaoh Horemheb, I have brought the king from Akhetaten, where lawlessness has jeopardized his safety." Of course, Meryra had told me that Akhetaten's body was missing, but these necropolis guards didn't know that.

The guard saluted. "My apologies, sir," he said, although his gruffness continued to show little respect. "It has been a difficult night and a long shift." He studied the document under torchlight and the way he ran his finger around the seal of the pharaoh made me wonder if the man even bothered to read the document.

After another salute, the guard stepped back to let our strange cortege through the gates. He waved two colleagues to lead the way to the tomb and then followed.

Although the top of the pyramid hill now shone like the sun itself, the ancient wadi that carved its way through the centre had such a chill in the air that I questioned whether this was death itself. No wonder the necropolis guards were so well paid. They spent their nights with the souls and no doubt the demons that preyed upon them. However, our discomfort was short as the gentle slope soon ended by an open tomb.

"Pharaoh Akhenaten's," the guard said gruffly, and I caught him making a slight hawking gesture as though the pharaoh's very name left a bad taste in his mouth. "Let's get this coffin in there and we can seal it up finally." As he spoke, he went to pull the coffin from the back of the carriage.

"I'll take it," I said, stepping in the way of the guards. Then I signalled for Thayjem to help and we lifted the coffin from the carriage.

"You can bring the canopic jars and the loose items," I said, nodding to the guards, "but don't touch the trunk."

Compared with the royal tombs in Akhetaten, I saw this one was simple and unfinished. With lanterns along the walls, we eased our way down steps into the antechamber and from there into the burial chamber. We placed the coffin into a golden shrine that seemed lost without a sarcophagus.

The guards hurried back and forth with the other items that I had brought from the royal tombs at Akhetaten. There was little of value, just family memorabilia from a different time and culture.

When they finished, I stood with them at the entrance and handed the necropolis guard a second document. This was the one Meryra had shown me, his royal mission.

I said, "I also have an order to take some old stuff into Tutankhamen's tomb." I hoped the guard wouldn't study the document too well. It had the pharaoh's seal, only this time it was the old pharaoh's and not Horemheb's.

"It's sealed," the guard said.

"Then get it unsealed, man!" I snapped back.

I left Thayjem to supervise and returned to the coffin in Akhenaten's simple tomb. Listening to ensure I was alone, I then lifted the coffin lid and said a prayer to Meryra lying within.

I adjusted the scarab on the mummy's chest and placed the electrum amulet beside it. My final act was to remove the scroll identical to Tutankhamen's from my satchel and whisper. "Go find your god, old friend."

The entrance to Tutankhamen's tomb was close to Akhenaten's. When I emerged into the valley I saw Thayjem arguing with the guard and stonemason responsible for closing the tombs. The entrance had been opened but there was only a small access hole in the doorway to the antechamber and the stonemason was refusing to make it any larger.

Inspecting it, I saw the gap was barely large enough to crawl through. From my satchel I took a small golden comb and palmed it to the stonemason.

I said, "I don't need to get into the king's burial chamber. I'm just responsible for delivering some funerary items to him."

There was a moment of hesitation and then the man nodded and turned to hammer and chisel more of the door away.

When I was happy the space was big enough, I said, "It's fine." Then I asked Thayjem to fetch the trunk Meryra had brought from Akhetaten. I took a torch and gripped the amulet, said a prayer to the dead and then clambered through into the room.

The light from the flames danced off the golden furniture crammed in the small space. For a moment I was frozen with awe. There was more wealth here than I could imagine. Then my heart jumped. The light caught two large figures: black men standing either side of the burial chamber door. It took a moment to register that they were statues, and I laughed at my skittishness.

Thayjem called through the hole, "Sir?"

I fixed the torch to a wall mount and took the first item that Thayjem passed me. Working quickly, we emptied the sack of the items, many of which had Tutankhamen's original Aten name engraved on them. After placing all the items around the room, I bowed to the two statues and apologized for using the faience necklace to pay for Meryra's mummification and the golden comb to pay the stonemason. I also promised that everything else Meryra had put in the sack for the king was now in the tomb.

Thayjem was back at the hole and called as he pushed a wooden chest into the space. I pulled it through and pushed it over to the statues. I opened the chest to show them the papyri within. "Your path to eternity is here, my lord," I whispered, and at that moment I was certain the boy king's ba was present. Rather than a chill in the icy chamber, I felt a surge of warmth and a sense of fulfilment. Beneath the Book

214

of the Dead, *I showed the statues the pile of papyri that were the words I had translated from Meryra's tablets. I closed the lid and dropped to my knees, arms outstretched in supplication.*

"My Lord Tutankhamen, who wore the crowns and bound the Two Lands together, who pleases the gods and is the son of Ra, I bring you the truth so that the gods may know the truth of your father and his queen and"—the words were formed by the quiet sound of my breath—*"the rulers who came after who do not have pure hearts."*

While Meryra's body was being embalmed I had returned to Akhenaten, found and decoded the old man's secret messages.

Pharaoh Ay had died and been buried with full honour, but Meryra had written that Ay had agreed to take the old way out and be replaced by Horemheb. Rather than be overthrown, he was buried as a pharaoh and had stolen Tutankhamen's rightful tomb.

The second message was that the tellers proclaimed that Horemheb was descended from the Great Ahmose and that Tutankhamen's wife, Queen Ankhesenamun, recognized him as the living god.

However, I told Tutankhamen that Ankhesenamun had sent a message to the Hittite king because she did not want to marry a commoner. Horemheb's claimed lineage was a lie and Ankhesenamun eventually married him only to preserve the true royal line.

I told Tutankhamen's ba *that he had been buried hurriedly with a shortened service led by Ay and without the instructions for reaching the Field of Reeds.*

I told him that Meryra had produced the missing spells and that I, his humble servant, had delivered them.

When I had finished talking, I sat completely still in that room full of riches, and listened. Silence engulfed me. Tutankhamen's spirit was there and I sensed he understood.

I also sensed that he would speak to me, like he had a great secret of his own.

But I waited long after my limbs grew stiff before I left. And he never said a word.

THIRTY-SEVEN

My slave ran to my side, relief on his face as I appeared from the dream temple. A glorious sun came over the distant hills and the ground turned to a burnished sienna colour.

"Master, I was worried…"

"That I wouldn't return?" I laughed.

"Not as the great Lord Yan-Khety," he said. "Maybe a lesser man."

"You think I'm great?"

Now Paneb laughed, his normal cockiness returning. "Well maybe one day, master. I have big hopes and expectations."

"I find that reassuring coming from you, my humble slave."

He was going to speak and I suspected he didn't pick up on my sarcasm. Or, more likely, he was about to overstep the mark with a cheeky response.

"Enough of dream temples," I said, cutting him off. "I know what I need to do." I was walking fast towards Akhmin, and Paneb hurried beside me.

"What?"

"Go to Waset. But first I need to earn something, otherwise we're going nowhere."

So I spent the day in the town square running my old court. As in Elephantine, there was a backlog of cases and I rattled through them. Later, I worried that I'd been more focused on the earnings than justice. I went over each case in my head until I was satisfied that the right decisions had indeed been made.

At evening prayers I asked for forgiveness and that my wife would have me back. Then, later, I spent time outside my home hoping to catch a glimpse of Nefer-bithia or hear her voice. But I didn't.

I spent the night in the same cheap accommodation with the same uncomfortable straw bedding as the night before but I slept well.

After prayers and breakfast we set up court again. However, before we began, a woman begged an audience.

"Do you remember me, my lord?"

"Senettekh—am I correct?"

She blinked her surprise. "Yes, my lord."

"You sold your daughter, Leti, to an officer of the merchant quay."

"His name is Piye," she said.

I nodded. "I judged that he had to find and return your daughter."

"And such a judgement was wonderful," she said with tears in her eyes."

"He hasn't done it?"

"My lord, he found Leti in Memphis, but the man who bought her sold her on and the new owner has asked a ridiculous sum. Piye has refused to pay."

"How much?"

"Twenty gold deben."

I shook my head in disbelief. He could buy a whole harem for that—or maybe a herd of good horses.

I said, "Piye doesn't have that sort of wealth?"

"No, and I could never save so much if I had my life a hundred times over."

People were now gathering for the start of the day's court. Paneb signalled that the first case should commence.

I took a breath. "I'm sorry, Senettekh, there's nothing I can do. This new owner's demands are ridiculous. All we can hope is that he comes to his senses. Inform Piye that you've told me and that he is not released from his duty to repurchase your daughter. He must keep trying until the price becomes reasonable."

She nodded and smiled weakly. "Thank you, my lord."

As she backed away I couldn't meet her eye. I suspected that she'd never see her daughter again and I felt her pain.

I ran the court for half of the day and realized my slave had prioritized the shorter, simpler cases. By midday I announced that the court would be ended for the day, and Paneb confirmed I'd earned enough to get us to Waset with plenty to survive for a week—although I insisted my next bed be better than the one I'd spent the last two nights on.

Waset never failed to impress me. Busy and exciting and with as many priests as normal city folk. It didn't have the exoticness of Elephantine, but that city was in three parts. Eastern and western Waset were the towns on either side of the Great River. And then there was the religious sector that we referred to as the City of a Thousand Gates because there were pylons and temples everywhere.

The grand vizier of the south had his palace in eastern Waset, but it was clear that the real power lay with the High Priest of Amun. The great temple and enclosure must have taken up around a quarter of the whole metropolis.

I saw many soldiers but none in the religious sector. They weren't allowed. And beggars weren't allowed anywhere in the city. I knew that the guards aggressively removed any vagrants and that was why none of the destitute village folk from the south ventured beyond the city limits.

I went into the public sector and prayed for many hours. I moved from courtyard to courtyard, shrine to shrine, getting closer to the inner sanctum. I wouldn't be permitted access to the holiest of places, but it was the high priest I sought rather than communion with the king of the gods.

By evening prayers I had still seen no sign of the religious leader. There was a hierarchy of priests and most were the lowly *wab*-priests responsible for most daily duties. However, I occasionally saw a *ka-* and *sau*-priest, but they were still all too junior.

I was about to leave when a *lector*-priest walked ahead of me. Following him, I waited until we couldn't be overheard.

"I seek an audience with the high priest," I said, and then introduced myself.

"Why should His Highness see you?" the man asked in a patronizing tone despite my nobility. Here, in the great temple, I had no status compared to a *lector*-priest.

I pulled the ring from beneath my robes.

His eyes narrowed. "You found his ring?" I could see that the man was probably thinking that I'd misappropriated it.

"The high priest sent a messenger," I said quickly. "Unfortunately, the man was arrested before we could speak."

The *lector*-priest took a long breath, his forehead knitted with thought.

I added: "Please just tell him that I am here."

After an incline of his head, the priest hurried away into the darkness.

Nothing happened for a long time. The public had gone and I saw only occasional *wab*-priests as I waited. I pretended to pray at a shrine and no one questioned my presence.

When someone finally came to find me, I jumped at their sudden appearance.

"Lord Khety?" he asked.

"Yes."

"Where are you staying?"

I gave him the address.

He nodded. "Go there and wait."

"The high priest will visit me there?"

But the man didn't answer and I was immediately alone again except for the sound of footfall on flagstones.

When I arrived at my lodgings, my slave told me someone was inside waiting for me. Only it wasn't the high priest. It was someone I would never have predicted.

THIRTY-EIGHT

"Lord Kheperure!" I said, astounded.

"You were expecting someone else perhaps?" the old man said, standing and offering his hand. "It's been a long time Yanhamu."

"I was just a boy."

"A precocious boy," he said, grinning.

I smiled in acknowledgement. This was the magistrate who'd signed the adoption papers making me Lord Khety's son and heir. He was also the magistrate from Elephantine. Could he be an emissary from the high priest? I waited for him to show his hand.

"So," he said in a raised voice, "what kind of host are you? Where is the wine you should provide an esteemed guest?"

I called my slave and instructed him to obtain wine. Kheperure chipped in with a specific request and Paneb hurried away.

Alone again, Kheperure said, "How did you get on?"

"In Elephantine? The high court case?"

"Of course," he said. "Tell me all about it."

So I went through the details, step by step, and he listened intently, nodded and frowned.

When I finished he said, "Did you question why the nomarch asked for you?"

"No," I said, and he nodded. I guessed he thought of me as arrogant and naïve. Maybe he was right.

"He didn't just choose you because I wasn't available. A lesson for you, my son, you should always question a man's motivation."

Sage advice. I nodded.

He continued: "You are well known as a good magistrate, but more than that. You are also known as being unconventional. Your sense of justice is not—how can I say this politely?—not always aligned with the Law of the Two Lands."

I nodded again. "I have always believed in the Law of Ra. It's been my guidance since I was a child, since I first learned of the law."

He put his fingers to his lips like he was praying or preventing the words from coming out. But then he said, "This is open to interpretation." He nodded. "Because the Law of Ra isn't written down."

"Because it doesn't need to be. Man's law—the Law of the Two Lands—is written and changed at a whim…"

"Be careful," Kheperure said seriously. "Such words can get you arrested."

"I don't mean it as—" My slave returned and I waited for him to pour wine and retreat before continuing. "I don't mean it as treason."

My guest tasted his wine and smacked his lips. "Lovely."

I toasted him and drank some of the liquid, slightly drier than I preferred.

He leaned close, although no one could have overheard anyway. "Treason is subjective. If the state believes you to be acting against it then you are guilty."

I was shocked by his tone. "I would never—"

"These are tense times," he said. "Whether you intend it or not, just be careful." Then he sat back and quaffed his wine. His face transformed with a jovial expression. "Now then, let's talk about this case of yours?"

"Which...?"

"The thefts from the necropolis of the nobles. Tell me again why Nomarch Userhat chose you."

"Because you were unavailable and, as you said, because he wanted an unconventional judgement... I don't know."

"Let me tell you about the mayor and nomarch. They are both friends and rivals. From what you told me, the mayor played you. He undoubtedly always wanted to implicate the nomarch's son and humiliate him."

"But I decided against calling Wesperen."

"The damage was done. Renseneb scored his point."

That's what the nomarch's officer had meant when he said, *I believe the mayor won.*

"Then why didn't he pay me?" I asked.

Kheperure laughed with genuine humour. "Oh, my dear boy. You have a lot to learn. Renseneb didn't need to reward you and Userhat never intended to pay you. The man is far too mean to part with his money. How much did he offer?"

I told him, and the old man laughed so hard that he started to cough.

I said, "It was too much, wasn't it? I should have guessed."

"Yes," Kheperure said after the coughing fit had ended. "The nomarch probably had something he could hold against you as well, I suspect."

I shook my head.

"Did he send you a girl?"

"A girl came but she was from the mayor."

Kheperure nodded thoughtfully. "How did you first learn about Wesperen's obsession with big cats? Did she sow the seed of him wearing a lion's head?"

I couldn't remember. She'd told me about a number of people including Kheperure, and she'd given me the dream powder. All I remembered of her was her sexuality and the golden chain around her waist. I had been such a fool on many levels.

Kheperure said, "The case is curious, but I suspect you have just been a pawn in a silly game of rivalry." I was about to agree when he called my slave and we had more wine.

After Paneb left us again, I changed the subject. "I was told you were in Memphis."

"I was."

"May I ask why?"

"A suspicious man may think that the mayor wanted me out of the way. The truth be told, I was requested by the grand vizier."

"Interesting…"

"Yes," he said.

I waited but he wouldn't be drawn further. I had the sense that it wasn't a legal case but something more serious, something that went to the heart of the state.

He turned the subject on to my adopted father and their history. I told him about my time in the army as a scribe and then my mission to take Pharaoh Akhenaten's body to the Great Field. I didn't

225

mention the secrets I'd learned from Meryra, and I judged that Kheperure had no inkling of the nefarious acts of Horemheb and his predecessor.

We were both drunk when my guest finally made a move. Astoundingly, I could hear the morning birds and saw the sky lightening. Dawn was less than two hours away.

He gripped my hand and arm warmly at the door. "Remember these are sensitive times," he said gravely. "Be careful, Yan-Khety. Be careful."

THIRTY-NINE

Whether or not anyone else had tried to visit during the night or morning, I don't know. I slept until midday and my head felt like I had a rock pressed against both temples.

I found that walking along the river and breathing fresh air helped, although I couldn't eat until much later. Across the water I could see the mortuary temples and the sacred mountain behind. Recalling that time when I'd travelled with the cart and collected Meryra's mummy before taking it to Akhenaten's empty tomb helped clear my mind.

When I eventually felt able, I returned to the great temple and looked for the *lector*-priest who I'd seen the night before.

I didn't find him, but a *wab*-priest pulled me aside.

"What are you doing here?" he asked.

I said nothing, wondering what he knew.

He said, "You shouldn't be here."

"Because?"

"That's all I've been told."

"I should wait at my lodgings."

He made a gesture that I read as confirmation then said something strange. "Water dries more quickly on a stone."

I left the temple and returned to my room. Paneb made me eat some bread and cooked eggs, and despite them turning my stomach at first, I began to feel better.

I waited and waited and we killed the time by playing senet. Of course, it would be unseemly for a noble to play with a slave, but we were in private and Paneb was different. We went way back, and for many years he'd been my superior.

We were evenly matched at the game, although he occasionally cheated, and it was only his humour that helped him get away with such behaviour.

I attended evening prayers at the temple of Mut, the mother goddess, and I prayed for my wife. I confessed my sins and told her that my heart was pure. I asked that we be reunited and be blessed with future sons.

As I left, I was reminded that Mut could also take the form of a lioness and that reminded me of Wesperen and the strange case at the cemetery.

I was still thinking of the case when a man stepped out of the shadows. Paneb drew his sword but I stayed his arm. Despite his appearance—a dark hood covering his head and putting his face in darkness—I sensed no threat.

"Water dries more quickly on a stone," the stranger said, and I nodded. The phrase had been a sign.

"Follow me. Your man stays here," the hooded man said, and he walked swiftly back into the darkness. After assuring Paneb that I would be all right, I hurried after the other man.

We took alleys and passages both narrow and dark until I was lost and I was sure that no one could have followed.

Finally, he darted into a doorway and I found myself in a tiny room that smelled of animals. I guessed it was either an old stable or was a storage room attached to one.

The man shut the door and fumbled in the darkness until he must have found a small oil lamp and I heard him strike a flint to light it.

As the flame caught, I saw that we were indeed in a stable, probably unused for many years, with straw that had started to rot. There were no windows, so we were alone and hidden.

I watched the man closely as he removed his hood. By now I had expected the high priest himself, but it was not. I had heard that the high priest was one of the oldest in the land—maybe sixty years. This man before me was younger by about twenty years, and despite his serious demeanour, he did not have the gravitas of a high priest.

"Who are you?" I asked.

"It doesn't matter. You have the ring?"

I pulled it from my robe and he nodded.

I asked, "You're representing—?"

He stopped me with a raised hand. "Don't name him. Yes, I am, and we should talk quickly. How much do you know?"

"About what?"

He took a breath. "Sit down."

We both sat on the dirty straw and he took another breath. I got the sense that he'd practised what he was about to say. But the next thing he said was another question.

"Do you know about Pharaoh Akhenaten?"

I knew many things that I'd learned from Meryra's secret tablets but I couldn't share them with this stranger.

"Assume very little," I said.

"Akhenaten was from the family line. The royal family descended from Ahmose the Great. Even when the Two Lands was occupied by foreigners, the royal family continued. Pharaoh Ahmose defeated the Hyksos and reunited the Two Lands."

I nodded. Of course I knew this. Anyone with a modicum of education was taught the history, particularly Ahmose's victories, as well as the great pharaohs who had followed.

"Amenhotep III—still before your time—was also a great leader, and like his forebears, he ran the country from this city. The ties between the priesthood and administration were almost indeterminable. His first son, Thutmosis, died and Amenhotep IV was crowned by the High Priest of Amun."

I nodded again.

He continued: "Amenhotep IV had been trained as a priest of Amun, and at first things continued as they had under his father. But then he changed. He became more and more obsessed with Ra-Horus on the horizon, the living sun disc."

"The Aten."

"Yes, and he began to reject the god whom he had served all his life. He did this physically too by moving the capital to the new city of Akhetaten."

"I know it. Mostly ruins now."

"I tell you this so that you understand what it must have been like for those of us who knew that Amun was the king of the gods."

"But Amun-Ra?" I prompted.

"We recognize that the Hidden One, Amun, is a manifestation of Ra. He is the spirit among us; he is Ra on his journey through the night sky. You cannot see him but he is there. I tell you this because although it is obvious, it wasn't properly explained to the people until after Akhenaten's death. And it helped Tutankhamen bring together a country where the south recognized Amun and the north Ra. Regent Ay, with Pharaoh Tutankhamen's authority, moved the administrative capital to Memphis and restored the religious capital at Waset—under the auspices of the High Priest of Amun."

I said, "All right, but what has this all got to do with me?"

"I'm just setting the scene so you understand the political situation."

I nodded, although I suspected this was a justification for what I was about to hear.

He said, "When Tutankhamen was born, Akhenaten had a male heir despite being born of a woman who was not from the royal line."

"Not Nefertiti," I clarified.

"Correct. And when Akhenaten died in his regnal year 17, Nefertiti became pharaoh. She was not appointed by the High Priest of Amun, but rather appointed herself as High Priest of Aten." He said this like it was acid in his stomach that burned a hole.

I said nothing, pretending I did not know about Nefertiti and how she was overthrown. How she and her people escaped to the Delta, were pursued and treated like outlaws.

"Nefertiti built monuments to Amun here, pretending her allegiance, but we knew it was false. She also married her eldest daughter, Meritaten, to continue the royal line."

"But they would need to have had a son."

"That's right."

"Not Tutankhamen? Are you telling me there was another son?" I asked.

"Yes. Meritaten had a son by her father. The boy was called Nebwaenra. He was Akhenaten's second son but a pure descendant of the royal line and should have been pharaoh rather than Tutankhamen." He swallowed.

I said, "Something happened, didn't it?"

"Nebwaenra was born in the year that his father died. We saw the terrible possibility of Atenism continuing beyond Nefertiti. We were told by the great god Amun that the boy needed to be removed."

"You had him killed," I said. "Not only that but you were behind the removal of Nefertiti and the rise of Ay."

He didn't deny it. Instead, he said, "Ay was never intended to replace Tutankhamen. We did not know that the boy would be so sickly."

"All right, so why all this cloak-and-dagger? How can I help the high priest?"

The man swallowed and looked at me hard through the orange flickering light.

"We were wrong," he said quietly. "We misunderstood Amun's instruction."

He paused, and I waited, feeling the tension between us.

Finally he said, "We believe the boy, Nebwaenra, didn't die. We believe the true pharaoh is alive."

FORTY

"Why?" I said, my throat suddenly desperate for a drink.

"Why do we think he's alive? Because we… we arranged for his death and were misled. The man tasked with eliminating the baby replaced him with a similar dead child. Everyone believed Nebwaenra was dead."

"Even his mother?"

"Possibly not. Meritaten may have been in on the deception to protect the child. It was a time of great tension and political fighting."

I said, "Ensuring that Nefertiti was overthrown and Tutankhamen became pharaoh with Ay as regent."

"Yes."

"What really happened to the boy?"

"A courtier smuggled him out one night. We don't know where he took him but it was from this city and we think he was held somewhere close. At some point later, the child was moved. We think he was being raised by a family loyal to Akhenaten and Nefertiti but something happened. Maybe they died, but the child was then taken by a slave and smuggled south, we think."

"A Nubian slave?" I asked.

"Yes."

"And you—your organization—is hoping to find him and usurp Pharaoh Horemheb? All because the High Priest of Amun isn't happy with the way things turned out?"

He said nothing.

"I can't be part of your little conspiracy," I said.

"We think you *are* part."

I stared at him. He was about to put into words what I was afraid of.

He said, "The child was about three years younger than his half-brother, Tutankhamen. How old are you, Lord Khety?"

"Twenty-six."

He raised his eyebrows.

"No," I said.

"We found the Nubian slave and sent him looking for the child—a man by now—a man of your age."

"No," I said again.

"He was with a troupe of actors. He died, stabbed through the throat, but not before he identified the boy."

I flashed back to the strange Nubian running at me and then dying at my feet after Paneb's sword had been stuck through his neck. The frothing blood and his mysterious words: *You... the boy.* You are the boy?

"He was mistaken," I said firmly.

"You definitely have the face," the man said. "You look like Tutankhamen."

I shook my head, almost laughed. "And that makes me his brother?"

"You have a scar over your right eye."

"That happened when I was four or five," I scoffed. "No, he—and you—are mistaken. Did this boy have a sister? I had a sister two years older. No, I am not the man you are looking for."

"He also had a birthmark on his right hip. Let me see."

Now I did laugh. "Hundreds maybe thousands must have a birthmark on their hip."

"It's different. It's three dots."

"This is ridiculous. I don't have a birthmark. Any kind of birthmark. I am not the one."

He stared at me.

"I can't be party to this treason," I said.

"Then I'm sorry," the man said, and before I knew what he was doing, he was lunging at me, a knife in his hand.

The blade caught in my robe. I twisted and grabbed his hand.

"What in Horus's name…!?"

We rolled and I flipped him over and pinned his arms on the ground.

He had fire in his eyes. "You know too much."

He continued to struggle under me. "Drop the knife!" I barked.

It fell from his grasp.

"Be reasonable," I said. "I may not want to join you. I may not support your treason, but neither am I about to turn you in."

He nodded and I felt him relax. The fire left his eyes and I judged rational thought had taken its place. But he tricked me. I don't know how he did it but one second I was sitting astride him, the next I was tumbling head over heels. I crashed into the side of the stable, and before I could get my balance, he was at me and we were grappling again.

Suddenly we weren't alone. I heard rather than saw people crash into the stable and I thought it was over. Other conspirators had burst in and I was a dead man.

But I was wrong. These were soldiers, lots of them, shouting and clashing their swords. A small room in semi-darkness and filled with armed men. I was hit. My arms, my body, my head. I saw blood spurt and I prayed. This was how it would end, and I would prepare myself for judgement and then for seeing my sister once more.

I stopped resisting and let my body go slack despite the pain. And then it all went black.

FORTY-ONE

Pain wracked my body like a needle in every muscle. But at least I wasn't dead.

I opened my eyes and found myself in a covered wagon. It was still night. There was blood on my clothes and I could see a gash on my arm, but it didn't look serious. The blood on my robe couldn't have been mine. I guessed it had been from the man who'd attacked me. He'd had a knife. Maybe he'd resisted the soldiers more than I had.

A chain ran through a ring on a thick belt around my middle. I moved to get more comfortable and felt the hands and knees of others claiming their small territories.

"There's been a mistake," I said to anyone who'd listen.

It brought chuckles from my fellow prisoners.

"We're all here by mistake," one grumbled.

"But I'm a magistrate!"

"What, and you think we're all peasant scum? I'm an administration officer," he said.

"I'm a *seb*-priest," another said.

"And I'm an *hour*-priest!" someone else said, as though scoring points in rank.

I peered at him through the darkness. It was hard to tell what he was due to torn and dirty clothes. My own were equally ruined.

More people called out their status, and I counted fifteen others, none of whom were commoners.

"Where are we going?" I asked after the bunch fell silent again, perhaps returning to their thoughts and fears.

"Pit of Repentance, I reckon," someone said.

I choked. It was a notorious prison for the worst offenders. I'd never seen it but everyone knew that you were thrown down there and no one ever came out again.

"They can't," I said. "I haven't been tried, for Sobek's sake. They can't do that."

"Oh yes they can," a voice said. "Treason doesn't need a tribunal."

"But I'm innocent!"

"And you think we're not?" the voice snapped back.

"I don't know," I said, trying to make eye contact with the other man, but he was a haze in the darkness. "What I do know is that there should be evidence of treason if the—"

Someone else scoffed, "They'll have no trouble making up the evidence!"

"These are terrible times," another voice mumbled.

Again we fell into silence, listening to the creak and groan of the wagon as we bumped along. Eventually I started to realize the cracks in the cover showed a lightening sky rather than being from the moon or stars. And when the sun came up, I almost laughed with relief, despite my situation.

The Pit of Repentance lay north of Waset. The sun came up on the right of the wagon, so we were heading south.

And then my humour changed. What if we were being taken away from the city for another reason? What if we were to be killed rather than imprisoned? I found myself listening to the road, trying to gauge whether we had left the main route south or were cutting along some other track into the wilderness.

Shortly afterwards, I heard beggars outside and figured we were either at or near my old village. We never stopped. The wheels kept rolling and the temperature kept rising.

Eventually men beside me started crying out for water. My own throat burned in desperation but I guessed we wouldn't get anything. And we didn't.

We were weak from heat exhaustion and dehydration when the wagon finally stopped. The sun had just set, and I knew we couldn't have reached Elephantine in the time, despite travelling faster than I had when I'd done the journey in reverse.

The cover was jerked back and a soldier ordered us out. We staggered and lurched, trying to coordinate our movements, keeping to the logic of our chain links. But the journey had affected our balance and coordination, and we tumbled out, awkward and dishevelled.

Beating us with sticks, the soldiers got us into line and started walking us to a ferry-raft. Now I was sure where we were going. Again I relaxed. Not far from the west bank was the prison of Behadet. Men returned from this prison. In fact, the necropolis guard, Nakht, found guilty of dereliction of duty, had been sentenced to a year in this place.

I looked along our line and couldn't see the man from last night. I figured that meant he'd fared worse than me. Much worse.

The morning sunlight made the walled prison look almost inviting as it appeared ahead. Our chain gang staggered for another half an hour until we were through the giant wooden doors and into a high-walled courtyard.

The thunk-clang of the doors as they shut behind us made my heart drop. It was like the scales of justice snapping never to be repaired.

We were unchained, because there was nowhere to run and the guards were armed with either spears or short sticks for hitting us. They all wore swords as well and I prayed I wouldn't see one drawn.

The chain binding us was removed and we were split into groups of four before being led into cells that would have been suitable for a single oxen rather than a group of men.

There was straw on the floor and a trough full of water. Despite its colour and things floating on the surface, we all drank to ease our parched throats.

Afterwards, we sat in the shaded room and stared at the baking courtyard. I saw that the other three men had defeated faces, like I'd seen before in the army. I was used to such conditions and knew the secret of survival was to accept my fate and wait. Watch for an opportunity and focus on any positive, no matter what it was.

At both sunset and before sunrise we were allowed into the courtyard to stretch our legs and do our ablutions. Once a day we got bread and our water was replaced. We learned to use the last of the water to wash ourselves just before changeover time.

I saw men beaten for crying too much or pleading for something. I saw a man die after he struggled into the courtyard, insane due to heat and light. A guard sliced his neck before his body was dragged away.

They left the pool of blood in the centre of the courtyard as a message I'm sure. We didn't need it. Only a crazy man would challenge his captors or face the fierce heat of the day.

The blood dried quickly and by the next day there was just a stain where a heart had once beat. I realized that there were stains all over the courtyard, and although I didn't intend it to, my unbidden mind counted fifteen marks where men had presumably died.

On the third day, more prisoners came through the gates, and our group of four became six. Later, the guards came in with an official—a weasel of a man with a long nose and whiny voice. He took our names, occupations and the town where we lived, before moving on to the next cell.

This was how I learned the name of the *hour*-priest who'd been in the wagon with me: Immaatra. Understandably, he led the prayers for our little group, and I found he did almost as much for the men's spirits as the arrival of bread and fresh water.

From this roll call, I discovered the names of all five other men. However, conversation between us was sparse and I felt they distrusted me.

That evening, in the courtyard, I walked with Immaatra.

"You're a magistrate," he said, when I asked about the way everyone looked at me. "Of course the others don't trust you."

"Because I'm a judge?" I said, astounded. "Surely I must be seen as fair and honest."

He laughed. "You think?"

"Yes."

"Well, they think you might be a spy. Why else would a magistrate be in prison?"

"Because of a misunderstanding."

"I remember your protestations from the wagon on the way here. We're all guilty until proven innocent."

"Are you guilty?"

"Look," he said, stopping. "You shouldn't discuss it. Keep your head down and pray to your god."

"And if he doesn't listen?"

"Then pray to Amun-Ra."

A week went by and more men were brought to the prison, until I thought we were overflowing. With six, our little cell was crowded. However, we became eight and then ten as more and more prisoners arrived at Behadet.

We could now no longer all lie down at the same time. I worked out shifts that the men obeyed. I also provided counsel. Although they may have suspected me of spying at first, I did earn their trust by talking and providing guidance. I avoided any talk of treason or other crimes, but focused on telling stories. Eventually the men started raising legal questions, and I even had other inmates approach me in the courtyard.

More out of something to do than real interest, I kept an eye out for Nakht, the necropolis guard, but I never saw him. Intrigued, I started asking other inmates and always got the same negative response.

I fashioned a game of senet on the ground and found small stones to play with. I considered myself as somewhat of a master of the game but met my match in Immaatra. It turned out that he spent many hours a day playing senet, and from him I learned new strategies.

He also told me things about life as a priest. I remembered the conversation I'd had with the conspirator prior to being arrested. He'd mentioned Amun and Ra, how they were manifestations of the same god. I idly brought the subject up.

The *hour*-priest smiled at first and then frowned. I was intrigued.

He spoke quietly: "They say Amun is a manifestation of Ra."

I nodded.

"You know Amun is the king of gods, and when Ahmose overthrew the invaders, he reinstated the god and—"

"And the high priest's power," I finished for him.

"Right."

"But the north and the capital worship Ra—"

"Being another form."

"With another high priest."

Immaatra nodded and then played a cunning move on the makeshift board.

I suspected then that he'd taken advantage of my distraction, but I didn't care. I'd never considered it before, but priests were men, and men had political ambitions.

Banging at the gates broke the quiet of the night and we looked out into the courtyard. Guards hurried and a receiving party quickly formed.

When the gates opened, a group of men entered bearing flaming torches.

I caught the faintest of glimpses. The light was flickering and the retinue large, but I knew the face of the main man who'd come in.

It was none other than Magistrate Kheperure.

FORTY-TWO

Overcome with relief and excitement, and before I could control myself, I called his name. In response, the guard outside our cell jabbed me with his stick and I fell to the ground, stunned.

Immaatra helped me up. "You know Magistrate Kheperure?"

"A friend of my father."

"Let's hope he shows you some leniency then," Immaatra said. "The man has a reputation…"

Not understanding him, I shook my head.

He said, "He's been charged with removing all and any threat. He's not here to judge, your father's friend is here to sentence."

I found it hard to believe. The priest's impression of the old magistrate didn't match up with the man I'd been drunk with little more than a week ago.

Over the next day, one by one, men were taken from the cells and did not return. Then, at the end of the day, before our exercise period, we saw the batch of men marched out of the prison.

Immaatra prayed and the others either shook with fear or wept.

Our night was broken by the plaintive cries of men who were sure of their deaths. I couldn't sleep and went over and over what I knew of the judgement and what I'd face.

I am pure. I am pure. I am pure, I kept reminding myself, since this is what Meryra had told me. I was guilty of killing an evil man and Osiris would understand. I was not guilty of treason, although I did not know whether such a crime would be considered. Of course, it depended on whether Horemheb was a follower of Horus and a true pharaoh.

At one point Immaatra prayed with me, and I asked, "Do you fear death?"

"Amun's judgement? No. It's man's judgement that I fear."

Morning came and I felt growing trepidation. Two men were taken from our cell. I realized each time that my hands were shaking.

The next to go was Immaatra.

None of them returned.

And then the guards came for me.

"Yan-Khety!" Magistrate Kheperure exclaimed as I was dragged into the room. "Everyone out!"

There must have been eight other men in the room but they exited quickly. Even the guards holding my arms let go when Kheperure waved at them.

I immediately sank to the floor, my legs suddenly devoid of strength.

Kheperure was at my side and helping me into a chair. He gave me a drink of beer, which I spluttered into and then apologized for my rudeness.

"I had no idea," he said.

I sipped at the drink and found my voice. "There's been a mistake."

"Of course," he said, shuffling documents on his desk. "First tell me that you are not a conspirator."

"I am not."

"You were found with a criminal, known for inciting trouble against the state."

"I had no idea."

"And yet you met with him secretly in a stable?"

Of course, the old magistrate knew. My details had been taken. I had been summoned. Was I therefore being played? Was he treating me with kindness to get at the truth of a crime he was sure I'd committed?

I was weak from lack of sleep and food. My mind wouldn't work. I hoped to think of wise words but all that I could say was: "I didn't know what I was getting into."

"I warned you."

"Yes," I said. "I was foolish."

"You had the High Priest of Amun's ring. How does that fit in?"

I took a sip of beer and tried to clear the fog from my brain.

"I was given it in Elephantine," I said. "I knew he wanted to meet. My curiosity was stupid."

Kheperure cleared his throat and his tone changed when he spoke again. "You are being charged with sedition. The ring suggests you are a ringleader."

He moved the beer out of reach.

"My lord, I am not! You have to believe me."

"Then give me the names of those who are."

"How can I? I'm not involved." I implored him with my eyes.

He shook his head. "For friendship's sake, Yan-Khety, give me something."

And so I told him everything that the stranger had told me. About how they thought that the pure

247

lineage from Ahmose had continued, that Akhenaten had a second son, one that should have been in power in place of Ay. One who could usurp Horemheb.

"We know this," he said.

"They think it's me."

"They think you are Nebwaenra?" His eyes bulged.

I forced a laugh, although I felt dizzy and sick rather than any good humour. "It's ridiculous."

"Why?"

"They based it on my appearance and age... and this scar. I pointed to the mark on my forehead. They said this happened as a baby, but I remember being about four. I was in the village. And I have... had a sister."

He was watching me closely, reading my eyes. "The village was south of Waset?"

"Yes." I paused, then feeling braver, said, "You know they thought the child was hidden in a peasant village?"

He nodded. "A criminal told Vizier Paramese and he appointed me."

"To destroy the villages?"

"That wasn't me. The army did that. I've tried to control their actions, but such is the concern..." He nodded, and I guessed he was trying to convince me of his innocence. "I have no influence over the army, and it could be that the vizier or even Pharaoh himself has instructed the general. The state is threatened and the state will defend itself."

I said, "Innocent people have died and will die."

"As is always the way," he said.

"But that is neither fair nor just."

"No, but that is the world in which we live."

Normally I might have argued with him, but I did not have the strength, and I also sensed he was still unconvinced of my innocence.

I said, "I am not Nebwaenra."

"And yet everything they say about you could be true."

"Except the birthmark. I was told the prince had a birthmark on his right hip." I pulled aside my shredded robe to show my hip. "No birthmark."

He passed the beer back to me and I took a gulp. I could see him thinking and I was desperate to get my own brain working. The magistrate needed an excuse to set me free. My protestation of innocence wasn't enough, nor was the story I'd told him. He needed conspirators or...

"There's another way," I said.

"Go on."

I desperately tried to think. The fog lifted now and again but the logic was just out of reach.

"I need time," I said.

"You have a day." And with that I was suddenly dismissed. The staff and guard returned and I was taken away. I passed a cell inside the building that had no light and smelled of death. I heard men's moans and guessed the others were being held there, perhaps before being taken out into the desert and executed.

But my quarters had a window and a bench for a bed. I was also given water and fruit. At first I tried to get my thoughts in order, to think about the dilemma rather than the solution. I wasn't sure what information I'd been told was relevant so I made notes in the dust on the floor. And then the sense of it started to come together: the politics, the religion, the men...

I moved to the bench and lay down. I didn't recall making that conscious decision, but relaxing, I thought, suddenly seemed to be a good idea. I closed my eyes and sleep sucked me into her dark realm immediately.

The next thing I knew, I was being shaken awake by the guard. From the shadows, I guessed the sun had moved through three stages. Ra was on his descent.

Ra was on his descent! It was as easy as that, I realized, although I knew having a plan and carrying it through was not always straightforward.

"The high priest thinks I'm Nebwaenra. Let me convince him I'm not," I said, facing Magistrate Kheperure.

"How does that help? They will search for another man—and I suspect it won't matter whether he's the true heir or an imposter."

And then I laid out my idea.

Kheperure softened, and I could see I had a chance, so I added that I needed the *hour*-priest Immaatra. He would get me access to the high priest and together we would convince him.

The magistrate thought and called for someone to bring us beer, and we went over it again and again until he was convinced—and he'd made sure I wouldn't forget.

Finally he stood up and embraced me. I was conscious that I must stink to high heaven but he didn't turn away.

"Well done," he said. "Lord Khety always said you were a smart one."

"We will leave in the morning," I said when his hug ended.

"Not so fast, young man. First of all I need to persuade the grand vizier of your plan. It only works if he—representing Pharaoh—agrees."

"Of course."

Before he let me go, he lapsed into conversation like we'd chatted in my lodgings. It was as though I hadn't been in this prison for ten days and he wasn't my interrogator. I raised the subject of the nobles' necropolis case, since I'd had many days and silence through which to contemplate. I said that the guard Nakht should be here and yet I could find no sign of him.

"I'll find him," Kheperure said. "Now, in the meantime, go and clean yourself up. You stink worse than animal dung."

FORTY-THREE

I was taken to a room in the prison that wasn't a cell. It had a bed and comfortable furnishings. It wasn't luxurious but was at least a thousand times better than the original cramped cell with its straw. After a wash I put on a clean robe and felt like a new man.

Later, Immaatra was brought to the room and eyed me suspiciously.

"You were a spy!" he said with venom.

"No," I said. "Sit down and let me explain." So I told him my story and plan, and he too saw the genius of it. All we had to do now was wait.

Four days later, we were collected by an official and walked out of Behadet prison. A small vessel awaited us by the river crossing and we set sail for Waset, where Magistrate Kheperure was waiting for us.

We were taken to the vizier's palace, washed and shaved by slaves and given new clothes. Dressed in my formal robes I was taken to meet Kheperure.

"You look and smell much better," he said, grinning.

"It was a good meeting?"

Before he answered, Immaatra was brought into the room and I noted that he had lost the gaunt look

I'd grown used to seeing. He no longer had the appearance of a man who had been in a prison, eating little and expecting to die.

Kheperure looked at the *hour*-priest. "Will the plan work?"

"Do you want an honest answer, my lord, or platitudes?"

"Honesty."

"I don't know. The plan is good, but who can second-guess the mind of the high priest?"

"The plan needs to work," Kheperure said. "The stability of this great land depends upon it. It depends upon the two of you." He fixed the *hour*-priest with eyes that could cut through a man. "Do not fail."

I was relieved that the old magistrate didn't use those same eyes on me, but I guessed the message was for both of us.

We talked through the plan and Kheperure clarified Pharaoh's terms. Finally content that we were prepared, the magistrate introduced us to a third man who would accompany us. The lowly official seemed normal enough, and we were told he'd been in the prison as well. However, this was just a story. I knew he'd not been there and was with us as either Kheperure's or the vizier's spy. He was there to ensure the encounter with the high priest went as planned. If it didn't... Well, I suspect he had a knife secreted upon his person.

Before we left the palace I sent a message to Paneb letting him know I was all right and would meet him at my previous lodgings soon. I didn't know whether he was still in Waset and suspected that he'd returned to Akhmin since I'd been gone so long. No doubt he'd assumed I was dead along with the man I'd met that fateful night.

Immaatra didn't take us through the main entrance to the temple complex. Instead, we circled east and came to a section that had been demolished. This, I was told, was where Akhenaten had built his arch, trying to link Ra-Horus-on-the-horizon, the Aten, with Amun.

Then we came to a walled section that was inaccessible from any other route and here we were confronted by temple guards. They looked like priests but carried swords. Perhaps because he was with us, they searched the *hour*-priest as well as us laymen before we were allowed to progress.

I was surprised that they didn't find a blade on our spy and saw a small smile in the corner of his eye. Perhaps he had another weapon or had skill enough to need no weapon. I didn't know, and I prayed that I would never find out.

After the search, Immaatra led us along galleried halls and through passageways until we came to another wall. A building within a building within the temple. Again we were searched and allowed to progress, and found ourselves inside the equivalent of a palace, only it had none of the finery or frippery of a royal or administrative palace. This was the heart of the high priest's administration, and we were told to wait for an audience.

We waited a long time, and I saw the shadows move from the right-hand wall to the left. I heard services and chanting and I was just starting to think that the evening prayer would start when a man came for us and said the high priest would grant us audience.

The only time I'd seen a high priest was when I'd collected Meryra's mummified body. The High Priest of Osiris had worn the traditional leopard-skin robe and swung incense from a flask.

The man who waited for us, perched on the edge of a silver and gold throne, was dressed in a flowing white gown with a golden trim. But its simplicity wasn't what first struck me. It was the man's age. He was much older than the sixty I'd assumed. The skin on his face looked like see-through quartz. Sunken eyes stared hard, small and black at me, and folds of thin skin made him look more fragile than cheap papyrus.

I had never before seen anyone so old and realized this high priest had crowned Akhenaten and some of his successors—although I couldn't be sure which. However, I did know that he'd supported Ay and then Horemheb. This was a supreme politician, who had tried to manipulate the crown of the Two Lands only to find his power less than he'd assumed.

Immaatra introduced us, and the way he spoke surprised me. Despite being an *hour*-priest, he was clearly in awe of his superior, maybe even afraid. He explained that we had been arrested and imprisoned for sedition and that we had only been released because of my connection with the magistrate.

The high priest kept his eyes on me and said nothing.

Immaatra explained that I had convinced Kheperure that I should act as an envoy. A flicker of a smile appeared on the high priest's face before he hid it.

I said, "I am not who you think I am."

"Who do I think you are?" the high priest finally said.

"The second son of Pharaoh Akhenaten by his daughter Meritaten. The boy called Nebwaenra, who was taken from Waset and raised by another family and later hidden and raised in a peasant village."

The high priest pursed his lips.

I said, "I am not that boy. I may have a family resemblance and I have a scar, but that scar came later, in the village, and I do not have the birthmark."

I showed my right hip and I saw disappointment in those small dark eyes.

"And," I said, "there was another boy. He was my age and I remember him. We called him Nebanni and he was not like the rest of us."

Now the high priest looked excited. "Yes?"

"He died," I said. "Half of our village died of the plague." I waited a beat. "I am sorry, Your Highness, but I know for sure that the boy is dead."

Despite this news, I could see his mind working, so I continued as planned. "You could keep looking for Nebanni, even find someone who could be him, and persuade the man to pretend he is the second son. But I will speak out. The state will use me so that everyone knows your man is not the true prince."

I saw the light fade in his eyes then.

"But there is another way," I said, about to pander to his vanity. "As High Priest of Amun, you are the most powerful man in the south and Waset is your capital."

His mind was working again.

I went on: "But you could be more powerful. You could control the whole country—second only to the pharaoh of course—just like in the old days."

Now his eyes were aflame with interest.

"Take this different path and you will be the high priest of the Two Lands, of Waset and of Memphis. You will be the High Priest of Amun-Ra."

FORTY-FOUR

All politicians crave power and the High Priest of Amun was not an exception. He accepted the second option with reluctance although I knew that he could wish for no greater accolade even under a new pharaoh.

Magistrate Kheperure had insisted that the high priest make it clear to his followers that the search for the lost pharaoh—as they called him—was over. The high priest said that his official acceptance of the appointment and the accompanying festivals would act as a clear message.

This is what we had hoped. The conspiracy against Pharaoh was over and I returned with my two colleagues to report our successful mission.

When I was alone with old Kheperure, he hugged me warmly.

"Can you ever forgive me?" he said.

"You had a job to do."

He let go and gripped my upper arm. "Thank Amun that it all worked out."

"Thank Amun-Ra," I said, and he laughed. Then seriously I said, "Tell me honestly. If things had not gone well, would your spy have killed me?"

"No," he said, and I believed him. "He was there in case your priest turned on you. He was also authorized to take action if the high priest was unreasonable."

"Kill the High Priest of Amun?"

He shook his head. "I could never confirm such an outrageous statement."

"It would have resulted in civil war."

"Perhaps. Thank Amun-Ra we will never find out."

He gave me a small purse. "For your journey home."

I said, "I'm still bothered by the Elephantine nobles' necropolis case."

"I checked the records for that guard—Nakht. He never arrived at the prison."

"Can you explain it?"

"He left Elephantine after the judgement but died on the way."

I shook my head. "I don't like it."

"So you aren't going home to Akhmin?"

I weighed the purse in my hand. "This will get me to Elephantine... if you don't mind me stepping on your toes."

"Go right ahead," he said. "You helped stop a war. The least I can do is let you step on my toes."

Paneb was outside my temporary lodgings when I left the vizier's palace. I'd never seen him so happy to see me before and was concerned he might try and kiss me.

He'd hurried back from my home in Akhmin as soon as he'd received the message and had brought fresh clothes in case I needed them. The clothes I had worn for the day were Kheperure's old ones and I felt more comfortable in my own.

"We're going back to Elephantine," I said as he packed my few things. He didn't comment.

"How is my wife?" I asked.

"Well."

"But…"

"You are not welcome back and she is still mourning the death of your child."

Before I caught a boat south, I found the shrine to Het where I'd cried for my dead sister and first met Meryra. There, I prayed long and hard for my wife and I prayed for forgiveness.

I paid for passage on a sleek merchant vessel that travelled swiftly against the current. Despite having seen it a number of times already, I still felt tears when I saw the fields of the villages south of Waset. There was no one working them anymore. Any of the few surviving crops had already been harvested. I wondered what Nabetu had traded my silver bracelet for and whether his people had any food left.

In contrast, the fields on the eastern bank before Elephantine had abundant crops. On the right I knew the northern commoner's necropolis was out there a few miles in the desert.

I disembarked at a short quay at the village where the ferries crossed the river. This was the site of the ferry disaster all those years ago.

After sending my slave on to secure me lodgings in the city, I found the owner of the bar—the man who'd been a boy when his uncle had died in the alleged accident.

"I want the truth," I told him.

He shook his head. "It was a long time ago."

259

"I need you to be a witness."

He shook his head again. "The case was closed. We need to get on with our lives."

"What are you afraid of?"

"Losing my life, my lord."

"I'll protect you."

"How can I trust you?"

So I told him he could decide when the time came. If he decided to give no evidence then so be it. However, he would see that I wanted justice to be done and I would protect anyone giving witness.

"With your life, my lord?"

"If that is what it takes," I said, and meant it.

When I left him I took the ferry across the river and stood on the eastern bank. People who had travelled on the same ferry now walked along a well-worn track towards the distant cemetery. Two men with eight donkeys tried to get business but no one took a ride. Except me.

We agreed a price and I asked one of them to accompany me.

"We're not going to the necropolis," I said to his surprise. "We're going south."

After a few hundred paces we came to the beehives. There were more than I remembered. And then the flower fields. Vast acres of red that I'd seen from the river.

This wasn't prime agricultural land but the flowers grew well here.

I looked around. Was my memory fading?

"Where is the village?"

"What village?"

"There was a village here. Years ago there were white pegs where the village ended and the honey farm land began."

"I've been here for five years, my lord, and there's been no village. You must be mistaken."

We continued south and eventually the flowers petered out to the odd, straggling one trying to survive on dust. We passed through desert and rock and there was no longer a path.

I could see Elephantine and the islands ahead. "How far to the nobles' necropolis?"

"So that's where we're going." He wiped sweat from his forehead. "Another three miles, maybe more."

"Have you ever brought anyone this way before?"

"Why would anyone do that?"

"Have you?"

"Not in the five years I've been doing this."

"Or your partner?"

"No. No one would come this way. It's too far and too difficult. And no noble—present company excepted—would make such a journey."

I gave him the date of the theft from the tombs. "What about on that night?"

"We don't operate the donkeys after nightfall. And anyway, the ferry service stops around sunset."

A little further and we approached the donkey owners who were across from the city. My guide waved a greeting to the other men.

"What are you doing?" one snapped at him. "This is not your business!"

"Just this once," I said. I dismounted and handed the second man a copper deben. "No offence intended."

"None taken, my lord," he said.

I asked him the same question about the night of the theft.

He shook his head slowly, as if processing the idea, then said, "The necropolis closes at night and we go home." He pointed south.

"Where's home?"

"Down there, about ten minutes' ride. For two more deben I will take you."

"No thank you," I started to say, and then a thought struck me. "Has your village always been there?"

"We used to live downriver," he said, and his colleague nodded.

The other man said, "We were forced to move years ago. It wasn't good land but better than now. City Planning forced us out because the honey farm was expanding. They took our land."

I paid them each another copper deben and thanked them for their time. Then I remounted my donkey and turned east along the track to the nobles' necropolis.

"Excuse the impertinence, my lord," the first donkey owner asked, riding at my shoulder. "But why all the questions?"

I wasn't sure, not completely, but a picture was rapidly forming in my mind. What I was about to do in the necropolis would confirm my biggest suspicion.

FORTY-FIVE

I asked the donkey owner to wait outside the necropolis and showed the guard my credentials. I walked around the cemetery as I had the first time I'd been there. I found the first tomb and saw the hole where the keystone had been levered out. Nothing had changed.

Unlike last time, I bent and inspected the hole and tried to move the stone. It didn't budge.

Then I located the second disturbed tomb and did the same thing. Again the keystone didn't move. Nor did it look like it had ever moved, such was the precision by which it had been replaced.

The third tomb was the old governor's and had been broken into from above. I located the hole over the burial chamber and pushed my arm into it. I moved my arm around and felt as far as I could. I wish I'd done this before. The crevice definitely narrowed at the point where my fingertips reached. Anyone getting down there would have been very slim indeed!

I removed a copper chisel from my bag and placed it beside the hole. Then I picked up a stone and struck the chisel gently.

The sound reverberated in the space below. I sat and waited. Nothing happened, so I repeated the procedure, this time striking a little harder. A small chip came off the rock.

I sat back and waited.

Nothing.

I looked up, said a prayer to Osiris, god of the dead, and struck the chisel hard. Bang! A chunk of rock came away.

A second later I saw the necropolis guard racing towards me. "What was that?" he shouted.

I raised a hand. "Just slipped. I'm all right. No need to worry." He pulled up just below me and I made a show of hobbling down from the rock.

"Foolish of me to go up there with a stiff hip," I said.

"Right," he said. He glanced up the rock and around, as though checking for someone else then back to me. I limped past him.

"Can I help you, my lord?" Now he sounded concerned for me.

I waved him away and continued to the gate where the donkey owner was patiently waiting.

"What did you hear?" I asked him as we rode back towards the river.

"Two bangs," he said. "A small crack, and then a minute later a much louder one."

"Yes," I said, "and this is daytime. This is daytime."

I paid the donkey owner handsomely for the ride and detour and hailed a boat that took me straight across to the city opposite.

I asked the boatman if he could remember the night of the tomb robbery. He said he could. A few boats operated at night, some taking people to the islands, some to the other side and the village upstream.

"Do you remember two or three men coming back that night with a bag or bags?"

He shook his head.

At the quay, I paid him and asked him to a find out if any of the other boatmen remembered anything. I promised to pay him well for negative information and double it if he found someone who could tell me something. I would return at sunrise.

My next visit was to find the Chief of Police.

"Did you tell the truth at high court," I challenged him."

He glared but tried to mask the offence he felt. "You should not ask me that!"

"Did you?"

"Of course I did."

"Where can I find the boy?"

"The witness?"

"Yes, the boy who heard the criminals planning their robbery."

He took time checking his records, although I was sure he already knew the answer. He gave me an area of the city: south-west.

"The house?" I prompted.

"We didn't find his exact home."

I squared up to him. "You aren't being very helpful."

He clenched his jaw. "You are not the magistrate of the first nome, my lord. You have no power here and I am a busy man."

"What are you doing that is so important?"

"Police work. Now leave before I have you thrown out!"

I backed down and walked out of his office and then stopped and turned.

"It's not over," I said.

He didn't reply.

From the Chief of Police's office I walked across the city and found the area he'd described.

From the trial I knew the boy's name, and I asked people I met. The responses were all negative. I widened my search and eventually found a stallholder who knew him.

"Why are you asking, my lord?"

"I'd like to see him," I said. "I have questions."

He shook his head.

"I will pay for information."

He shook his head again. "I would love you to pay me but I haven't seen him for days."

"How long?"

"Since the court case."

"Did you see him after the court case?"

The man thought and then shook his head again.

I asked more people, but anyone who knew him said he'd gone away or they hadn't seen him since the case.

Widening my search, I got no success for an hour and decided to give up. I located Magistrate Kheperure's house and knocked on the doors. I didn't expect him to be home, but when we'd parted he'd offered me lodgings. I presented his authority to his head servant and was treated like a fine guest.

Despite the nice quarters and linen, I found the night long and restless. I didn't like what I had learned today but it all made sense. I just needed to confirm one more thing and that was at the quay.

Before sunrise I was there waiting for the boatman from the day before. He arrived grinning.

"I have found someone with information," he said.

I paid him the basic fee I'd promised and said I'd pay the rest for the information.

He led me along the quay to another boatman, who tied up his boat and scurried towards us.

The first man said, "This is the boat owner who took three men from the east bank on that night."

"Who were they?" I asked.

"I don't know, my lord," he said.

"So what can you tell me?"

"I picked up three men in the dark. They had bags."

"How many?"

"Bags? Three. One each, my lord."

"How big were these bags?"

He looked at my shoulder bag. "About that size," he said.

"Anything else you can tell me? Were they nobles?"

"I don't think so. It was dark, my lord."

"What hour was it?"

The second man looked at the first.

I said, "Don't look at him, he wasn't there."

"Sorry, my lord, I... er... it was... the eighth hour. No maybe the ninth. I can't be sure because I wasn't checking."

"But the Khnum temple bells sound every hour."

"Er yes... I had been drinking and..."

"Enough of the lies. For this nonsense I'll pay nothing." I turned to the first man. "Did you ask everyone or just come up with this trickery?"

He lowered his head. "I asked everyone and no one saw anybody that night," he said. "I apologize sincerely, my lord."

I handed them both a piece of copper. "Well it's your lucky day," I said, "because I'm in a good mood." And I was. What they had confirmed completed my picture. Now I had two visits to make.

FORTY-SIX

First, I met with the nomarch.

"No hard feelings," he said, accepting my bow.

I tried to look surprised, as though the very thought would never have crossed my mind. "You are the nomarch of the first nome," I said, my voice dripping with deference. "I am a mere magistrate and owe you a debt of appreciation for inviting me to the Great Hall."

"Yes," he said, nodding.

I waited, and he watched me with patient eyes although I guessed his mind was racing, considering angles and possibilities like the politician he was.

I said, "The case has troubled me ever since."

"It has?"

"I feel we became distracted by the lion thing and I wondered whether that whole scenario had been… shall we say, constructed?"

"By the mayor?"

I feigned surprise. "Yes!"

He nodded. "I've wondered about the same thing. However, the case is tried and judgement written."

"Perhaps there is another way to correct things, my lord."

His eyes narrowed and he tried to mask his interest. "What do you have in mind?"

"Meet me tonight at the Hall of Records."

He frowned. "Why there?"

"Somewhere neutral," I said with a shrug. "It was the first place I found available. Be there at the second hour this evening."

He asked me some questions but I got away without giving him any straight answers and he remained intrigued.

My next visit was to the mayor's office, and I said the same thing about the case troubling me.

"Or is it the money? I hear Userhat still won't pay you."

I waited a few beats before trying to look guilty—as though he'd seen through me. "Perhaps my motivation is somewhat influenced by that."

"You want revenge," he said with a sneer.

"Will you help me?"

"I won't go directly against him."

"I don't need you to."

"Then what do you need me for?"

"Just turn up and listen," I said. "Be there at the Hall of Records tonight. Second hour."

Waiting until the second hour of the night was difficult, but I couldn't rush this and was dependent on someone else. I prepared a table with drinks and three chairs. It was set up like a cosy evening between three friends.

The mayor arrived early and kept tapping his fingers together with ill-concealed excitement. I poured him some wine, and while he drank he tried to prise information out of me.

I deflected all of his questions and was relieved when Nomarch Userhat finally turned up, late. With an impassive face, he nodded to us both and took the third chair.

"Thank you for coming and for humouring me," I began. "I think my favourite wisdom is that a proud man can be a fool. A fool to others and a fool to himself."

Both men nodded, pretending they were only vaguely interested. But I knew they were. They had come here and both expected to score points over the other man—to prove him to be a fool perhaps.

I continued: "I'm going to revisit the high court case. And I'd like to do it like a mock trial and be hypothetical."

"Fine, providing you don't take too long," Mayor Renseneb said, pouring himself some wine and then addressing Userhat. "At least this wine is of good quality."

I'd remembered the wine that Magistrate Kheperure had requested when we'd met in Waset, so I'd purchased enough for an army of visitors. For myself, I poured watered-down beer and took a sip. Now that I finally had these two senior men in front of me, I felt nerves constrict my chest.

"Get on with it," Userhat snapped grumpily, but I could see it was an act, and he also poured himself wine.

I held up my rod of office. "So we'll do this as though it's real and like in the high court—if you wish to speak then take the rod. Agreed?"

They both muttered agreement, both secretly smiling.

"Good. So let's go over the crime. Two men—"

"Possibly three," the mayor interjected, but he was then turned on by the nomarch.

"The rule is you must have the rod to speak!"

I nodded and casually waved my hands, as though I really didn't care that much. "Otherwise we just walk away and let this lie. If I'm to get to the truth we need rules."

Both men nodded.

"You can speak later, once I've finished, My Lord Mayor, but for now, the start of the story is that there were two men. They travelled across to the east bank of the river by boat and there they used donkeys to travel to the necropolis of the nobles." I paused and took another sip of beer. Both men were watching me intently.

I continued: "They somehow slipped past the guard and located the tombs they intended to rob. They got into the first two by levering open the entrances by locating the keystones. Afterwards they replaced the stones so that it would only look like the tombs had been disturbed if you looked really closely and knew which was the keystone.

"They then went to a third tomb—one belonging to a governor, but more importantly his wife. Here they had to tunnel in through the roof to get into the burial chamber.

"Afterwards they snuck out again and rode—"

The mayor wanted to interrupt again but I shook my head. I guessed he wanted to point out the celebrations that attracted Nakht, the guard.

"—rode back on the donkeys and crossed the river again. They then quickly disposed of the treasure somehow. However, a young boy had heard them planning the crime and the men were arrested."

Userhat took a slug of wine and secretly smiled at me.

I said, "But there are so many problems with this story. Firstly, there's the question about the young boy's motivation. Why inform the guards about the criminals? For his trouble he received several lashes to the soles of his feet. But let's not worry about this minor point. Of more concern is why the Chief of Police didn't locate the boatman or question Nakht, the necropolis guard, straight away. If you recall, it was my visit to the necropolis that uncovered Nakht as a witness."

Renseneb nodded thoughtfully, while Userhat looked at me unblinking.

I said, "What really troubles me is why this was? So I asked the donkey owners and men at the wharf. The boatmen didn't recall transferring two—or more—men on that night. Neither did the donkey owners."

Finally, I yielded the rod to the nomarch. "We are used to such things. Like you said of the young boy witness, sometimes people are reluctant to admit what they know."

I took the rod back and said, "And sometimes people tell a lie to cover up a truth. But we'll come to that. My biggest concern was Nakht. Even if he was incompetent, he would have still heard the criminals removing the stones and chiselling into the governor's tomb. I tested it during the day and the clash of stone on stone brought the guards running. At night the sound would have seemed very loud."

Renseneb was nodding again and, leaning forward, focused on my words.

I opened my free hand. "So this is where I'd like to get hypothetical. Let us say that the crime never

273

happened. The criminals never took the boat to the east bank, never got on donkeys, never made any noise in the necropolis and never carried a heavy bag of treasure back on the donkeys and boat. Which also means that the booty was never disposed of either— which helps explain that conundrum. You see, if they did have it, then such a quick disposal must have meant there was someone ready to receive it. And that person would need to be in high office. The items wouldn't be disposed of. They would be used and displayed."

Now Userhat was openly smiling. "I think you are onto something."

I raised the rod and he fell silent, the corners of his mouth still upturned.

I said, "My only true witness who could tell me what really happened was Nakht. And I believe he was murdered to keep him quiet."

Userhat's smile vanished.

I said, "Let's introduce two new characters, Cup and Stone. These two nobles are great rivals. Perhaps it's a game for entertainment, perhaps it's more serious, but there is something that sets these two men against one another.

"Like in the game, cup-stone-water, the stone can break the cup made of pottery. So let's suggest that Stone wants to break Cup and so he invents a crime. But he doesn't make the connection obvious, not until the high court is in session and a witness provides the details of a stolen item. This item could be linked to Cup." I didn't need to spell it out. I was referring to the silver necklace with sapphire and emerald gemstones. I had seen the mayor's wife wearing something very similar the time I met her.

"However, Cup is not easily beaten and he had his own trick. He made sure that a new witness would be found who would point the finger. This would be Water. The cup holds water but the stone sinks. This witness points the finger at Stone—or rather his son. It was a stroke of genius," I said.

Now I saw a glint in Renseneb's eye. He appreciated being referred to as a genius. The nomarch had chosen me because he thought I'd think there must have been a third man involved who could dispose of the booty and then realize that the mayor's wife was wearing the necklace. I suspect a search of the mayor's house would have uncovered other treasures allegedly stolen from the tombs. Maybe even the golden sword.

However, Renseneb had made sure I found about Userhat's son, his obsession with big cats and pretending to be the god Maahes. It had neutralized Userhat's plan.

Userhat said, "And you promised that no further action would be taken in that regard."

The hypothetical scenario was over. I said, "The theft from the tombs would have been almost as unconscionable as the claimed debauchery and impersonation of a god."

Renseneb said, "So there was never a crime."

"Yes there was," I said, feeling more emboldened now that I'd laid everything out. "But not the theft from the nobles' tombs. Nothing was ever taken. The two men who were executed were lying about it. However, they were undoubtedly criminals and I think they were persuaded to go along with this pretend crime believing they would be treated less harshly. Of course, they were wrong."

Userhat shrugged. "They confessed. Their punishment was appropriate."

"What about the boy?"

"What about him?"

"Was he killed too?"

Userhat turned his mouth down like he had no idea.

I said, "I couldn't find him so I couldn't ask why he reported the two criminals. Of course, Nakht was also disposed of, so I can't ask him either. So their deaths, covering up the lies, was the real crime."

The mayor's eyes shone briefly until I spoke again.

"It would make both Cup and Stone guilty," I said. "The boy was part of Stone's story and the necropolis guard was Cup's—he wanted me to go there because it was a member of his staff who took me and Nakht's story implicated Stone's son."

"Fine," Userhat said. "Who had access to all of these men?"

"And the boy."

"The Chief of Police," Userhat concluded. "I have always suspected him. He's a cunning man who may have set this whole thing up—tricked us all."

"How so?" asked the mayor.

"Think about it. We record that a crime was committed and therefore it was. So later, the Chief of Police re-enacts that crime and walks away with all the goods. All he would need to do is make sure his own guards are on duty and remove the items while allegedly repairing the tombs."

"Very clever," Renseneb agreed. "The Chief of Police is guilty. After all, he knew all of the criminals and he had custody of the necropolis guard we sent to Behadet prison."

I looked at Userhat. "It'll be your word against his."

The nomarch snorted and I knew the chief didn't stand a chance. Maybe he wouldn't even dare implicate the nomarch. Maybe he'd use fake names like Cup and Stone, like I had. He'd lose and he'd die.

I'd have liked a confession from the mayor and nomarch, but I wouldn't get it and I didn't expect it.

Which was why I had something else up my sleeve.

FORTY-SEVEN

The mayor and nomarch were enjoying themselves and had quaffed a vast amount of the wine. They joked and talked of things that meant nothing to me, and I waited.

Finally, during a quiet moment, I said, "Years ago I came here as a magistrate's assistant."

"Did you?" Renseneb said, as though I'd said something immensely interesting.

"It was a case of a ferry disaster. Some people died and my master concluded that the ferryman was to blame. We fell out over it because I was suspicious that the rope had been cut."

"Was there evidence?" Userhat asked, suddenly sobering up.

"No," I said. "But we failed because we didn't get to the heart of the motive for the crime."

Userhat said, "What motive could there be? The ferryman was charged with neglect. The rope frayed and snapped. It was his responsibility to ensure his ferry was safe."

The nomarch clearly knew the case well despite appearing to be ignorant initially. I said, "We should have also thought about who had died."

"Some locals. They were crossing to visit the commoner's necropolis on the other side."

"That's what we assumed," I said. "We failed, and it troubled me for years that justice wasn't done that day."

"It happens," Renseneb said. "When you get older, and wiser, you appreciate that you can't solve every problem."

"It's often a matter of compromise," Userhat said. They raised their cups to one another, both drank and relaxed again.

I looked at the mayor, hard. "You know why we're here, in the Hall of Records?"

"No."

"What I discovered was that you were the City Planning Officer before you became mayor. That's a big step up, but don't comment. No need. Not just yet."

Renseneb drank more wine. So much for him being wiser! If he'd had any sense he'd have guessed what was coming and sobered up. Instead, he kept quiet and studied me nervously.

I said, "And you know what's an amazing coincidence? The previous planning officer was killed in an accident."

Neither man said anything.

"The ferry disaster," I continued. "He died in the very same ferry case that my master was investigating."

The mayor looked like he was holding his breath. Userhat clenched his teeth.

I said, "I never thought it was an accident."

Userhat said, "That was Magistrate Khety's verdict."

I ignored him. "At the time, I suspected it was about the ferryman and extortion—sorry, I mean unofficial taxes. However, what if it was nothing to do with the ferryman? What if the motivation was to kill the planning officer?"

"That would be unconscionable," Userhat said. Renseneb breathed deeply.

"And then I thought: what if it was so that Lord Renseneb could become the planning officer?"

"Ridiculous!" the mayor grumbled.

"Yes," I said, "because there's something else that I confirmed in here: you used to be the Overseer of the Waterways. I thought I recognized you. It's been a long time, and you're—shall we say—much fatter now, but it was you."

The mayor took a sharp intake of breath at my rudeness, but I didn't care what he thought.

"And do you know what's so odd? The role of City Planning Officer is of lower status than that of Overseer of the Waterways. Why take a step down? Demotion? I don't think so. There's no evidence here in the records that you made a mistake as the Overseer of the Waterways. You weren't demoted. No, the move was deliberate and premeditated. You killed the planning officer so that you could take the role."

There was panic in Renseneb's eyes. He looked from me to Userhat.

The nomarch clapped his hands. "Very funny. It's a good story. Well done, Yan-Khety. You deserve payment for your services after all."

"Thank you," I said, "but I'm not finished. Before we investigated the ferry disaster, we dealt with a minor planning issue. In those days, I didn't understand. I saw beehives and a honey business. I also saw flower fields providing food for the bees. And that's what I didn't understand. Because now I see a much bigger flower field. And where a village once was, there is now an operation that dries the poppy pods and grinds them to make dream powder."

They were both looking at me again, their faces frozen, probably wondering what I was about to say.

"You own the poppy fields," I said to Userhat.

He pulled a fake smile. "It's no secret, Yan-Khety."

"And it was the source of your fortune. Am I right?"

"I won't deny it."

"And particularly so since its expansion."

He nodded, took a sip of wine and tried to look relaxed.

"And how did you manage to expand, my lord?"

"The villagers moved away," he said.

"The villagers were removed," I said forcibly.

"I couldn't comment on that."

"But Mayor Renseneb could, couldn't you, my lord?"

Renseneb said nothing.

"Did the previous planning officer refuse to help? Is that it?"

Userhat shook his head. "This is circumstantial evidence at best."

Looking at Renseneb, I said, "You arranged for the ferry rope to be cut. The accident killed the planning officer and the mayor demoted you into the vacant position. The two of you have always worked together—you planned this together."

"Rubbish!" Userhat shouted.

I said, "I have a witness. This witness heard the overseer demand the ferry's guide rope be cut."

Renseneb shook his head. "No one has ever made a claim against me."

"No," I said, "because they were too afraid. People know how you"—I pointed at Userhat—"treat witnesses."

The nomarch shook his head, disgust on his face.

"Nakht, the necropolis guard, is just one example."

"That was the Chief of Police," Userhat said. "We've already established he's guilty of that crime."

Renseneb said, "I didn't have anything to do with the ferry guide rope."

I called over my shoulder. "Step forward."

Out of the darkness came the man I'd met in the bar near the ferry crossing. His head was bowed and his nerves showed.

"Is that the man who ordered the ferry lines be cut?"

The man raised his head, looked directly at Renseneb and said, "Yes."

I dismissed him and the barman rushed away, undoubtedly still worried that he'd done the wrong thing. I was determined that he wouldn't be punished for his honesty.

Userhat said, "So you have a witness. So what?"

"His word against mine." Renseneb stood up.

"It's enough," I said.

"No it's not." Userhat scoffed. "You can't bring a case against us, Yan-Khety. You are just one man. A magistrate, I'll grant you. Magistrate of the ninth nome"—there was derision in his tone—"and you can do nothing."

"And you're very naïve," Renseneb said. "Why do you think the nomarch chose you for the high court case? It was even more fun because you were so easily manipulated."

"By both of us," Userhat added, and now both of them were standing, glaring at me. Two against one. "In fact, I believe I have a witness that you planned to rob the tombs. That's why you revisited them. And another witness from the prison—the necropolis guard was taken there and you killed him."

I shook my head. Based on what I'd learned about these two men, I was sure they'd construct a case against me. I'd be tried and convicted and murdered.

"Guards!" Userhat shouted. I'd suspected he wouldn't come alone. His guards would be waiting outside in case he needed them.

"Not so fast," a voice called from the darkness. I heard footsteps and breathed with relief. I'd delayed as long as possible but he'd finally arrived.

Magistrate Kheperure stepped up beside me.

"Guards!" Userhat shouted more loudly, and finally the doors behind me burst open and armed men rushed in.

"Arrest them!" Userhat screamed, pointing at us. But instead of arresting us, the guards encircled the mayor and nomarch.

Userhat blinked, suddenly realizing the men were being commanded by Kheperure.

Renseneb retched and spittle ran down his jowl.

Kheperure said, "The two of you will be taken to a holding cell until Paramese, vizier of the south will see you. You are charged with murder, extortion and manipulation for your own personal gain."

When the two nobles had been led away, I sank back into my chair. Kheperure poured me a large amount of wine and I gulped it down. He pulled up one of the other chairs and patted my shoulder.

"Well done. You might be a bit unconventional and rough around the edges, but one day you might be ready for my job."

FORTY-EIGHT

Kheperure came to my lodgings the following day with four armed guards and a wagon.

Paneb panicked, thinking I was about to be arrested again, but he couldn't have been more wrong.

"For your journey home," Kheperure said after we embraced. "Compliments of the nomarch."

He looked serious as he pulled back the cover on the wagon and showed me what was underneath. A chest too big for one man to carry with comfort.

"It's the payment that Userhat promised you. He's got no need of his treasure now, so it was just and fair that you should be paid. You can't keep the guards I'm afraid, they'll just travel with you for protection."

I gripped his forearm in thanks.

I said, "I assumed you'd need me to stay around for the trial."

He shook his head. "I have a better witness. The Chief of Police was willing to confess once he heard that I'd arrested the nomarch. You were right about the two criminals; they didn't rob the tombs but they were guilty of theft. The nomarch promised them leniency if they pled guilty to the nobles' tomb crime. They thought they'd be convicted but allowed to escape. The mayor promised to pay the necropolis guard to lie about the debauchery and lion god. He also arranged for the man to be murdered on the way to prison."

"What about the boy?"

"The police chief said he was a genuine witness."

"Did they kill him too?"

"That was the intention, but no one's seen him. Looks like he had more sense than the others and ran away."

More than the wealth inside the chest, the news that the boy was alive lifted my spirits. However, when it came to arranging transport north, the incredible wealth meant that I could afford a comfortable and fast vessel.

Because of my armed guard, the boatman was happy to travel through the night, and because of the current, we arrived in my hometown of Akhmin the following day.

However, I didn't stop for long. Instead of disembarking, I sent Paneb to find the quay officer Piye. I also asked him to find another, smaller chest.

"Have you had success?" I asked Piye as he stood before me. "Have you returned the girl you bought and sold? Have you returned Leti to her mother?"

He swallowed guiltily. "No, my lord."

I pointed to the gangplank. "Get on board. We're going to Memphis."

He may have considered running but eyed my armed guard and thought the better of it. After protesting about having no luggage or precious metal, he walked onto my boat.

Paneb was about to board when I stopped him. I told him to remain in Akhmin and await my return. I transferred some of the gold into the smaller chest and asked my slave to take the other to my home and my wife.

He was unhappy that I was travelling on without him and his protection, but he had to accept my order and I saw him standing on the quay until he faded into the distance behind us.

I made Piye sit in the sun, on deck. An hour later, I took pity and let him find a more comfortable spot. It would be a long journey and I needed him when we got to the capital.

We stopped once to purchase more provisions and eventually reached Memphis after two and a half days and travelling through the night.

The sight of the great pyramids never ceased to amaze me. Like golden mountains they came up on the horizon and just grew and grew. I believe the Great Pyramid was about half the height of the mountain in western Waset, but these were made by human effort and all the more astounding for it.

While I watched from the prow, I thought of Paneb and how my wife had received him. Would she welcome the wealth inside the chest or reject it as sullied by my infidelity?

I would have liked Paneb to have been with me. I always enjoyed his company and occasional counsel. However, he didn't appreciate art and architecture. "I'm just a slave," he would tell me. "I'm here to serve, not marvel at chunks of stone." It reminded me that men see things differently. I was driven by justice, whereas Piye, the quay officer, was more interested in wealth. It seemed that I was in a minority most of the time.

Just before we docked, I found Piye sulking below decks.

"I can't afford to buy the girl back," he said. I knew because he'd said it many times by this stage.

"Did you try again?" I asked. "The girl's mother said the new owner demanded twenty golden deben."

He shook his head. "I haven't got round to it. The man is crazy. I got no sense that he'd negotiate."

"Why?"

"Perhaps he likes the girl more than gold." He looked uncertain, like he wanted to say something but felt uncomfortable.

"What?"

"I was wondering why. Why are you so insistent that we should come here? She's just a girl after all."

I felt no compulsion to explain that her situation reminded me of my sister. Thousands of girls were bought and sold, but somehow the story of Leti touched me. Perhaps it was because her mother expected her back. But more likely it was the timing: the strange incident with the Nubian and later Sadhu reminding me of when I was a boy. It seemed right.

"Some things are just meant to be," I said, as a pilot boat came alongside and our boatman requested a landing place on the high noble's quay.

"Who is he?" the other man called back. "Who's your passenger?"

"Lord Khety."

That made me smile. Neither of these men knew who Lord Khety was—and indeed it had been my adopted father rather than me—and yet money proved status, and who was I to object?

Memphis was a sprawling city, bigger than Waset but with a smaller permanent population. However, with merchants and travellers and soldiers, the daily numbers, I was told, exceeded a hundred thousand souls. The city was also a jumble of commerce and administration and religion. Unlike Waset, the northern capital didn't have a religious city within the city. Temples and monuments were everywhere. Which was a good thing because they provided reference points for ease of navigation.

Of course, officer Piye had been here before and knew where to find the new owner of the girl, and he led me and my small retinue.

The owner turned out to be a high administrator for the pharaoh, although I saw no sign of Horemheb or any of his most senior advisors.

The man's name was Djehuty and he loved himself.

He wore clothes that I suppose were the latest fashion and make-up around his eyes like a girl's. When he greeted me, his hand was limp and his flesh soft.

"With some make-up you would look quite attractive. In fact, you remind me of—"

"I'm grateful for your kind words," I said, more generously than I felt. "However, I have little time and would like to come to the point, if you forgive my rudeness."

Djehuty looked at Piye, smiled, and then looked back at me. "You've come for little Leti."

"I have."

"The price is twenty-five golden deben."

I shook my head. "That is ridiculous."

"I think not. I think she's worth it, otherwise you wouldn't be here." He gave instructions to a servant and within minutes there were a dozen young girls in the room. They were all very pretty, in a natural way: good features, fine bones, nice skin colour. They also stood with style. The same style: one foot behind the other, hands behind a straight back, chin slightly raised. I judged them both elegant and confident. Not really what I'd expected. Not like other such groups.

Djehuty called Leti's name and one of the girls stepped forward. She didn't have the same poise as the others, but she was stunning even for one so young.

I looked at Piye and he nodded confirmation that this was indeed the girl I sought. "Leave us," I said.

He blinked surprise then left the room.

Djehuty sat in silence, a slight smile playing on his lips. I'd misjudged him and his motives. He was not a man who particularly enjoyed the pleasures of the fairer sex. Nor was he someone who collected beautiful girls as a demonstration of his wealth. He moulded girls into elegant ladies. They might be commoners but they could pass for courtiers, even royalty themselves.

I said, "I'll be honest. I'm a single man. My motive is purely selfish."

Djehuty let his smile broaden. "She will be worth a fortune as the bride for a prince. The best deal I can offer is twenty-one gold deben."

"She may be worth a fortune in the future, but not yet," I said. "She needs years of training first. I'm a magistrate with prospects but I'm not a wealthy man yet. I can stretch to ten."

"Then come back when you are."

"How long before she's ready? How much training to be the wife of a prince?"

"Two years should be enough."

"And she'll be on the edge of puberty. Girls change. You'll be gambling that she won't lose her shine. I'll give you twelve."

We continued like this until we settled on seventeen golden deben. Still an absolute fortune, but I'd been prepared to pay more. However, the less I spent on the girl the more it left for a second part of my plan.

FORTY-NINE

I purchased a boatload of grain and paid the merchant to deliver the shipment to the villages south of Waset. The man thought I had spent too long in the sun, since there were no official towns or quays for miles beyond Waset, but when I paid extra, he happily agreed.

With little precious metal left in my small chest, I needed no more protection. So, I sent the four guards with the merchant to ensure he delivered the grain as instructed. I considered leaving Piye behind to make his own way home, but by the time I reached my boat I changed my mind. It would have been petty and cruel since he had nothing to support himself.

Sailing against the river current meant it seemed an interminable journey home. I discovered that Piye was reasonable company and fairly good at senet. By the end of the journey I wouldn't have called him a friend, but I decided he was someone I could trust and would trust me.

As the walls of Akhmin hove into view, I felt excitement rise within me. The love of my life was here, and now that she would have seen the wealth I'd received from Elephantine, and that I'd completed my quest, maybe, just maybe, she would forgive me and we could move on.

However, Paneb wasn't standing on the quay awaiting my return. Despite telling myself that it was unreasonable to expect him there, it felt like a bad sign.

Leti's mother wept as the girl rushed into her arms.

"She's untouched," I said, and the mother cried even more.

When they finally stopped hugging and kissing, the mother started scrabbling in a box. "I managed to save twenty-six copper deben," she said. "How much do I owe you, my lord?"

"Nothing," I said. "Seeing you and Leti reunited is payment enough."

Before I could stop her, the mother fell to her knees and kissed my feet. Then she blessed me.

As we left, Piye thanked me too.

"Why?" I asked. "Because I didn't make you pay?"

"No. You have restored my faith in human nature," he said. "If you ever have the need, then I'm your man." Then he also prayed that the gods recognized my good heart and that I would have a fulfilled life.

Despite the exceptional well-wishes, I still felt great trepidation as I entered my courtyard. And I immediately knew something was wrong. My servants and slaves hurried into position. One came to remove my sandals and wash my feet, but I waved him away.

Paneb wasn't there and neither was Nefer-bithia.

"They have gone, master," Sadhu said breaking from his studies.

"Where?"

"Elephantine. By boat, three days since."

I heard him ask if he could join me, but I was already leaving. Although unseemly for a magistrate, I ran. I left my house and hurried to the quay.

Thank Horus! My boat was still there, although the boatman was about to depart. He'd picked up five paying passengers and I became his sixth.

"Elephantine," I said, and he just nodded as though it was the most logical thing in the world.

FIFTY

My stomach churned with worry for the whole journey. Was my wife all right? Had she gone insane? Why go to Elephantine? At least Paneb was with her for protection.

And then as we pulled into the amazing city, I realized I had no idea where she would be or whether I had missed her. Might she have been and turned around? I cursed my stupidity. Why hadn't I checked every boat going the other way?

I paid the boatman far too much, since he had been returning anyway and had other passengers. However, my mind was a mess and I handed over the gold without a thought.

Exotic goods were being loaded onto a merchant ship ahead of me. Beyond that, animals were being goaded into pens for the market. I heard prayers and music across the water. Had she sought a temple? Could that be where she'd gone?

I doubted she would have crossed to Great Elephantine Island and the temple of Khnum. Could she have gone to one of the smaller temples? Hathor didn't have a temple here but further south was a small temple on an island just before the cataract.

Philae and the temple of Isis. Isis, the goddess of many things, including motherhood.

That would be where she'd gone.

I hailed a sailboat and paid for swift passage to the island.

She wasn't there.

The beautiful temple and shrine for Osiris were on the smaller of the twin islands. I searched every nook and cranny. I studied every face hidden by a cowl but she definitely wasn't on the temple island. Nor was she on the larger one.

Despondent, I travelled back to the city and found myself outside the nomarch's palace. Magistrate Kheperure's assistant found me there, and minutes later I was gripping the old man's arm in greeting.

"Back so soon?" He grinned. "I'm not ready to hand you my robes just yet." And then he stopped smiling and frowned. "What's wrong?"

"I can't find my wife," I said, and I explained what had happened.

Together we walked through the city and searched for Nefer-bithia. Kheperure introduced me to nobles and officials, but they all said the same thing. They hadn't seen her.

While we walked, the old man updated me on the case and said that it had been judged. Both the mayor and nomarch had been stripped of their titles and property.

"And Paramese has asked me to be the new nomarch!" Kheperure said.

"Congratulations."

"Maybe. I haven't decided," he said. "I think I'm done with politics."

We were back near the nomarch's palace when a young man bowed to us. I thought I recognized him from the trial, and he confirmed he was a city administrator working for the old nomarch.

"I can't guarantee your job," Kheperure said gruffly.

"My lord," the man said, bowing to both of us. "I was given a message in case I saw Lord Khety."

"Yes?" My heart raced.

"Your wife," he said. "She came here asking questions."

"And she's gone again?"

"To consider her future. She said you'd know where she'd be."

I thanked the man and bade farewell to old Kheperure before running back to the quay.

I entered the grove of sycamore fig trees on the outskirts of Waset. Goats sheltered here from the sun and the air had a stillness that seemed timeless. I could visualize that special moment many years ago when I'd carved Nefer-bithia's name into the bark.

Also, I remembered when I'd returned from the army, uncertain of my future. I'd come here to find her then. She'd left me a message carved under her name telling me she was in Akhmin. Would I find another message now?

I approached the tree with trepidation. Goats trotted out of my way annoyed that I'd disturbed their peace. With my eyes barely open, I reached for the bark and found her name with Akhmin written beneath it. And nothing else.

There was no new message.

"Hello," a voice said, and I almost fell over.

"Bith!"

She had followed me into the grove and now stood ten paces distant, her face impassive, her arms by her side.

Despite my weak, trembling legs, I rushed to her and then stopped short. I wanted to grab her and hold her and profess my love, but she remained impassive.

And then she threw her arms around me and we cried.

"I am so sorry," I mumbled into her cheek.

"No!" she said, pushing me to arm's length. "I have been so foolish. I listened to that stupid priestess when I should have listened to my heart. I should have known you didn't do anything—"

"But I—"

"No." She looked at me sternly now, and despite her focus, she was still beautiful. "I went to Elephantine. To the nomarch's palace."

I nodded. Of course I knew.

"I met the girl from the harem."

My heart stopped. The girl. Tihepet.

She said, "Paneb knew a eunuch who introduced me to the girl. She told me what happened. She told me what a good man you are and how she tricked you."

"Tricked me?"

Nefer-bithia pulled me in close again. "Nothing happened. She was told to seduce you but you rejected her so she pretended you had."

"I love you," I said, overcome with emotion.

"But you should have told me the truth."

"I tried."

"Not about the girl, I mean about the treason. About the high priest's claims. About the one they call the lost pharaoh."

298

"What was there to tell?" I said. "The boy wasn't me. They were looking for a man with a scar from my village, but it wasn't me.

"What a shame! I could have been your queen. I could have been worshipped."

"You are my queen and *I* worship you."

I put my arm on her shoulder and we walked together out of the grove. We were back together. We were wealthy. We would go back to Akhmin and move to a house in the higher noble's sector.

"Are you sure you made the right decision?" she asked later. "You could have pretended to be the missing son."

"The rituals, the politics, the manipulation by others. Yes, I made the right decision—for both of us."

"Good," she said with finality, "then we will never talk about the lost pharaoh again."

FIFTY-ONE

BCE 3122 – five years earlier

Perhaps it was tiredness, but in the darkness of Tutankhamen's tomb, I sensed time swirling around me. I put my hands on the rock-hewn ground and my hands seemed disconnected like they weren't mine. My fingers tingled and then I could no longer feel them. I lost sense of where I was. What was up and what was down. And then I heard a whisper.

"I see you," it said.

"Who are you?"

"You know who I am."

"Lord Tutankhamen, Neb kheperu re—"

"I prefer Kanakht."

Victorious bull, *I thought. An unfit name for the pretty boy with weak legs. However, I politely replied, "I didn't know, my lord."*

"My ba *appears to be trapped here. Do you know which way I should go?"*

"I have brought you the instructions and spells, my lord." I tried to point at the Meryra's chest but my arms didn't work.

Annoyance gave an edged to his tone. "Why were they not here?"

300

"My lord, I have a terrible tale to tell. You were murdered by your vizier Ay so that he might be Pharaoh. He also ensured that you would be trapped here so that Osiris would never know." Then I told him that Ay had killed himself and that Horemheb had become Pharaoh. I also told him about Meryra and how he had rescued the mummy of Akhenaten, Tutankhamen's father, and buried Nefertiti. After I finished my story, there was a long silence and I thought that Tutankhamen's *ba* had already gone.

Then he surprised me by saying, *"I know you don't I?"*

"No, my lord."

"You have a birthmark on your left hip. Three dots."

I said nothing.

"You were taken away as a baby so that my kingship would not be questioned."

My head spun. "No, I—"

"See you in the Field of Reeds, brother," he whispered and was gone.

"Not for a long time," I said when I could finally speak. *"Not for a very long time."*

Left and right. Easily mixed up. A fifty-fifty chance that may have saved my life. If the High Priest had seen the birth marks on my left hip, my life would have been very different. I was content with my deception although lying to my wife gave me many sleepless nights. Perhaps I should have told her, but I was not prepared for the consequences should anyone else discover the truth.

So I wrote my story but excluded the conversation with my brother's *ba*.

Nefer-bithia and I were contented—for a while at least. Because that was before the authorities took my Nefer-Bithia away and before I became the Keeper of Secrets.

Acknowledgements

Although my mother wanted me to write Yanhamu's story for children, I'm grateful because it inspired me to write this tale. I'm also grateful to my wife for continued support of my crazy passion that is writing.

Thanks to Pete Tonkin and Richard Sheehan, my unofficial and official editors. Your contributions are greatly appreciated.

A final thank you goes to Egyptologist Lauren from *Books Beyond The Story* for her enthusiastic reception of *Map of the Dead* and also for providing support with some of my Egyptology research.

Yanhamu first appears in

MAP OF THE DEAD

When Alex MacLure's friend and colleague dies he is
determined to carry on her research into ancient Egypt.
He finds she has left him a coded message and, as he tries
to make sense of it all, he discovers she was murdered.
And now the murderer needs to silence him.

With only a few clues and a mysterious object, Alex
follows a trail from London to Cairo. He must crack the
code and expose a shocking and inconceivable truth
before the secret is buried for ever.

*"A page turner, blending historical accuracy with thrilling
and imaginative plot twist and turns"*

"Up there with the best of Wilbur Smith. A gripping read
from modern day to ancient Egypt."

*"The market is seriously lacking something of this
magnitude...Brilliant!"*

Yanhamu also appears in the second book from the
Egyptian series

SIGN OF THE DEAD*

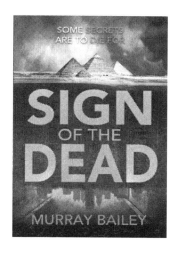

Atlanta, Georgia. When a body dump is found, FBI
Special Agent Charlie Rebb thinks a serial killer has
resurfaced. Called the Surgeon by the media, his telltale
technique has everyone wondering why. But then the murders
seem to stop again.

Cairo, Egypt. Alex MacLure is contacted by a student who
thinks he's uncovered a conspiracy involving the pyramids. He
asks for Alex's help to piece together a message using new
discoveries. But the student disappears and Alex is arrested for
a murder. Meanwhile, the special agent sees a sign that the
Surgeon is now in Egypt.

MacLure links up with Special Agent Reed to track down the
killer. As he decrypts an ancient story, MacLure realizes this is
a race against time. The Surgeon must be stopped before he
completes his terrible and startling mission

* Previously entitled Secrets of the Dead.

Read on for an extract of Yanhamu's story from

SIGN OF THE DEAD

1315 BCE, Badari

The large crowd fell into an expectant hush as they awaited the judgement. Magistrate Yan-Khety sat in the shade of the awning and adjusted his purple sash.

"Sir, they are waiting," his assistant whispered.

Let them wait, Yanhamu thought. Make the guilty man sweat.

He cleared his throat. And, as was the custom, he summarized the case before pronouncing judgement. "The defendant, Theshan, was commissioned by the accuser—a minor nobleman called Rudjek—to build an extension to his house. The defendant obtained agreement to the design and construction and built it in accordance with requirements. In fact, he finished the building ahead of the three months he promised. The accuser paid for the build—although we heard that this was paid a month later than agreed. However, we also visited the site and found that part of the structure has moved and appears unstable. The accuser therefore demands repayment of the money and reparations for the problems and anxiety caused."

Yanhamu stopped and glanced at the slave, Yuf, who was listening so hard he'd stopped waving the ostrich feather fan. The slave realized his error and immediately began fanning again.

"The case would appear straight-forward," Yanhamu began.

"As is the Law of the Two Lands," Rudjek said with a smirk. The crowd muttered their agreement, perhaps hoping for a severe punishment.

"Quiet!" Yanhamu shouted, knowing that most of the people were there to see blood rather than justice. He was weary of the show that such cases often became. He was in the insignificant eleventh nome, where the wine was bad and the accommodation worse. It made him irritable and he knew he needed to remind himself that he was here to do the right thing, however unpopular.

"I have heard witnesses speak as to the character of the defendant. I have heard other customers express satisfaction with his work. I have also learned that the original price he quoted was rejected and that the accuser, Rudjek, insisted on a lower price and sourced the building materials himself.

"Theshan, the defendant, says that he expressed concern regarding the materials, although Rudjek denies this." Yanhamu looked at both men's faces and could now see the truth. "My judgement is that Theshan should rebuild the extension so that it is sound and of good quality and so repair his reputation." The defendant lowered his eyes in acceptance. But Yanhamu wasn't finished. "However, I find the accuser guilty of bringing this case when it is his own fault. He provided substandard materials and insisted that the construction should go ahead despite Theshan's concerns. He will therefore not only provide any additional acceptable quality material

2

required for the rebuilding, but he will also pay the defendant for those repairs. This is my judgement."

Rudjek clenched his teeth and then muttered something. A guard stepped forward.

"Don't disrespect the judgement," he growled at the minor noble. "Or you'll find yourself in prison."

Rudjek slunk away without another word and two guards brought forward the next defendant. It was a Nubian, as black as coal, although he was small for a man from that country. He was accused of using pig meat in his pies. Pig was only eaten by the peasants, because it was blamed for the plague that had killed hundreds over the years. Yanhamu knew this all too well since his mother had died this way. It was a serious crime to pass off pig as another meat. In another nome, under another magistrate, the crime might have been punishable by death. Yanhamu prayed there was no evidence of such a crime.

He listened to witnesses' statements and then had twenty pies opened and inspected. Yanhamu himself prodded at the contents with a stick.

"What is this?"

"A mixture, my lord. Beef, chicken, goat and..." The Nubian swallowed hard, as though the words wouldn't come out.

The crowd remained tense.

"What is it?" Yanhamu bellowed.

"Dog, my lord." He nodded with contrition as he said it quietly

There were gasps in the crowd and a woman fainted.

"Not pig?"

"Oh no, my lord! Never!"

Yanhamu waved his assistant to bring him a pie. He stuck a finger in and tasted it.

"My lord?" the assistant whispered, alarmed. Nobles would never eat dog meat.

Yanhamu repeated the procedure. "It's not pig, it is indeed dog," he announced a moment later.

He asked for the witnesses again and questioned whether the pie seller had made any claims as to the contents. All of them admitted that he had not. They were sold as meat pies and that's what they were.

Yanhamu dismissed the case, saying, "The pie seller is not guilty of including pig meat. However, I suspect he will never sell another pie in this nome."

As the defendant was led away to the hisses of the crowd, the assistant leaned in.

"My lord, how did you know it was dog meat? You could have risked your life if it had been pig."

"I'll explain later. What's the last case?"

"A man accused of selling dates past their best."

Thank Thoth, Yanhamu thought. He dreaded the thief who would need to lose a hand or a rapist who would have his testicles crushed. But this was a simple case and Yanhamu quickly passed judgement. The man received five lashes, much to the satisfaction of the crowd.

Even before the assistant began to dismantle the stage, Yanhamu was up and heading for their accommodation. The eleventh nome tribunals were over for another month and he was ready to go home.

As he packed the magistrate's things, the assistant asked about the day's lesson.

"First of all, Sadhu, I believed the man when he said it wasn't pig."

"How could you read anything in that black face?"

"His eyes told the truth," Yanhamu said. "And I know that most towns-people have never tasted pig so

4

could easily mislabel something different. Second of all, your lesson for today was observation."

"I observed you tasting either pig or dog. Neither of which is appropriate for a noble such as yourself, my lord."

"No! The observation was that I inserted my middle finger in the pie but licked my index finger."

When he arrived at his home in Akhmim, old Paneb opened the courtyard door and bowed. He took his master's coat and washed his feet.

"Is Nefer-bithia here?" Yanhamu asked the slave.

"In the drawing room, master."

Yanhamu noted hesitancy. "What is it, old friend? Did she have a difficult case?"

Paneb dropped his head and held his hands wide. He wasn't going to say, so Yanhamu walked into the house with trepidation.

"Bith?"

His wife rushed to him and kissed him hard.

He laughed. "I'm grateful, but why the extreme affection? I thought you'd had a bad day."

Nefer-bithia pointed to a scroll on a table. It had an unbroken royal seal. She said, "Have you done something wrong, Yani?"

"Probably!" He laughed again, although this time it was forced.

Two strides took him to the table and he snatched it up. It wasn't Pharaoh Horemheb's seal but the vizier of Waset's. He hesitated and then broke it open.

"What does it say?"

"I'm being summoned by Vizier Paramese."

She looked pale so he put his arm around her. "It's not about one of my judgements. This is a call-up."

"But…"

He quoted: "In the name of Pharaoh Horemheb, rightful ruler and descendant of the great Ahmose, one who reunited the Two Lands, Mighty Sword, destroyer of her enemies the Nine Bows, King of Upper and Lower Egypt, you are ordered to present yourself for duty—"

"Why?"

"Because I was once an officer, second class. This is a call-up because I am a veteran officer."

"To fight?" She still looked pale.

"It can't be, sweetheart. I was in communications and special missions in the last war. Perhaps I'm needed for training or advice."

"When?"

"Tomorrow." He held her tight until the shadow of the sundial told them it was time to pray. "One good thing," he said as they went to an upstairs room where they could witness the setting sun. "If this takes more than a month, I won't need to do the tribunal at Badari."

"Great," she said. "That means I have to do it. And knowing your wayward judgements, I'll probably have to retry your old cases."

But it wasn't for a month. When he arrived at the garrison outside Waset, Yanhamu found himself in a queue of thirty other veterans. They were destined for Canaan, to take back Egyptian land. And they were going there as an army.

1309 BCE, Akhmim

The courtyard was strangely dusty and silent. On the last leg of his journey, Yanhamu had witnessed a barge capsize. It had been carrying salt. His crew immediately prostrated themselves and prayed, requesting protection against the bad omen. Yanhamu didn't believe such silly superstitions. He knew the gods were above petty warnings like spilled salt. Even though their only son had been still-born, he didn't believe it was a judgement by the gods. It was life. Good things happened and bad things happened. The gods were far too busy making sure the heavens moved, the annual flood occurred and the harvest was bountiful.

As a boy he'd worried about Het's judgement the day he took too many duck eggs. Foolish childish fears, that's all they were. It's what separated the intelligent from the commoners. It's why they needed good magistrates like him and Nefer-bithia.

That's what he told himself, and yet, as he stood in his desolate courtyard, he wondered whether his world-view was mistaken. Had the spilled salt really been a bad omen?

It took him just a couple of minutes to confirm that the house was deserted. Nefer-bithia had gone and there was no message, nothing telling him why she wasn't there. He sat down on the edge of the well and thought.

He'd been away for almost six years. The armies had moved north. They took land and retreated. They built garrisons and fortifications. They policed the lands and then fought. They overcame the Caananites, they fought skirmishes with the Ibru and finally drove the Hittites out of Ugarit.

He'd started as officer, first class and ended up leader of Three Osiris—the Blues. They weren't as respected as the Reds or feared so much as the Blacks, and that suited Yanhamu. He'd been strategic and survived. Unlike his old colleague Thayjem.

In the last war they'd been simple communication officers, translating and scribing. Thayjem wasn't a fighter. Neither of them was. But his old friend had found himself in the front line officer, second class in a Red unit that had been ambushed by Ibru. That enemy did not understand or abide by the rules of war. They attacked in small groups and thought nothing of dirty tricks.

Transporting wagon-loads of dead Egyptians back to Egypt was the closest Yanhamu had come to returning home during those six years. On that mission he discovered that the dead officer in his care was none other than Thayjem.

It was a long, arduous journey and the bodies stank before they were half-way home. But they were to be buried in the soil of the Two Lands. That was all that mattered. Then the dead could find their way to the Field of Reeds. It was the promise made to all Egyptian fighters no matter how lowly.

"My Lord Khety, is that you?"

The voice snapped Yanhamu out of his reverie. He sat up and looked at the young man standing in the courtyard doorway. Sadhu.

"By Sobek, it is you!" Sadhu gasped. "May I come in?"

Yanhamu beckoned the young man over. "You've grown up," he said.

Sadhu smiled wanly. "And you have grown grey, master. I hardly recognize you."

"Where's my wife? Do you know?"

Sadhu lowered his eyes. "I have returned everyday hoping to find you so that you might know. So that you wouldn't come here and think the worst. Not after you have fought for our safety and defeated our enemies."

"I see you've got no better at coming to the point."

"A lot has changed since you've been gone. Egypt—at least Upper Egypt—has changed."

"Where is she?" Yanhamu bit back his frustration with the man. "Just tell me."

"She's gone." There were tears in Sadhu's eyes now. "She was taken away."

Yanhamu stood up. His heart, though weak, thudded against his chest. "Where?"

"I don't know."

Yanhamu could see the young man was losing it so he calmed himself and led him into the house. In the kitchen he found a bottle of unopened wine and poured them both a cup. They sat at the table and drank two before he spoke again.

"Now, start at the beginning and explain what you do know."

"The vizier of the south…"

"Paramese?"

"He's just calling himself Ramses now."

"Go on, what did Vizier Ramses do?"

"He has been Pharaoh's voice here in the Upper lands and he has been making new laws. Although he says they are old laws of the First Ones. He says they are the Law of Ra."

Yanhamu knew about the Law of Ra. He'd sought it his whole life after his first encounter with Meryra the scribe after his sister disappeared—taken by the gods because of her beautiful soul. And when he had found the law of man he had found it sadly lacking. So, he thought, perhaps Vizier Ramses has addressed the disparity between justice and law.

However, Yanhamu's hope was soon dashed.

Sadhu continued: "There are many changes. We must now all worship Amun and Ra, whether we are from the north or south. Only the men are permitted inside the temples. Women must pray separately. Married women must cover their heads and mouths so as not to encourage infidelity. Any married woman found to be acting lewdly will be stoned. And lewd behaviour has been interpreted as just looking at a man a certain way!"

Yanhamu shook his head. This was a strange interpretation of the Law of Ra. He feared the worst when he asked, "So are you telling me that Nefer-bithia has been stoned?"

"Oh no! What I haven't explained is that the new law also precludes a woman from certain jobs. Of course, women must work and satisfy their husband's needs, we all know that, but Vizier Ramses said something new. He decreed that no woman could take high office."

"Like being a magistrate?"

"Yes."

"So my wife stopped acting as a magistrate and went where?"

Sadhu poured himself another glass and glugged it down. "No, my lord. Your wife refused to accept the ruling. She wasn't so foolish as to refute it in public but she carried on. She wore your beard of office and—although clearly a woman—said she was a man. After all, she explained to me, Pharaoh Hatshepsut was a woman. She also said other pharaohs were originally women too. She said a person could, by their office, change their sex."

"And she carried on."

"In the name of Lord Khety. After all, you weren't here and it had been her father's name."

"What happened?"

"They came for her. Three moons ago, they let her open the tribunal in Abydos and then the local Nomarch stepped forward as the first case and accused her of being a woman and breaking the law. The crowd would have stoned her to death if it weren't for the guards. I was hit on the head and body, and your wife took some stones too. But the city guard encircled us and the prefect tore off her beard and gown. The last I saw of her was as they marched her out of the square. I was too much in shock…"

Yanhamu placed a calming hand on the young man's arm. "You could have done nothing. Where is everyone else? Where are the slaves?"

"Taken by the state."

"Poor Paneb."

"My lord, the slave Paneb is dead. The soldiers killed him." He started to cry. "And I am sorry, my lord for your wife is surely dead too."

"No!" Yanhamu stood, his hands clenched. "They wouldn't dare. Despite this new law, she was still a

11

noble of high birth and they would not spill her blood. If they wanted that then she could have been fed to the mob. No, they wanted her alive." He thanked the young man and marched out of the house.

"Where are you going, my lord."

"To find her!"

"Good," Sadhu said, hurrying beside him. "Then I'm coming with you."

Yanhamu beat hard on the Nomarch's door until a guard opened it. He was still wearing the insignia of a Blue army officer and the guard immediately saluted.

"Where is Nomarch Amethu? Tell him Lord Khety, past magistrate of the eleventh nome, officer of the army of Horus, has returned from the northern wars and demands an audience."

The soldier saluted once more and hurried away. Yanhamu didn't wait to be asked. He marched through the courtyard to the Hall of Records. He was met by a gaggle of scribes and was reminded that this was an administration centre. The Nomarch was just an administrator.

"Where is he?" Yanhamu bellowed.

The panicking men in white robes drew back and then one stepped forward and bowed.

"My lord, the Nomarch is not here. Lord Amethu is at the merchant's quay."

Yanhamu didn't wait for any more information. He turned on his heel and raced out of the Nomarch's office, through the town towards the river. As soon as he reached the quay, he spotted Amethu stepping off a barge. The soldier from the office had beaten them here and was already speaking to the Nomarch.

Yanhamu waited for Amethu to approach him. The Nomarch bowed, not low, but enough to show respect.

"Where is she, Amethu?"

"It's funny how quickly the people turn."

Yanhamu grabbed the other man by the tunic. The soldier stepped forward but Amethu waved him down.

Yanhamu said, "Funny how quickly the people turn? You turned on us, Amethu!" He pulled the Nomarch closer and glared into his face. "We once called you friend."

"I was just following orders."

"Where is she?" he asked again.

"I don't know. I honestly don't know."

"Did you cast her into the Pit of Repentance?" Yanhamu found the words hard to say. It was a dungeon close to the desert where the convicted were dumped. Food and water was passed down but no one ever came up. The stench of death was said to be more foul than the waters of the underworld where Apep plotted against Ra.

The Nomarch held up his hands in horror. "Oh no, Lord Khety. I could never... No, I was just acting on orders from the vizier. I merely carried out his orders. He arranged for her to be taken from here."

"Vizier Paramese?"

"He's calling himself Ramses these days."

"So I hear. Well, I don't care if he thinks he's Ra himself!" The men within earshot gasped but Yanhamu continued: "Will I find him in Waset?"

"That's where your wife was taken."

Moored close by was a single-sailed small boat. It looked sleek and fast.

"For hire?" Yanhamu said as he boarded her. "I need to get to Waset quickly."

The pilot bowed and quoted an extortionate price.

"He'll pay," Yanhamu shouted, and pointed to Nomarch Amethu. "Isn't that right?"

The Nomarch looked uncomfortable but nodded agreement, and within seconds the sail-boat cast off and began tacking against the Nile current. Sadhu sat on cushions at the rear while Yanhamu stood on the prow. He leaned forward as though urging the boat on could make it go faster.

At the palace of the vizier, Yanhamu was forced to wait for an appointment. However, when he was finally called forward for an audience, it wasn't the vizier but another court official who met him. It had taken the little boat almost two days and Yanhamu's rage had subsided. He was tired from lack of sleep but knew that calm would work better than confrontation.

"I asked to speak with Vizier Ramses," Yanhamu said after polite introductions.

"I am sorry but he is not here."

"That is a considerable shame since I have travelled so far." Yanhamu took a breath. "When will the great vizier return?"

"It is unknown."

"May I enquire where he has gone?"

"He now resides in Memphis."

"But his lordship is responsible for Upper Egypt."

The court official seemed to relax. Almost conspiratorially he said, "Of course you are correct... at the present. Who knows what Pharaoh has planned for the future?"

Yanhamu didn't know what this meant except that he would need to deal with someone else if he was to find out where Nefer-bithia was—if she was still alive. He took an offered drink and smiled. "Perhaps you have the power to help me."

The man smiled back. "If I have the power then it will be freely given. However, you should speak with Chancellor Memephat."

Yanhamu had another long wait before he was led through the halls into the Room of Judgement. Ordinarily, the vizier would have occupied the ornate chair on the stage. But the overweight man in flowing gown was the chancellor.

Yanhamu bowed as he was introduced.

"Ah, the great Lord Khety," the chancellor said and raised a hand. It was plump, like a plucked, overfed duck, and every finger had a gold or electrum ring.

Yanhamu stepped forward and pretended to kiss the hand. "You honour me," he said.

"It is an honour to meet the real Lord Khety." The chancellor smiled and Yanhamu felt an imagined knife to the gut.

"My wife was the genuine Lord Khety. I was in a foreign land fighting for Pharaoh, who is the Two Lands. My wife had every right to use my title."

Chancellor Memephat shrugged. "I'm afraid the law changed while you were away. It is now a crime to assume the office of a man. These were the old laws, passed down by the gods."

Yanhamu wanted to challenge the nonsense but there was clearly no point. There were guards behind the stage, and on either side sat two large cats with spots. Although docile, the threat was subtle. The chancellor must have seen his gaze.

"They are beautiful are they not? A gift. Faster and sleeker than a lion. More intelligent than a dog."

Yanhamu looked into Memephat's cold eyes. "My wife is beautiful and intelligent. I have been told she was brought to this city. Where would I begin to look for her?"

The chancellor held his hands wide, causing a ripple of fat under his arms. "I am afraid I do not know all cases or persons. Perhaps if you would like to take the Lodging of Nobles, I will enquire."

Yanhamu nodded. He tried to smile, although the knot in his stomach tightened with frustration. The man was telling him to wait for an indefinite period. "I would just like to know that she is alive."

"Oh, of course. I fully understand, Lord Khety. Please, take the lodging and we will send you a message as soon as an answer is available."

Five days passed before a messenger came to the Lodgings of Nobles asking for him. He'd spent the time in his room. Sadhu had visited him daily and brought food and wine. He spoke with enthusiasm about the excitement and gaiety of the city and the wonder of the temples in the adjacent City of a Thousand Gates. The boy had never been to the great third nome before. But his enthusiasm was lost on his master.

They travelled together with the messenger but it wasn't to the vizier's palace. They were taken to a small house in the artisan centre of town. Memephat was sitting under an awning drinking milk and eating cake when they arrived. He waved away his servant and pointed to Yanhamu. The message was clear. This was a private meeting and Sadhu was to wait outside.

"I trust you are well," Memephat began.

"I have found the lodgings to be most acceptable."

"And the entertainment?"

"Ah, unfortunately I have been unable to sample the delights of the city. However, my assistant tells me how much he has been enjoying the sights and pleasures."

The chancellor held out a plate. "Please try some of this honey bread. I have it imported from Punt." After Yanhamu took a small sticky slice, Memephat continued: "So, as I was saying, the women are very beautiful, no? Now that the married ones must wear a veil, it is easier to choose the available fruit."

"I am sure they are. However, my wife..."

The man showed a touch of irritation at Yanhamu's directness but didn't comment. Instead he tightened his lips in a faux smile. "My lord, I am saying that perhaps it is time for you to find yourself a young maiden."

"I am married."

"Ah yes..." Now the official grinned. "Aren't we all but the law allows for a man—"

"Where is my wife?"

Again the tight-lipped smile and then the shake of his head.

"A shame, I could arrange for an attractive mistress." He held up a placatory hand as Yanhamu started to stand. "Lord Khety, I see that you are determined, but I can do nothing about it."

"Is she alive?"

"You would like to see her, yes? But it is impossible."

"How much will it cost me?"

Memephat turned up his nose like there was a bad smell. "Please, there is no need for crudeness. Perhaps a gift? Do you have any leopards?"

"I will give you my property in Akhmim. It has twenty rooms, a courtyard ten times the size of this one and has a view of the Great River."

"In the lowly ninth nome? How many slaves can you throw in?"

"All my slaves were confiscated by the state."

Memephat's smile told Yanhamu that the man already knew about the slaves.

Yanhamu said, "I have returned to claim what is rightfully mine. I am Lord Khety, and when the slaves are mine once more, I will gift them to you."

"Alas it is too late. Your slaves are gone. Sold or dead." He smiled, although his small dark eyes stayed cold. "Perhaps gold?"

"Half my salary in gold is yours, great Memephat."

The chancellor nodded slowly, as though considering the bargain. "Half your gold for ten minutes with your wife. All your gold for thirty minutes. I'm sure you understand that these things must be arranged and funded."

Memephat smiled naturally for the first time. He held out the Rod of Agreement—an ivory bar with golden scrolled tips. Both men gripped it, sealing the deal. Between nobles it was as good as a signature or independent witnesses.

"Come to the palace tomorrow," Memephat said. "Not the main gate. You will find a small door in the west wall. Be there at the hour of Sais, before sunrise, and you shall see your wife."

"Small door, west wall," Yanhamu said, his head light with relief.

"Yes," the man said still smiling. "It is the way to the vizier's private harem."

1309 BCE, Waset (Luxor)

The nocturnal hour of Sais was the false dawn. It was said that at this hour, Seth would lead the four serpent goddesses to ward off the final dangers that might threaten sunrise. In the pits, the shadows, the ba-souls, and the heads of those to be punished are destroyed one by one.

As Yanhamu touched the grain of the tamarisk door he felt the same portent. Beyond this door was either a new day or the pits of eternal darkness. Of course, he hadn't slept. Memephat had said he would see his wife. It wasn't until after the meeting that Yanhamu had realized the chancellor had not been clear. When he'd asked if she was alive, Memephat had said it was impossible to see her and then he'd accepted the financial agreement. Yanhamu knew of such trickery and he kicked himself for falling for it. Nefer-bithia could be dead.

At the precise moment of the hour, Yanhamu knocked. He then placed his shaking hands behind his back.

The door was immediately opened a crack.

"You are Yan-Khety?"

It had been a long time since his name had been used without a title. But he wore a simple grey gown with no symbols of office or status. Memephat had said it was for discretion but Yanhamu knew it was a gesture of control. The chancellor wanted him belittled. He had taken everything that Yanhamu owned and now he was taking his pride.

"I am he," Yanhamu said, and the door opened wide. He stepped through into a courtyard. The man who closed the door behind him had a spear and a lifeless face.

Yanhamu swallowed. "I am here to see Nefer Khety."

"This way."

The path led under an arch into a garden. Even in the grey light of pre-dawn Yanhamu could see its beauty. There were circular beds of flowers and manicured trees that were like sleeping storks. They walked on and came to another arch over soil that had been freshly turned. There was a spade.

Oh Anhuris, strong and good protector! Yanhamu prayed. My Bith has been taken to the afterlife. His legs gave way and he fell to his knees. They were going to dig up her body so that he could see her. That was Memephat's trick.

He felt a rough hand under his arm pulling him back up.

"You only have thirty minutes, and you don't want to waste it sniffing the mud!"

Yanhamu staggered on, confused. "She's alive?" he managed to say.

The guard chuckled. "Of course, you idiot! Why would anyone in their right mind pay to come in here to see a dead girl?"

They went through another courtyard and, for the first time, Yanhamu saw the walls of the palace. Two storeys up was a balcony with an ornate screen.

"Wait and watch and be quiet," the guard said.

Yanhamu waited. Nothing happened for five minutes except the honk of unseen geese beyond the next wall. He was about to complain when a shadow moved on the balcony.

"Bith!" Yanhamu shouted. He would have shouted again but a rough hand clamped around his throat.

"Silence, or this is over right now!"

Yanhamu nodded and the hand was released. He could see more shadows and then the screens were pulled back. Ladies stood above him and stretched and yawned. One opened her tunic and showed perfectly formed breasts. The guard chuckled.

They glanced down, and Yanhamu suspected the show had just been for them. The women moved and more appeared, but he couldn't see his wife. And then she was there, as beautiful as the day they had married ten years ago.

"Bith!" he screamed. At the same time, he twisted away from the guard.

"Yani?"

"I'll get you out, my sweet. I'll—" but his words were smothered by a hand.

"Vizier Ramses," she called as he was dragged away. "Tell the pharaoh he's holding me!"

Ramses was no longer a vizier. He was now referred to as the Deputy Lord of the Two Lands, as well as Pharaoh's right-hand fan-bearer. He'd built a palace in Memphis bigger than the vizier's palace in the south. There was a great deal of construction going on, continuing the recognition of Memphis as the state's capital, whereas Waset and the City of a Thousand Gates was the religious capital. Amun in the south and Ra in the north. United as one god Amun-Ra, making Egypt great again. But all the wealth and power and joy were alien to Yanhamu. He'd spent a week travelling back after Sadhu had persuaded him to leave Waset.

His wife wanted Yanhamu to speak to the pharaoh, but that would be impossible and pointless. So, Yanhamu's initial plan was to raise an army and break into the vizier's palace. He was sure he could find ex-Blue soldiers who would follow him.

"And if you gain a victory, if you are reunited with your wife, what then?" Sadhu had said.

"It will be over."

"Yes it will," he had said with wisdom beyond his years. "You will be hunted down and destroyed. You cannot fight the state and expect to survive."

"But justice is on my side!"

"Tell that to Osiris when your body is dumped in the pit."

So Yanhamu and his assistant had travelled north to the capital and they had plotted. What does a man do when he has nothing? He creates something from that nothing.

Yanhamu requested an audience with Deputy Lord Ramses and within two hours was taken to the Great Hall.

Yanhamu almost stopped in his tracks as he approached Ramses' throne. The man could have passed for the pharaoh if he had worn the two crowns—the red and white of the Two Lands—rather than the lesser blue one.

The man squinted at him, and Yanhamu was reminded that he was not a young man. His eldest son—now Master of the King's Horses—was at least Yanhamu's age.

"Is that you, Yan-Khety? I don't recognize you."

"Time has passed."

Ramses nodded.

Yanhamu said, "And you, my lord, have been recognized as a great leader. I remember when you were commander of the king's army."

"And you were once a translation officer in the Black and rose to the status of leader of 250, for the Blues." The way Ramses said it was with contempt rather than as an accolade. Then he smiled. "You bring a message. What's this I hear about secrets?"

"I have secrets to tell."

Ramses smiled again. "Yes?"

"I know what happened to Pharaoh Tutankhaten."

"Tutankhamen."

"And his father."

"So?"

"And Pharaoh Ay."

Ramses clapped his hands and bellowed, "Leave us!"

There must have been thirty men in the room, and within seconds, Ramses and Yanhamu were alone.

"Are you threatening me, Khety?"

"No, my lord, certainly not! I am offering you my services. The pharaoh must have a Keeper of Secrets and I know that since the royal line was broken, the secrets have been lost."

"I am a descendant of Ahmose who could trace his origins back to Horus Himself."

"You are Pharaoh Horemheb's cousin."

Ramses nodded, and Yanhamu saw something in the old man's eye. Something wasn't quite right although he doubted he'd ever find out what it was. The deputy said. "Go on, then. Tell me what you know."

So Yanhamu told Ramses what he had learned from Meryra, who had served Akhenaten and

Nefertiti. He told the deputy that, after her husband's death, Nefertiti had ruled using the name Smenkhkare. She had married her own daughter to continue the blood-line and wait until Tutankhaten—as he was originally called—was old enough. They had enemies, not least of whom were the priests who saw themselves undermined and impoverished by the heretic pharaoh. With their support, Ay—the boy's paternal grandfather, and of no royal blood—took charge as regent.

"He poisoned Pharaoh," Yanhamu said. Even after so many years, he still found it hard to say. "He also performed the Opening of the Mouth incorrectly and made sure the pharaoh could not find the Field of Reeds."

"What else do you know?"

"I know about Pharaoh Horemheb, how he persuaded the usurper Ay to take the old way and die with honour. However"—now he spoke quietly because he knew that his words were tantamount to treason—"he desecrated the tombs of Akhenaten and Ay."

Ramses shook his head. "This is terrible."

"And they are secrets, my lord. I have said them to no other but yourself—" Yanhamu took a breath. Everything that he had planned now hinged on what happened next. He said, "Descendant of Horus, future pharaoh of the Two Lands, you must know the facts."

Ramses said nothing for a long time. He fixed Yanhamu with his eyes and Yanhamu tried to look like a trusted servant. Eventually the deputy said, "You have gambled with your life, Khety. Either you should be put to death immediately for your lies or you should become my Keeper of Secrets. Which should it be?"

"Keeper of Pharaoh's secrets," Yanhamu replied.

Ramses shook his head. "But I need more. The secrets you know are nothing and of no use. I need the true secrets of the past."

"You need to be assured of Osiris' blessing and of guaranteed eternal life," Yanhamu said. None of the rulers since Amenhotep III, Akhenaten's father had been given the appropriate respect and shown the way to the Field of Reeds by their successors. And eternal life was what it was all about.

"Then you must prove yourself," Ramses said with finality. "Find me the truth."

Sign of the Dead is available now in paperback and ebook

murraybaileybooks.com

IF YOU ENJOYED THIS BOOK

Feedback helps me understand what works, what doesn't and what readers want more of. It also brings a book to life.

Online reviews are also very important in encouraging others to try my books. I don't have the financial clout of a big publisher. I can't take out newspaper ads or run poster campaigns.

But what I do have is an enthusiastic and committed bunch of readers.

Honest reviews are a powerful tool. I'd be very grateful if you could spend a couple of minutes leaving a review, however short, on sites like Amazon and Goodreads.

Thank you
Murray

Printed in Poland
by Amazon Fulfillment
Poland Sp. z o.o., Wrocław